BUTCHER, BAKER, CANDLESTICK TAKER

BUTCHER, BAKER, CANDLESTICK TAKER

Book One of the Spokane Clock Tower Mysteries

PATRICIA MEREDITH

Games Afoot, LLC

This book is dedicated to my grandfathers:

Leroy Hammond, who taught me to eschew obfuscation,

and Eugene Rizzo, who taught me determination
and perspective.

Great men of words, intelligence, and faith—I know they
are smiling down on me with pride.

Think of fire.

Think of the sound. The roar, the rumble, like a rushing river rising. Then *pop*. The crackling of the kindling as the catch ignites. The sputtering as the tendrils of flame *snap*. The breath of the blaze as it burns. *Sigh*.

Think of the flames as they quiver. They are eager, begging you to join them in their darting dance of decay. Come, caper and cavort with me. Frisk, frolic, skip, and gambol the night into morning. It may be your last.

Think of the colors. Their simplistic splendor. Let them leap and whirl before your eyes, sparking and tripping on the air in a fantastic masquerade. The exquisite glamor of conflagration.

Think of the heat. The sizzle of skin as it burns flesh. As the muscles contract and pop and the weight sloughs off. As the tissue curls and the meat leaves the bone.

Think of the ash. Black and flaky cinders mixing in the grayish gravel of crumbling bone.

Am I getting warmer?

One

Monday, April 15, 1901

Spokane, Washington

Bernard Carew's face was melting. The heat was too intense. His insides were slowly boiling, like one of Mrs. Hill's attempts at chicken and dumpling soup. Soon he'd be nothing but mush, and then what would happen to Roslyn?

With a grunt, he rose out of the claw-footed tub and wrapped his dripping wet, embarrassingly hairy body in one of the towels hanging on the rack nearby.

He hadn't been able to sleep, so he'd thought he'd try one of his wife's tried-and-true remedies: a hot bath.

But he wasn't used to the sensation. Completely engulfing his body in a tub of water heated within new pipes that ran through his home was too odd for him. He hadn't taken a bath since he was a child, when, as the oldest, he'd been forced to take the last bath in the house, even though he was only two minutes older than his brother. Thomas always did get great pleasure out of watching Bernard empty the tub of the grime he'd left behind while he stood warmly wrapped in a towel before the large cookstove.

Bernard grumbled aloud as he moved to the porcelain sink in the corner and studied the effect of the bath's steam on his mustache by the light of the Argand lamp.

From now on he'd stick to the bowl and pitcher, that was for darn certain.

A few swipes of a comb through his dark black hair and mustache brought things back to the way he preferred them. He grunted in satisfaction and turned to don his blue-and-white striped pajamas.

The reason for his lack of sleep soon resurfaced, however, and he sank onto the covered toilet seat, his wet towel still in his hand.

He was thirty-two, he had a wife he adored, a modern house with indoor plumbing, he had finally earned detective...

And he was already floundering. He'd accomplished his dream, but so far it hadn't brought him the satisfaction he'd longed for.

Instead, it had brought a thousand new problems, not the least of which was the fact that McPhee, MacDonald, McDermott, and Burns had taken on plenty of interesting cases in the months since Bernard had made detective with the Spokane Police, but had as yet only handed him stick-ups, robberies, and thefts, which were plentiful, but boring to a mind like his and left him wondering if he'd get to keep his badge.

It didn't help that the other detectives seemed determined to keep him an outsider of their little group. Not that they'd been rude, per se—just some jovial pranks as a sort of hazing. When he'd set up his new desk, he'd mistakenly let them see his favorite Sherlock Holmes novel amongst his possessions.

"*A Study in Scarlet*?" McDermott had laughed. "You know the great Holmes is dead, right?"

Bernard, a man of few words, hadn't replied. He'd grown up in the police force—his father and grandfather having paid their bit of life behind the badge—and so he knew the brutality, in some ways first-hand, that often accompanied police investigations. In Sherlock Holmes's deductive reasoning he saw a future where crime could potentially be stopped before it even happened. A world where there was no more cruelty, and only peace and understanding... Well, he knew it was a far-off future, if ever, but with new technologies springing up every day from the telephone to the automobile, it was possible to let himself believe that someday he might live in a world where communication, logic, and reasoning resulted in a more peaceful time in history. To that end, he had taken to using more of Holmes's skills in problem-solving, instead of his fists. And he'd earned detective. So he must be doing something right.

Bernard stood and hung up his towel, carrying the lamp back to bed with him, then returning almost immediately because he'd forgotten to pull the plug so the tub could disgorge its soupy concoction.

Finally, he blew out the lamp and climbed into bed beside his wife, whose placid face seemed to laugh at his inability to find rest.

With a sigh, he rolled over and tried something else he hadn't done since childhood: counting sheep.

* * *

One. The Red Rogue almost dropped the clock when it began to sound the hour—by Red's account, half an hour too early.

Two. The clock was an antique. Simple in form, elegant in feature, distractingly alluring in sound.

Three. The chimes were really quite...mesmerizing. Red's train of thought kept skipping off the track.

Four. Red ran a gloved hand over the smooth finished oak of the sides and back, trying to...what was it again? Oh, right. Stealing.

Five. Pondering for too long the idea of still taking the dysfunctional clock—time seemed to slow as the chimes continued bewitchingly—

Six. The thief decided that it was best to leave it behind if it was going to chime without reason, which would certainly not be helpful during the getaway portion of the evening.

Seven. No matter. The thief had already passed on an appealing sculpture of a Japanese samurai on his warhorse, due to its weight and sharp edges.

Eight. The clock was still in the thief's hands. Where did it go again? Right. Mantelpiece.

Nine. The thief returned the clock and ran a gloved finger along the smooth marble, checking for areas where there was a lack of dust or a slight rise that might indicate a false panel.

Ten. Ah, Lady Luck. Light fingers felt the ridge between the cherry blossoms gracing the mantel's top right corner and the carved ornamental story told in panels beneath.

Eleven. Before pulling ever so slightly on the branch of the tree, the thief took a moment to attempt to shake clear the chimes of the clock once more—they seemed to be worming their way into corners of the mind.

Twelve. Red was gratified to hear the low grating sound of marble on marble that indicated a hidden drawer sliding open. With a steady hand, one borne of years of practice, Red removed the drawer completely and quietly, and placed it gently on the mantel.

Silence. The chimes were finally through. Thank God for that. The thief quickly removed the ornate peacock-blue enameled necklace and sapphire earrings within, then placed them in the hidden pockets of the long burgundy overcoat, which had been modified for just such use, tucking them alongside a miniature Alfred Daguet butterfly box and four pure gold geisha candlesticks.

Red slid the drawer smoothly back into the hole with a soft *shik.*

Time to go.

The Red Rogue moved swiftly through the room, carefully avoiding the grand ebony dragon bench in case the overcoat snagged on a claw or tooth. But wait, what were those staring from above the bench along the wall? Masks? Little bit creepy those masks.

And yet, one of them spoke to the Red Rogue.

The mask in question had a white, laughing, dog-like face surrounded by long red hair and whiskers. The thief grinned at it and gently tucked it inside the lining of the overcoat.

It was so kind of this home to offer up such a unique collection.

But now it really was time to be going.

Furtive steps brought the thief to the pocket doors between the parlor and the hall. Sliding the doors open gently, Red checked to ensure the odd clock hadn't woken the household. All was quiet. Slipping through and closing the doors softly, the thief scurried down the hall, past three or four more pocket doors that called for exploration but would have to wait for another night.

The thief opened the door that led down the servant stairs and into the bowels of the house. The door opened and closed on well-oiled hinges—no one wanted to hear servants coming and going—which made descending all the more ingenious in its simplicity.

The thief made straight for the door at the bottom of the wood shaft designed for sliding cordwood down to be collected beside the furnace. Red had quite happily discovered that a thin thief was the same size as a bundle of wood, and now passed through what had been a locked door at the bottom of the shaft—most likely in place to deter such things from happening, but nothing a quick lock-pick couldn't handle—and locked the door once again. Then up the shaft Red carefully climbed, stopping only once to un-snag the hem of the burgundy overcoat from splinters of wood.

Once out, the Red Rogue closed the latch to the small iron door that marked the shaft from outside, then darted along the edge of the drive toward the carriage house, heading for the acres of forest surrounding the private parcel of land tucked away out of town—a forest that would no doubt one day be delivered to the very same shaft the thief had just exited.

The thief's movements blended with the wind blowing through the pine trees that lined the sides and back of the property. Coming to a long stone wall, Red quickly leapt up and sprang out onto the open lawn that led back toward the forest. A low run took the thief to the forest's edge where Red paused in the shadows, crouching on the ground for a moment, considering the night.

Then, turning swiftly, Red disappeared into darkness.

* * *

Archie Prescot was unable to resist his first morning impulse to wind the pocket watch that lay on his bedside table. It had become an unbreakable habit at an early age, and now, at the age of twenty-nine, it didn't feel like something worth the effort of changing.

He placed his fingers around the knob and turned. Once for his father, once for his mother, and once for God in heaven.

His mother had taught him that, and the phrase still slid through his mind whenever he wound the watch. It had once been his grandfather's, though now it resembled its original appearance only in the most mechanical sense. He'd never liked the idea of a self-winding watch; by winding his own watch he felt like he had some measurable control over time. In his nimble fingers he could hold time at bay, correct it, soothe it and its hold on him.

Then again, every watchmaker possessed these skills.

He turned his pocket watch over in large hands with fingers so fat no one would assume he could manipulate such fine things as clockworks.

By the dawning light just beginning to creep through the window, he studied what he could make of his reflection in the casing, though it required he hold the gold surface practically at the end of his nose. This angle made him look ranarian—a word that unfortunately was a perfect descriptor of himself, especially once he put on the round glasses that seemed to magnify his near-sighted eyes.

He'd come across the word while reading once and it had stuck with him, and occasionally leapt out at him whenever he shined his grandfather's pocket watch to the point his own frog-like features stared back at him, for that was the meaning of the word. Then again, anyone might look frog-like when viewing their reflection in the casing of a pocket watch.

But the rest of him was no better. He was pear-shaped, with a bottom that spoke to his many hours spent seated at a desk hunched over movements, dials, faces, and hands too tiny to be seen without special glasses. His short black hair was curly if he let it grow too long, which made it extremely unfashionable and difficult to manage. It didn't matter if he parted it down the middle, as was the current fashion, or to either side, it still liked to spring up into little curls around his ears. To make matters worse, he couldn't seem to grow a mustache for the life of him, and if he did manage to get a few sprouts of fur above his up-per lip, that was all it appeared to be: fur. And no one wanted to talk to someone with a little black caterpillar attempting to nab their attention the whole time.

He lay back down in the strange bed, wide awake too early to rise but too late to attempt a return to what had been an uncomfortable sleep, as seemed to be common for him whenever he moved to new lodgings. This time he'd only be here a few months, till the end of summer, or at least, that was the plan, but Archie well knew that the best-laid plans of nicer men... Wait, was that right? No matter, the fact was all plans—the well-laid and the not-so-well-laid—had a tendency to go awry. Just look at how he'd ended up lying here, boarding in the home of a detective and his wife almost 3,000 miles from home.

From a young age he'd been fascinated by his father's ability to "tame time," as he put it. It had been many years before he'd learned his father was simply a watchmaker. To Archie, he'd always seemed to be more like a medieval wizard, capable of unspeakable beauty one minute, and hurtful devastation the next. With his hands he could create, molding time into the shape of a clock, but with his words he knew only how to tear down and destroy.

And yet, Archie couldn't hold back his interest in the tenuous link between sound and time, and so, early on, he'd sat at his father's workbench loving how he could manipulate each steel comb and pinned barrel combination into a chime that was unique. Some said Archie had the gift. He had never thought of it as such, however, as he knew how much time, energy, and effort had gone into learning the art. He was like a violinist who appeared capable of playing the most intricate symphonies without pause, though in reality his fingers had once grown numb with practice, the tips blistering to the point of bleeding before callousing in just the right places.

But he wasn't a violinist, he was a clockmaker—a much more time-consuming occupation.

He chuckled to himself at his little joke as he rolled over.

It was thanks to his gift he had been hired to design the new clock tower feature for the Great Northern Railroad Depot in Spokane. He'd had little to say in the matter. His boss at Seth Thomas in Connecticut had heard they wanted a weight-operated clock in the new depot in Spokane and had told Frost and Granger of Chicago, who'd been drawing up the plans, that Archie must be the man to design it. And so by mail, telegram, and even telephone, Archie and the other contractors from across the nation had exchanged ideas and plans until the day came for Archie to make his way clear across the country, all the way from the great state of Connecticut to the much younger state of Washington to complete his sketches for his unique handcrafted tower clock.

Archie tossed back the other direction, debating whether to get up. He didn't want to bother the entire household on only his third morning.

Finally he gave in and hoisted himself out of bed, putting his glasses on in order to find his clothes. Once clothed, he picked up his satchel and pulled the strap over his head and across his shoulder, checking to ensure all the contents were safely confined within, before sneaking down the stairs and out the back door. Then he turned and began making his way toward the incline of the hill to the south as the sun rose overhead in parallel.

* * *

The house was in mourning. Dark, gray shadows crept out from the acanthus leaves decorating the corners of the ceiling and crawled down the walls, daring the light to peek through the heavy maroon drapes shrouding the windows.

Marian Kenyon ran her fingers over the anaglypta wallpaper as she walked down the hall and into the front parlor. The pattern of stylized crosses and flowers took her back to a time when she had finally become tall enough to reach them with her fingertips, and had taken to running her fingers along the embossed wall whenever she walked through her home.

She hadn't found it in herself yet to pull back the draperies. What was the use? There was no one to see anyway. She often preferred a lack of companionship, though other twenty-three-year-old women might think her odd because of this. Everyone else had sisters, a mother, or at least girlfriends to sit with after the passing of a family member, but Marian just had herself.

And Nain's empty chair.

The daisy-printed Sheraton armless parlor chair stared at her, the black eyes of the flowers boring into her like the awkward stares of children who don't know any better. No matter where she turned her gaze or where she stood or sat in the house, she could feel those eyes following her, judging her, questioning her thoughts and feelings, much as her grandmother had done in life.

No, that was wrong. Nain had never judged her, even as the world around her had. The orphan. The girl who didn't belong. The girl without a family.

Her grandmother had offered her a home, a heart full of love and compassion, and she'd accepted it. And then she'd thrown it away in one furious moment of independence.

"I'm going to Seattle."

"Nonsense. Whatever for? And however will you afford such a venture?"

"I'll find a way."

And she had. And she'd been gone for five years. And she'd never said goodbye.

She turned from the chair and drifted into the dining room. The baskets of once-fresh flowers were tired and brown, drooping over the wicker sides and resting against the grand oak tabletop, which had only just begun to collect a thin layer of dust. She ran her finger along the edge of the table as she continued padding her way on bare feet toward the dark kitchen.

The cast-iron range in the corner seemed to draw all the light and heat out of the room and into its tightly closed matte-black doors. Marian leaned down and used the front of her long, wool dressing gown to guard her hand as she wrapped her fingers around the steel handle. Nain used to scold her for doing so...

She let down the grate and sifted the ashes and cinders, thinking back on the first time she'd thought she was old enough to start the fire, and had instead only managed to cover herself in a fine cloud of black ash. Oh, what a mess...

She laid the fire now, putting in a few handfuls of dry shavings in the bottom of the grate, then layering small sticks of pinewood, then a few cinders, watching them glow as they nestled into the tempting bits of wood, and finally on top she put a few small lumps of coal. Then she opened all the drafts, closed all the covers, and lit the fire with a match. She knelt there for a short time, watching the cinders and coal light gradually before adding a few more lumps to ensure a nice, hot fire. Then she closed the cover and left the fire to do its work.

She rose and crossed to the sink, filling a kettle with cold water and returning it to the stovetop to boil. She almost settled into one of the simple wooden chairs beside the maple kitchen table, a table ingrained with indelible scratches and marks made from so many pots of chicken and dumpling soup, bread rolls, apple pies...but she couldn't stand the memories and let herself meander back out into the front parlor.

The chair was waiting for her.

She stared at it, daring it to say something in Nain's voice.

And yet, at the same time, almost wishing it would. Anything.

Don't change horses in mid-stream.

Fear the Greeks bearing gifts.

Robin Hood could brave all weathers but a thaw wind.

"All right, all right!" Marian finally said aloud, her voice dry and shaky after days without use.

She threw her petite frame down into what had been her chair—a bentwood rocking chair with an ornate curled design—drawing her knees up to her chest and hugging her arms across her legs like she had as a child. She hadn't worn a corset in days, either. Come to think of it, she couldn't remember the last time she'd gotten properly dressed or gone out into society or answered knocks on the door since returning home...

"I know what you're thinking," she told the chair. "But I'm not going out. What's the use? This town hasn't changed in five years. It'll all be the same as it was before...a bunch of small-town, judgmental, petulant busy bodies eager to tell me what to do with my life now—"

She stopped, her voice cracking.

She'd been sure she'd run out of tears by now.

Apparently not.

But like all tears, there came an end. She rubbed the back of her hand across her wet eyes, letting her feet fall back to the ground. She stood and returned to the kitchen, making her morning cup of tea—a habit she'd been unable to break with the Seattle trend toward bitter coffee—then came back to the hearth in the parlor.

Marian sipped her tea slowly, lifting the china cup gently to her lips, holding the saucer with a steady left hand, just like her Nain had taught.

If only she hadn't arrived too late to see her buried. The only part left to play was to open the home to receive guests wishing to offer condolences in the form of letters, flowers, and words of encouragement.

So now Marian should have been seated sipping tea in a black dress, nodding her head and welcoming the latest visitor. Instead, she sat in her nightgown and robe, drinking tea by herself, the front door locked and the curtains still closed, talking to a chair and staring into the black eyes of daisies.

Why don't you tell me what you're afraid of, they seemed to say in her grandmother's voice.

The truth escaped from her lips before she could stop it. "I don't know if I can do it without you..." Marian had always thought of herself as independent. But it wasn't until Nain's passing that she realized she'd continued to think of her as a place of

safety, somewhere she could fall should it—the future and whatever that held—not work out. But now all that was gone. She was
alone. Completely alone.

But then a chuckle followed. "Well, perhaps not completely
alone. I do have your chair."

She laughed softly at herself, straightened her back, and sat
properly, away from her chair back, feet on the floor, hands
folded in her lap around her cup and saucer. She actually felt
more comfortable than she thought she would.

"Perhaps you're right. As you'd say, Nain, 'If ifs and ands were
pots and pans, there'd be no work for tinkers' hands.' Perhaps it's
time to see if Spokane has changed."

* * *

Miss Mitchell had declared the front parlor must be "spit
spot" at all times in case of guests, and so Eleanor Sigmund began
her day as usual in the room that took the longest thanks to the
amount of Japanesque memorabilia decorating every surface.

Miss Mitchell had declared with every new piece that Eleanor
should take time to familiarize herself with its purpose and history, to ensure she knew how it should look when it was properly
cleaned and displayed.

Miss Mitchell had declared this, and it was so. This was
Eleanor's life, working as the lone housemaid in a large home.
And she accepted it for what it was.

She even enjoyed it. She'd found great contemplative peace
in the Japanese art that now filled Miss Mitchell's home, spilling
out beyond the front parlor. To dust the items one by one was a
rhythmic, meditative dance that allowed her freedom of move-

ment from one area to another, instead of crawling backward on her hands and knees—which seemed to be not quite so willing as they'd been before she'd turned forty—scrubbing her fingers raw, as she'd have to do later. It was a comparatively easy way to begin the day.

She started with the impressive black cabinet in the corner. It was black as night, made from ebonized cherry wood, inlaid with brass flowers on the doors and along the top and bottom on the outside. Inside, the cabinet doors and drawers were lined with blood-red silk embossed with golden cranes and flowers.

Beside the cabinet was a folding screen also of ebonized wood, with gilt decoration along the top and six painted panels of swallows and wisterias against a muted brown background.

Next to the screen sat a dragon bench made of pure ebony. The serpent-like lizard writhed along the back, forcing its tail and its head into armrests on either end. Eleanor pressed her feather duster into the cracks of the scales and the intricate carvings that seemed to bring the creature to life.

Above the bench upon the wall were *noh* theatre masks hanging across an artistic rendering of *kabuki* players enacting a scene from a play. Eleanor identified with the masks because she, too, often felt she had to switch hers out from moment to moment, depending on who she was speaking to. Her favorite of the masks was the chubby, comical one because it made her smile to look at it. The others were almost disturbing, ranging in gender: lovely woman to ugly witch to samurai warrior, emotion: from sad to happy to angry, and even in species: from monkey to dragon to fox—

Wait.

Where was the fox? It was quite distinct because of its red tufts of fur around a white dog-like face. Usually it hung next to the accompanying bright fans dancers would wield as they danced in the New Year, but now there was only a gaping hole where it had once been.

She turned around and her gaze fell on a table where stood a bronze sculpture of a samurai on his warhorse set upon an onyx base. It was flanked by an ormolu glass vase and—where was the Daguet butterfly box?

Eleanor turned from side to side, picking up gold-threaded cushions with stylized cherry blossoms and bamboo shoots, throwing open the doors to the black lacquered chest on a gilt-wood stand embossed with scenes of Japanese homes and geishas.

Her heart found her toes along with all the energy in her body.

With slow, heavy steps that seemed to echo the grandfather clock in the hall resounding the early morning hour, she made her way to the mantelpiece of the fireplace, deftly triggering the secret drawer with the marble branch.

She pulled it all the way out and stared despairingly at the emptiness inside.

* * *

Archie entered quietly through the back door of the small house where he was currently boarding. He was thankful for the lack of inquiry into his whereabouts from persistent mother figures who cloaked themselves in the guise of "housekeeper," as he'd found to be the case in many places he'd boarded in

Connecticut. He had chosen this location for his summer stay because it was let out by a police detective and his wife. The brother who also resided here seemed to work late hours, and Detective Bernard Carew and the missus were of the private sort, like himself, which suited Archie wonderfully.

He was surprised, therefore, when upon entering the front hall he heard the soft *squeak* of wheels and then received a greeting from the flaxen-haired Mrs. Carew.

"Good morning, Mr. Prescot. I hope your morning has started off on the right note," she said as she rolled her chair toward him, a card on her lap. She held this out to him once she was within arm's length. "A card was sent for you by messenger."

He took the calling card. It was lettered in cursive with "Miss Gladys Mitchell" across the front. On the back, above her address, where the time would have been listed, she had written "at your earliest convenience" and along the bottom in small print she'd added, "The clock is broken."

Shock crossed Archie's face but it was quickly replaced by a flush of disappointment.

On his journey cross-country aboard the North Coast Limited, an angel had visited him in the form of Miss Gladys Mitchell, a rather wealthy patroness of the arts in the very town he was traveling to. Unable to sleep one night, he'd made her acquaintance in the dining car, and they'd found they had enough in common to fall deep into conversation. Before he knew it, she'd offered to test one of his latest inventions, something that pushed the boundaries of what sound could do—the invention he'd just happened to bring with him, since he'd hoped to find the time to tinker with it more when he wasn't working on official projects. He'd delivered the clock to her house only yesterday and had hoped to hear from her sometime before he returned home at the end of summer.

"Mrs. Carew, you are the pinochle of politeness," said Archie, placing the card into his black vest pocket.

"Isn't it a bit early to be playing games?" came Bernard Carew's gruff voice as he joined them from the bedroom. He was still straightening his tie as he leaned down to kiss his wife's cheek. He was a grizzly bear of a man—broad, tall, and thick. His heavy black mustache and matching eyebrows were surely a deterrent to any criminal who happened across his path, and his gaze probably forced truths out of the most defiant.

But with his wife he was as kind-tempered as Kipling's Baloo in every manner.

"I think Mr. Prescot meant 'pinnacle,' dear," said Mrs. Carew kindly.

Archie blushed. He did have a tendency to say the wrong word at the oddest moments, especially when he was feeling flustered. And to hear his clock was broken already? His heart sank. Perhaps it was simply God's way of popping his pride a bit.

"I do hope the messenger did not interrupt your own morning," said Archie, glancing from Mrs. to Mr. and back again. "I would hate to think my private business was encroaching upon your home life."

"Not at all, Mr. Prescot," Mrs. Carew said brusquely, her voice reminding Archie of his boss back at Seth Thomas, who lived by the belief that busy bees were the standard to which all men must aspire. "I rise with the housemaids, never one to waste life with unneeded sleep when there is work to be done."

"And I've overslept as it is," said Bernard, reaching for his hat and coat off the stand in the hall.

"You really should eat something first, dear," said his wife, but the detective shrugged and shook his head.

"I'm sorry, my rose." He pecked her on the cheek once more, even with Archie standing there watching. It was nice to see a couple who didn't mind showing a little affection before a stranger. "I promise I'll be home for dinner. Have a good day, Mr. Prescot." He tipped his hat and was out the door before Archie could reply.

He turned back to Mrs. Carew. "Thank you for taking the message for me. I shall attend to it immediately. I am sorry you had to bring it to me."

"Actually, as my companion is abed not feeling well, I thought I might join you for breakfast. It was mere happenstance that I met you on my way."

"I am sorry to hear Miss Gillen is ill. Please do let me know if I can be of any assistance to you."

"Nonsense, Mr. Prescot. I cannot have my guest replacing my companion. I am perfectly capable of buttering my own toast and getting myself hither and thither."

Archie smiled. It had taken someone pointedly asking him if he found it difficult staying in a house with an invalid before he realized that most people might view Mrs. Carew as such because of her chair. His own grandfather had lived his life atop crutches after losing his left leg to an infection. Like Mrs. Carew, he'd never let it slow him down.

Archie poured himself a cup of milk with just an inch of bitter coffee before sitting with Mrs. Carew to attempt enjoyment of the household cook's simple breakfast: mealy baked cinnamon apples, undercooked oatmeal with sugar and cream, watery eggs, burnt ham, and toast with un-pitted cherry jam. They ate in un-encumbered silence until they were finished and Archie took his leave.

With breakfast sitting a bit too heavily in his belly, he climbed onboard the streetcar a few blocks east of the house, clinking his five cents into the collection bin before taking a seat in the back. He soon found himself attracted by the elegant pocket watch held by the man seated across the aisle from him. It was a Seth Thomas, probably made around 1889, encased in embossed gold that glistened from cleaning. The man was watching the minute hand tick slowly around the face with the air of one counting the seconds in between, so Archie didn't disrupt his meditation. Instead, he pulled his gaze away to study the passing neighborhoods as the car glided up the steep hill on the south side of town. He was increasingly impressed by the smoothness with which an electric tram could travel, so much so that he would have pulled out his sketchbook if his stop hadn't come up so quickly.

He disembarked at 29th, finding himself on a dirt road where the houses thinned and turned back into the forest of pines and maples that had once covered this entire area. He came to an iron gate and a long drive, which he walked up with confidence, knowing he was expected, though he recalled his trepidation on his first visit just a couple days prior.

The grandeur of the house still amazed him as he approached. Built in a rambling Tudor style, the house boasted a white stucco exterior crisscrossed with dark brown timber on the second and third floors, red brick and sandstone on the first, steeply pitched roofs, and mullioned windows, unique in their colored glass. Ornate brick chimneys rose above the slanted roof—he counted four just on the house from this side, and one on the carriage house tucked away to the west. It was the sort of house that transported one to someplace more like a Grimm fairyland than Washington.

He walked up the long white front porch—complete with anomalous columns that didn't seem to go with the rest of the house—to the imposing front door, taking in the stained glass windows on either side portraying bright white cherry blossoms against a vibrant blue sky. After ringing the bell, he was admitted by a tall and impressive butler who took his hat and coat before leaving him in the front parlor.

He may have only been in Spokane for two days, but already he'd noticed the fascination with Japanese art that seemed to be leaking across the city. Archie was pretty sure the headwaters of the leak were in Miss Mitchell's front parlor.

The black furniture, wooden panels, and rich colors were simple and elegant; the intricate design-work practically hidden along the edges was eye-catching and mesmerizing. The inked art showing birds on bamboo, waves in the ocean, and red flowers against black backgrounds was graceful and winsome. Or would have been, if it hadn't been *everywhere*. Every surface had been inlaid with images of scholars, geishas, bamboo trees, and cherry blossoms.

As Miss Mitchell swept into the room dressed in bright yellow, however, he reminded himself that she had proven to be a highly intellectual woman capable of lengthy discourse on technological subjects. Her fashionable beauty and tastes were only the most obvious part of her.

"Mr. Prescot, welcome. Thank you for coming so quickly," she said languidly, in direct opposition to her words. He'd forgotten the deep, slow way she spoke, like she had all the time in the world. Which, with her money, she probably did. "I'll come straight to it: last night I was robbed."

"Robbed, Miss Mitchell? Already?"

"Yes. Robbed." She clasped her hands before her and he realized she was wearing some new fashion cut to look like a Japanese kimono with bloomers. Her clearly defined legs and bare ankles above soft shoes were less of a distraction than they might have been if the situation hadn't been so serious. "You understand what this means, of course?"

"My idea did not work…"

"Indeed." Miss Mitchell waved her hand, the gold on her wrists twinkling, toward the clock on the mantelpiece, whose hands were stuck at a minute to twelve.

"May I?" Archie asked as he stepped toward the fireplace.

Miss Mitchell nodded, drifting toward a small table in the corner and helping herself to a decanter of auburn liquid. He lifted his clock carefully in his hands, allowing the minute hand to reach twelve and waiting for the chimes to sound off.

They were melodious and mesmerizing. He felt himself getting drowsy as he considered the problem. What problem was that again?

"Mr. Prescot, would you mind?"

Archie turned sluggishly to see that Miss Mitchell had her hands over her ears.

He set the clock back on the mantelpiece, popped open the glass over the clock face, and forced the minute hand back around to a minute to twelve, resetting the mechanism. The chimes stopped.

Miss Mitchell let her hands fall, collecting a crystal glass with an inch of liquid in it. "I'm not certain I quite understand why you thought this would deter thieves. All he'd have to do is cover his ears."

"Yes, but how many thieves do you know who'd expect a clock to start sounding twelve chimes when it's not midnight? I strongly suspect the thief considered stealing the piece, then replaced it on the mantel to avoid anymore outbursts of noise." He stopped, realizing he'd spoken without thinking, and nodded his head slightly toward the woman who was clearly a class above him. "Ma'am."

"Never mind the 'ma'am,' Mr. Prescot. I would hope you'd respect me enough to speak to me as your equal in matters of technology." She draped herself across the settee, her glass in one hand. She took a long sip before saying, "Explain it to me again and perhaps I can help fix it."

Archie tried to hide the doubt that leapt across his face by studying his hands.

"Yes, well..." He paused, preparing his thoughts in an orderly procession, like the mechanism of his clock, before pushing his glasses up his nose and meeting Miss Mitchell's pursed lips and expectant gaze. "Well, see, inside there's a brass ball track and it's precariously balanced: any movement makes the ball go down the track, hit a pressure plate, and roll into a basket, setting off the chimes. After the pressure plate is hit, the gears wind to set the chimes off, which takes one minute, so they'll go off at 'midnight' even though it might be any hour but twelve. When the chimes sound, the repetitive frequency, tone, and melody are meant to hypnotize the thief to sleep, so they can be apprehended upon discovery. Though the hour hand does not move, the minute hand continues around the face and stops at a minute to twelve, resetting the mechanism. As the minute hand turns, the basket moves along the track and returns the ball back into its original placement."

On the most basic level, at least, that was how it worked. He was suddenly aware of how he'd been waving his hands about crazily while attempting to explain the inner workings of something he knew to be as complex as a typewriter.

But to his astonishment, Miss Mitchell appeared to have followed this description and was nodding her head in approval. "And all that fits into a mantel clock. Mr. Prescot, I must say, I am quite impressed."

Archie beamed and stilled his hands, but before he could thank her for the compliment she continued.

"I also must admit, I liked the reminder to live life as though it all ends at midnight, like something out of a story, but perhaps therein lies the issue. Perhaps the clock must work as a clock, so the thief gets farther away before the chimes sound?"

"Perhaps." Archie turned back to his clock.

"Or perhaps the chimes need not lull the thief to sleep, but instead must be loud and irritating enough to alert my staff of an intruder?"

"Perhaps." He delicately closed the front, admiring the beauty of his own design.

"Or perhaps you're a regular Wisenheimer who thinks he's got it all figured out?"

Archie pivoted away from his clock quickly, his arms dropping to his sides as his neck reddened.

"I apologize, Miss Mitchell." Perhaps she wasn't as impressed as he'd thought. "Thank you for allowing me to test my invention in your home. I am sorry it did not work as I had intended." He could feel the heat climbing from his neck to his cheeks as his voice and head lowered like a disciplined dachshund. "I can remove it, if you'd prefer..."

"No need, Mr. Prescot." His head shot up again as he pushed his glasses back up his nose. She finished her drink and smiled at him. "I enjoyed seeing your idea brought to life. If no one had taken a chance on my designs, I would not be here with you today, able to support you as a patroness."

Archie's eyes widened. He was suddenly very aware of his hands again and was unsure where to put them. Behind his back? In his pockets? "Well, knock me over with a fetter. My patroness? You would be willing to...? You'd do that for me?"

"Indeed, Mr. Prescot. With a wave of my hand, I could make all your ideas come true." She stood, leaving her glass on a side table and crossing to stand before him. Close to him. A cloying scent of roses wafted from her. "On one condition: that you be willing to involve me in your process and would consider my critiques when I share them."

Archie dipped his head immediately, still amazed at the gift this woman was bestowing upon him. "Of course, ma'am. I would be delighted to hear your perspective."

* * *

It took Marian until close to midday to finally escape the darkness of the quiet house in Browne's Addition.

She might've blamed it on the fruitless search for her button hook before resorting to her fingers or the time spent re-binding herself into a corset—though she actually enjoyed the return of its supportive hug around her middle—or the mad attempt to contain all of her auburn curls in one pinned bun at the back of her head while also maintaining the adequate pompadour required to meet the current fashion.

It even might have been the fact that after all this time, she still had no mourning jewelry or black dresses of her own, being one whose complexion didn't work well with black, and one who decidedly avoided the popular morbid obsession with death. This meant, however, that if she intended to go out into society she would have to go through her grandmother's own mourning ensembles to find something that fit.

For someone who avoided the idea of death, Marian had found it incredibly difficult to pick through the jet-like dark brown wood of the bog oak jewelry her grandmother had preferred. And then to make a selection from the dull choices of crepe dresses with their deep black silk gauze, crimped and stiffened into a texture that would only irritate her skin...

But it really wasn't any of those things that slowed her pace this morning. It was the memories that came with them. The memories of Nain telling her even as a little girl that a woman must always have a mourning ensemble handy.

The idea had always sickened her. To own a mourning dress

in the current fashion—and those fashions changed every sea-
son—seemed to Marian a way of supporting an industry that
made its money on death, a decidedly disgusting fact. To force
those who'd just lost their loved ones to shell out another several
dollars because society dictated this year one must be seen in
bombazine instead of paramatta—well, it was a very Victorian
ideal. And this was America. And a new century. And as of January and Queen Victoria's death, wasn't this actually a new era
anyway?

But, if she didn't wear black, and happened to pass one of her
Nain's dear friends, well...she'd do it for Nain.

But she'd still wear her forest green overcoat.

And so, finally, Marian stood on the front porch and inhaled
a deep breath of fresh, brisk April air and the smell of pine
before making her way to the nearest stop for the streetcar to
downtown.

Marian was proven right immediately: it was the same old
Spokane. As the streetcar rumbled along Riverside, she caught
sight of the standard Salvation Army parade: three musi-
cians—two women and one man—and not a single person on the
streets stopping to listen, though they sang and yelled and called
down fire and brimstone on anyone who dared pass by. Signs
advertised "umbrellas for just $2 apiece" and "shaving 25 cents."
They passed numerous carriages with young men seated between
two young ladies out for a midday ride, the horses used to the
clang of the streetcar by now. Along the edges of the road raced
many a bicycle rider—working men and women—most of them
rushing to the canteen for their hour-long luncheon break, no
doubt.

She took in the city as she stepped off the streetcar downtown. In her absence, Spokane's rail yards had taken over Havermale Island at the head of Spokane Falls, for which the city had originally been named. The cacophony of clanging streetcars, *clip-clop* of horses' hooves, rumbling wheels of carriages, ringing bells of bicycles, not-so-distant train whistles, and the reverberating *clash* of metalwork from construction sites was almost too much.

Amidst the noise and city smells rose the magnificent brick, stone, and terra cotta buildings that had grown out of the devastation of the Great Fire back in 1889. Thirty-two blocks of downtown had been destroyed, but by destroying the old, the new had been given its head, and out of the ashes, the phoenix of Spokane had risen. Of course, at that time it had still been Spokane Falls.

Marian walked toward the namesake of the city and let the roar and rush fill her ears. Drowning out the city sounds. Letting her soul rest in the thundering of the waterfall.

She'd missed this. There was nothing like it in Seattle.

She wished she'd brought her camera out with her after all. It had been too long since she'd felt its ponderous weight between her hands. The monolithic task of attempting to capture nature's beauty in a small frame had helped give her a sense of control in a world that often was as un-capture-able as the falls before her.

She hadn't touched her camera since Nain's passing...

Finally, with a sigh, she turned her back on the river and considered where she'd go next.

Her first thought was to go to the New York Kitchen on Washington—her favorite place to eat luncheon before—and was saddened to find that it had been replaced by something called the Pioneer Restaurant. She was still debating on whether to attempt the new place when she nearly collided with a man hurrying along the sidewalk.

"I'm sorry, miss, I didn't see you there," the gentleman said smoothly.

His voice was too oily, and his suave, debonair charm seemed to be at odds with something in the man's green eyes.

"Good day, miss," he said, tipping his hat to her. "Mr. Cecil Sigmund, at your service, Miss..." He removed his hat entirely and bowed, revealing a head of shocking curly hair the color of an orange tabby cat.

"Miss Kenyon," Marian said slowly.

"Ah, you must be the granddaughter of Mrs. Kenyon, then. So sorry for your loss," he purred.

"Um, thank you. I am sorry, but how did you know my grandmother?"

"You know Spokane—a small town striving to be a big city. I'm afraid I must be on my way." He tipped his hat to her once more and continued along, pulling leather driving gloves out of his overcoat pocket and onto his hands.

Marian gave an involuntary shiver as she watched the tabby cat saunter north up Washington toward the Falls. Then she turned around and headed south toward the ten sets of railroad tracks that cut straight through downtown. She recalled her grandfather complaining about the tracks, saying they required one to plan an extra quarter-hour travel time in case of delay when attempting to reach destinations in the center of town. It wasn't the time delay so much as the smell and noise of the engines that bothered her. But nothing could be done, nor would be done, about an industry that was the cause for all the booming life coming into Spokane.

Once across, she kept going, wending her way through the streets past tall blocks of businesses and lodging houses. Soon she was out of the main city, amongst residential homes, and found she was hiking up the hill to the south, out of the valley where Spokane's downtown nestled along the river. She walked along the roads of her youth like a woman with a purpose, though she had none. She dismissed the idea of taking the streetcar that seemed to be traveling her way up Grand, deciding what she needed was a refreshing walk.

In Seattle she had always enjoyed the exertion of energy required to get places. She'd never been one to sit demurely by, nor one to pay for expensive carriages or even streetcars. When she'd first arrived in Seattle she hadn't had more than her meager savings, and so she'd accustomed herself to living frugally. And the lifestyle had stuck.

Roughly two miles later, she began to slow down as she realized she'd come to Montrose Park, and felt that this was where she'd meant to come all along.

Here was an island of quiet amidst the roar of a city with growing pains.

Mirror Lake still sparkled with small laughing ripples that mirrored the deep April blue sky, sweeping meandering ducks from one end to the next. Three yellow ducklings followed their momma in a v-shape, the proud papa in the lead. Wild flowers edged curves in the lane in yellows and purples and pinks, and the fruit trees and hawthorns were just starting to bud in premature anticipation of warmer weather. Adventurous couples bundled in cloaks and overcoats found warmth in the brisk morning air by walking swiftly along the paths. The sun was just bright enough overhead to give hope that spring had begun, though her Nain would say, "It is not spring until you can plant your foot upon twelve daisies."

The small path that wound around hills and through spring foliage guided her gently to where the wild roses made their home, giving the park its name. She took a deep breath as though the flowers were in bloom, though she knew it would be another month or two before they would appear. Wild roses. Her grandmother's favorite: "Beautiful in bloom, but sharp enough to protect themselves."

The stillness.

The solitude.

It met her heart in just the right place. She found an available bench where she could sit quietly and take it all in—for about five minutes before someone interrupted her calm by stomping through the underbrush behind her.

She stood and peered through the trees, reaching for her chatelaine purse whilst attempting to determine whether she needed to make a lady-like escape. Then she saw it was only some overweight man with a satchel slung over one shoulder; in the palm of his right hand was a small box with a grooved brass horn, and with his left he was turning a miniature crank on the side. His hat was an older-styled black homburg that wasn't fitted to his head properly because it squashed his ears down slightly on either side—either that, or his ears were just of the size and type that did not work well with a homburg. He wore thick glasses that made his brown eyes appear somewhat frog-like, and had a thin bit of fur growing above his upper lip that looked like a caterpillar trying to escape out of his nose.

Altogether, a very un-worrying man.

"Ahem," she cleared her throat, raising her hand in a small wave.

The man looked up at her sharply. "Ah! I'm terribly sorry! I didn't mean to disturb anyone. I'll just find another bit of woods, then."

"Whatever are you doing?" Marian asked curiously, taking a small step forward.

The man stopped where he was and looked to his left, then his right, then back at Marian, as though trying to think of a good answer.

"Just out for a stroll?"

Marian heard the question at the end of the statement. She brushed a stray curl behind her ear. "I'm afraid, sir, you'll have to do better than that. No one goes 'strolling' through the woods with a strange weapon in their hands."

"Oh, no! No! I promise you it isn't a weapon," the man said quickly, pointing the funnel-shaped horn toward Marian. She leapt hastily out of the line of fire. "I promise!" He quickly pointed the horn toward the ground. "Would you like to see it?"

Marian looked about to see if there were any witnesses. No one. And she hadn't seen anyone nearby as she made her way through the park. But then she considered the heavy-set man and figured, perhaps impolitely, that she could always outrun him. Besides, she really had nothing to lose, and she was extremely curious about what he was doing... As her Nain would say, "There is nothing lost by civility."

She met the kind brown eyes behind the glasses.

"Is it a recording device?" she asked by way of an answer.

His wide-eyed gape of surprise told her she was right before he nodded. "Well, knock me over with a fetter, yes, actually." The man started crunching out to her.

Marian ignored the malapropism and continued in her curiosity. "It looks like a Graphophone or phonograph, but I've never seen one so small."

"You surely haven't. I hadn't either till I made one myself." The man beamed proudly. "The manufacturers of the original Graphophone are located in Bridgeport, Connecticut, just south of my home in Thomaston. It was surprisingly simple to take a larger one apart and figure out how to make it smaller for personal use."

"'Simple'? I doubt that. Otherwise, the company itself would have made some themselves by now."

The man's cheeks reddened and his shoulders straightened.

"What were you recording? Your stomping through the brush was too loud for you to be attempting to capture birdsong."

"Actually, the stomping is what I was recording. I've been collecting different resonation frequencies to determine a solid vibration pattern that will work for an idea I've got."

"I see."

"Well, actually, for all intensive purposes, you *hear*," the man said, blushing and smiling in a manner that indicated he was trying to be humorous. "Did you know every person's footsteps are unique? Given the different shoes they wear, the size of their feet, and the weight upon those feet?"

"That makes some sense, I suppose." She lifted her skirts slightly and contemplated her own boots. The salesman had sold them to her as being made from some new material. All she knew was he'd told her they would make her steps quiet, something she preferred over the incessant *tap, tap, tap* of heels.

"Ah, the new 'gutta-percha' boots," the man said, following her gaze. "I've heard of those. Such an interesting material. It's a gummy substance that can be heated and then hardened into a tough latex rubber. It's used in many ways: mourning jewelry, canes, walking sticks...shoes." He pointed.

Marian laughed. "Well, I didn't know about all that, but they've certainly proven their five dollars' worth. They've been so comfortable I haven't even considered my feet until this moment." She clicked them together now and only heard a soft *squeak* in return.

"Inducibly."

Marian smiled. Spokane still had its characters.

* * *

Archie smiled in return. Spokane had such characters. Where else would he find two women who were actually interested in science? Things seemed to be shaping up very well for him in Spokane.

"I'm Archibald Prescot," he said, sweeping off his best hat.

"Marian Kenyon." She gave a small curtsy, tucking a stray curl behind her ear as she rose. The dark green of her coat made the green of her eyes feel all the more intense as she regarded him.

"So, what do you do when you're not frightening young ladies by stomping through the underbrush?"

"I'm a clockmaker. I was sent here by the Seth Thomas Company in Connecticut to design a tower clock for the new Great Northern Railroad Depot."

"That's quite a mouthful," Miss Kenyon said. Her smile carried into her eyes. "How long will you be in town then?"

"I just arrived a couple days ago, actually, and plan to stay through the summer, at least, to ensure my design ideas will work with the tower they've planned. I hope to create a new sound for the chimes."

"Don't all clocks sound alike? They all go *bong* as far as I know."

Archie gave a small laugh. "Not my clocks."

"Excuse me? Your clocks don't go *bong*? Do they *tick tock*? Whatever is the world coming to if our clocks stop *ticking* and *tocking*?"

He chuckled. "My clocks still *tick* and *tock* if that's any help. As that's a mechanical noise, I'm not sure how to do more than dampen it. But the chimes themselves, well, listen to this."

He tucked the small Graphophone back into his satchel and pulled out his pocket watch and held it out to her. She stepped toward him and reached out but then pulled her hand back, as though half expecting it to shock her.

"It won't bite."

She arched an eyebrow before taking the watch carefully in her hands.

"It's heavier than most watches," she said, turning it over in her hand and taking in the simple embossment around the edges.

It was 14K gold, but he knew that wasn't what made it feel heavy. Inside, he'd managed to fit twelve unique chimes on one rotating wheel.

"Open it," he encouraged.

She popped open the cover and the soft, tinkling sound of wind chimes emerged.

"One o'clock," he said.

She looked up at him, the watch face hidden behind her fingers. "How did you know?"

"Each hour's chime is a different sound, so I can know what time it is without looking at my pocket watch, and without the monotonous *bongs*."

Her mouth actually swung open. What a great reaction. He hoped he could surprise her more.

"That's what I hope to do with the clock tower, as well. I want to record different songs in a variety of sounds for each hour, and at each quarter-hour it should play a quarter of the song. If every hour a different song rings out, no matter where you are in Spokane, when you hear the bells, you'll know what time it is before the *bongs*, if they're even still necessary."

Her eyes widened. The green in them darkened when she was surprised.

"That is...incredible!"

Yes, he definitely wanted to show her more.

* * *

Eleanor wrung the chamois skin out of the warm water and rubbed the windows in the living room, wiping them down afterward with a dry cloth.

Next, she grabbed the paraffin oil lamps; there were exactly thirteen in this room alone—she had to ensure there were always exactly the same number, thirteen being an unlucky number, and therefore to have any fewer would naturally signify something devilish was in the works. It took her several trips to carry them all downstairs to the kitchen. There she filled three large pots with cold water, placed the lamp chimneys in the pots, and placed them on the stovetop, turning the gas up on the range so the heat would gradually warm the water until it reached boiling point.

While the chimneys warmed, she refilled the lamp bottoms with oil and replaced the wicks on those that were getting too short. Once the water boiled, she turned off the burners and removed the kettles to the sideboard, out of Mrs. Curry's way, to let them sit in the water until it was cold before removing the glass.

Eventually, she knew, these lamps would no longer be required, as Miss Mitchell had already had the house built with electrical wiring in the walls—something Eleanor thought unnecessarily risky. She did not know why Miss Mitchell had not as yet made use of the sconces, but she did know it was better not to question those above her station.

She returned to the living room with her broom and dustpan in hand and began the sweeping of all the wood floors and carpets. After sweeping them, she took out the kerosene oil and a woolen cloth to polish all the hardwood floors, rubbing first with a small amount of oil followed by a clean cloth. Then on to the furniture, using equal parts linseed oil and turpentine to give them a beautiful shine. The piano keys were a simple matter of being rubbed with—

"Ah, the sweet smell of alcohol."

Her spine straightened. She kept moving her hand, but the cloth was barely touching the keys.

A jacketed arm wrapped around her waist and her entire body stiffened.

"Good afternoon, my dear."

His voice. A fox speaking to a chicken couldn't sound more seductive yet frightening.

She turned out of his arm, keeping her eyes focused on the embroidered rug at her feet, her hands clasped before her, still holding the cloth and bottle of alcohol.

She had a brief vision of throwing the alcohol in his face but it passed quickly.

"Good afternoon, Mr. Sigmund." She curtsied to her husband.

He reached out and grabbed her arm, roughly bringing her wrist up to his mouth to kiss it, inhaling the scent that was drifting up from the cloth. He sighed.

"It won't be long now, my dear," he purred, using his other hand to tuck under her chin and force her eyes to meet his. "We'll be able to leave this coop soon enough and you'll never have to clean again."

His eyes—so green. The Irish red curls of his hair peeked out from beneath his chauffeur's cap. He'd been so handsome once. But his nose was now wrinkled in a permanent sneer that pulled up the edges of his mouth. Even his smile was patronizing.

She allowed him to look at her, but wouldn't let her true feelings show in her eyes. Her fear she'd keep locked away in her heart, though she realized her hand was gripping the bottle of alcohol so tightly it might crack. She tried to force her fingers to relax but they weren't responding.

He patted her cheek, but then gripped her face, forcing her head to the left and then to the right.

"You should be more careful. A pretty face like yours shouldn't show such blemishes."

She flinched as he tapped the bruise hidden just below her hairline behind her ear. She'd tried to twist her hair this morning in a way that left enough looseness to cover the yellow and purple mark but apparently she hadn't been successful.

"I'm sorry." She tipped her head and averted her eyes as soon as he let go of her face.

"I'm going out. Don't wait up for me."

She nodded as she studied the carpet, not really hearing, praying with all her heart that he'd just leave.

When he finally let go of her wrist, he left behind his handprint.

* * *

Archie was having an extraordinary day. It seemed that nothing could go wrong.

He'd spent the most delightful midday discussing the science of sound with Miss Marian Kenyon, a young lady of incredible affinity and understanding. He'd noted the sad undertones of her later dialogue in the garden, and her black mourning jewelry beneath her green coat, but he'd also noticed how she attempted to keep the conversation focused on him and not her, and so he'd allowed it. Who was he to argue with a lady, after all?

He'd been asked to return to Miss Mitchell's home that afternoon to meet with another inventor she was patronizing, which was why he'd gone only so far as Montrose Park to spend the intervening hours. What luck he had been there at the same time as Miss Kenyon!

As he made his way back now, he considered which notes he'd share. His Big Idea, the one he'd been working on in his spare time for the past two years or so, was one he didn't intend to share at this first meeting. But should he find an encouraging, intelligent, inquisitive mind, much like Miss Kenyon's but in the head of another inventor, he might reconsider.

His idea was so simple, really. In a small chamber filled with water he would set a tuning fork at the wide-mouth end of a funnel, the small end focused on a gear, which was connected to another gear connected to another gear, as gears were wont to do. What Archie hoped to figure out was what combination of chambers, tuning fork, water volume, and gears worked together in the correct order, size, shape, resonation, frequency, and decibel in order to get sound wave vibrations to make the gears move. A "sound engine" of sorts.

It would take years and years of research, of course, but with the rise of the automobile—of which there were a growing number back home, and yet none, at least that he'd seen, so far in Spokane—he felt his engine just might be a perfect companion to run the things. It'd be better than those smelly gasoline engines or those dangerous electrical engines. He'd even come up with a name for them already: the "cot"—short for Prescot.

He was ushered for the second time that day into the overwhelmingly Japanese front parlor, but this time he was left alone as the grandfather clock struck three o'clock in the hall. He took a moment to admire the items displayed around his clock that he'd missed before, unable to stop himself from picking up an ornate blue-and-white vase with an intricate story portrayed around it, following the trail of a woman in a kimono who walked along a river sadly, but then appeared to be happier after talking to a fish. He set the vase down and turned to his clock, running a finger along the face.

Archie wondered what the other inventor would be like. Would he be interested in what Archie liked to call "sound theory"? Or would he be reticent to allow another inventor near his patroness? What if he saw Archie as a threat rather than a counterpart? Perhaps he'd sabotage his work to avoid sharing Miss Mitchell? What if this was exactly like how Tesla and Edison had begun?

"You must be Mr. Prescot," said a sonorous, smooth voice like cold steel.

Archie jumped, searching for the origin of the voice. And then, like an optical illusion, a man stepped from the far corner of the room, walking in a slow, sure manner.

How long had he been standing there? The man had blended into the room, becoming one with the masks on the wall and the dark furniture.

He had skin the color of Archie's morning coffee, and was ageless. The soft crinkles around his dark eyes might have been age lines indicating half a century, or might have been laugh lines indicating youth, though the short black beard encircling his mouth and outlining his round face indicated somewhere in between. He wore a simple white collared shirt, with the sleeves rolled up above his elbows, revealing forearms marred by hard work of some sort. Incongruously stuck in the belt of his black suit pants hung what looked like a phonograph horn on the end of a gun.

The man offered a thickly callused hand to Archie, bending slightly at the waist as he did so, his eyes resting on Archie's pocket watch that hung from a chain across his vest. Archie took the hand in greeting, also half-bowing out of respect. As they unclasped and rose, Archie noticed his eyes. If eyes were the windows to the soul, his were closed with shutters.

Archie was unsure how exactly to respond since Miss Mitchell hadn't revealed the name of the inventor he was to meet. He was saved the question.

"I am Hayate Matsumoto." His voice was so deep, so fluid, like a river babbling over small rocks. The man waved an inviting hand toward the cherry blossom-embroidered settee as he took a seat on the ebony dragon bench opposite.

Archie had never spoken to someone from Asia, though he knew enough to understand it was incorrect to think of the Japanese as the same as the Chinese. A mysterious island native, from a land that had only in the last fifty years opened its borders to allow a freer exchange of ideas, this Mr. Matsumoto was as unquantifiable as a new element. He wondered what sort of inventor this man was, but guessed it had something to do with the weapon at his side.

"I'm sorry." Archie realized he'd been staring and forced his gaze onto his clock, the sight giving him a focal point to rest his thoughts and steady his heart.

"I understand you designed the clock on the mantel." Archie

looked back at Matsumoto. The man was smiling, and suddenly his eyes didn't seem quite so shuttered.

Archie took a deep breath. There was no need to be intimidated by a man he did not yet know, nor unsettled by the color of his skin. He was a person, a scientifically minded person just like himself. He hadn't understood precisely how sound traveled when he'd first heard a clock chime, and yet now he had one that could lull a listener to sleep. Who knew what the future might bring from a partnership with this man?

"Yes, I did," he said as he sat upon the settee. "Did Miss Mitchell tell you what it does?"

"Yes, but she did not need to. One touch and I could tell it was crafted with care and attention. A man's work should always reflect his inner thoughts."

Archie pushed his glasses up his nose. "It's only my first attempt at an idea to do with the effect of chimes, but I've always been interested in sound and its intricacies. And what work do you do?"

"I also find myself working with sound, as it happens. Sound waves, to be more precise."

"Oh?" Archie's eyes glanced toward the gun-shaped item in his belt and wondered what research required self-defense.

"I use sound waves to move around the room," he said, turning his head toward the doorway.

Archie raised an eyebrow, but just then the butler entered with a tray set for tea. He set it down before Archie—which he thought odd, given he was the guest and from what Miss Mitchell had said, this inventor was her boarder. Shouldn't he pour the tea? Perhaps etiquette was different out west?

In response to his questioning glance, however, the butler said, a bit rudely in Archie's opinion, "As Mr. Matsumoto is blind and unable to pour, would you like me to do so for you?"

Archie jerked and glanced back to Matsumoto.

The blind man looked at the butler. *Looked.* "Thank you, Jennings. Please." He waved a hand toward the tea indicating the butler should pour, though Jennings must have only seen it from the corner of his eye, as he was resolutely avoiding looking in the Japanese man's direction.

"I'm sorry, how can you do that?" Archie asked in amazement, staring over the maroon ceramic teapot at Matsumoto. "How did you know he was standing right there?"

"Close your eyes," said Matsumoto. His eyes focused unnervingly on Archie as Jennings began to pour the tea.

Archie raised both eyebrows.

"Please," said the cold, fluid voice.

Archie obeyed, and as soon as his eyes closed, Matsumoto said, "Thank you."

Archie almost opened his eyes again in surprise.

"Now, listen to the room."

"I'm sorry?"

"Listen."

Archie sat silently, feeling like an idiot, his eyes closed to the world around him. But the longer he sat, the more he heard. Jennings breathed next to him, his hands clinking the cups and saucers and plinking sugar into them—one, two, three, *four*—as he served. The fabric of Matsumoto's pants rustled as he adjusted his legs. The fireplace creaked, the fire crackled, and a grandfather clock *tick-tocked* out in the hall, slow, methodical. The sound brought to mind his own workshop back in Connecticut.

He opened his eyes and smiled. "I see what you mean. I've actually done a similar thing when working on clocks at my desk, but I never thought to do the same in public. To be honest, the world seems too loud to hear anything worth listening to these days."

Matsumoto nodded. "The world around us vibrates with sound. If we would only pause to listen, however, we might see better."

Archie wondered.

"In part that's why I've chosen to work out here on Miss Mitchell's property, because of the quiet. Miss Mitchell, as my patroness, has also provided me with a workshop where I can craft, test, and research my ideas."

"Craft?" Archie asked. What crafts could a blind man do? he wondered.

"Yes, I am the son of a sword-maker, and although my father was most distressed to realize his son was born blind, he did not let that stop him from teaching me the family trade." Matsumoto held up his scarred hands and Archie winced, understanding now why they must be so callused. They were marred in a manner that told Archie he was serious, though it was difficult to believe a blind man could work a forge. Archie couldn't imagine fixing clocks without his sight, much less creating a sword from burning metal.

"What saved me from complete disfigurement was my discovery early in my training that by clicking my tongue in a certain way, and listening to the resonance of the items around me,

I could distinguish the location of an object, and perhaps even what it was."

Archie's jaw dropped. He was so distracted by Matsumoto's story he hadn't even noticed when the butler had left, though he'd done so after serving Archie his tea and pointedly leaving Matsumoto's on the table. Archie reached forward and offered the cup and saucer to Matsumoto, who took it gratefully before continuing.

"It was many years before I made the connection between my gift and the discoveries of others into the matter of sound waves, and I realized that my technique means sound bounces."

"Bounces?"

"Yes," Matsumoto said simply, taking a sip of tea and then replacing it on the table. No doubt it was too sweet, if the amount of sugar cubes Archie had heard Jennings adding earlier was to be believed.

"Is that the work Miss Mitchell is patronizing?" Archie asked.

Matsumoto nodded. "In a way. I am currently attempting to find ways to direct sound, as I imagine if I could make a tool that produced more clicks at a higher frequency, I, or anyone, could 'see' a more detailed image of what I cannot see."

"That's amazing," said Archie, taking a sip of tea.

"I also wonder, if sound bounces, if it could be used to push gears in a motor."

Archie almost spat out his tea. "That— Wow. That'd sure be something." He stopped himself from expounding. He couldn't believe it. Once again someone had beaten him to his idea. How was that possible?

"This is my latest attempt," said Matsumoto, pulling out the gun-like funnel object from his belt and presenting it like a gift to Archie with a slight inclination of his head. "Please, hold it, but do not press the trigger."

Archie set down his cup and saucer and took the odd gun in his hands carefully, turning it over one way then the other.

"This is a 'sound gun' built around the idea that sound waves spread out like ripples from a stone in the water," the Japanese inventor continued.

Archie found himself nodding.

"I have recently discovered that higher frequency sound waves do not spread out as rapidly as lower frequency. Therefore, I should be able to focus the sound and send it toward one person or object, like I do with my clicks," explained Matsumoto. "What I do not have as yet is a way of producing the originating sound wave in the gun itself, other than putting the funnel up to my mouth or a phonograph. I have been testing with tuning forks struck by a hammer when you pull the trigger, but they do not seem to be strong enough to produce an effect."

Archie nodded as he listened.

"Miss Mitchell tells me you are going to help with this, that you are a sound scientist."

Archie couldn't stop the surprised laugh that bubbled out of him. "Well," he choked, "I guess that's one way of putting it. I'm a clockmaker."

Matsumoto didn't blink.

Archie considered the man, then the gun, then the man again.

"So, you're hoping to make something that produces multiple clicks at a high frequency that could be shot from a gun like a bullet?" Archie asked.

"Yes," Matsumoto said, nodding, his unseeing eyes excited.

But Archie wasn't sure what to say. Hearing something similar to his own idea presented in this way actually sounded ridiculous.

Archie stopped turning the gun. It had been his luck in life to arrive at ideas a step behind someone else. Look at how far this blind blacksmith had come on his own. This man seemed to think Archie had something to offer, but Archie wasn't so sure. Perhaps he was better off sticking to the clock tower and then returning to his clocks in Connecticut. Though then he'd never be remembered as anyone but the designer of the Spokane clock—and even then only if it was never torn down to make way for some newer, more useful invention.

In his mind, Archie pored over his own diagrams and sketches in an attempt to determine if he had something to offer this man, or if he was arriving too late to be of any use, as usual. Matsumoto *was* offering to include him; in fact, he seemed to think he held in his head the other half of the equation. If they worked together...well, maybe even the "cot" would be possible someday.

* * *

Marian had never struck up a conversation with a complete stranger before. And there was no better word to describe Mr. Archibald Prescot. A stranger stranger she'd never met.

But he was kind and funny in his way (she smiled recalling his "au reservoir!" as they'd parted), and he'd helped her forget her troubles for a couple hours at least.

She was grateful to him for that. As her Nain would say, "The unexpected always happens."

She sat in the small Owl Cafe and gazed out the window at the passing faces heading down Howard and Main in the glow of the setting sun. Mr. Prescot had recommended the place based on an ad he'd seen in the paper and she'd been very pleased thus far with the nightly special of chicken pot pie. She suspected they used thyme in their seasoning like her grandmother had done.

Nain had always prided herself on her tasting skills, down to her ability to tell how many days old an egg was even after it was cooked.

"Don't tell me this is fresh off the farm when it has clearly spent five days in the back of a truck getting to my table. In this day and age, when one can order anything from anywhere and have it delivered within the week, I expect more from 'local' produce."

In this day and age...

Oh, Nain. For someone so forward-thinking, why in heaven's name had she questioned Marian's ability to fend for herself in a city like Seattle? What would Nain say, knowing her Marian had finally left the house only to walk directly into a chance encounter *alone* with a strange man. And made friends.

She could see her now, seated before her, wiping her mouth daintily with a napkin and slipping a few extra biscuits into her enormous quilted handbag.

"Someday everyone will have a bag this size," she'd say.

"What on earth can a woman need to carry with her at all times that wouldn't fit in a chatelaine?" She prided herself on her ability to carry everything she could possibly need in the little silk purse that hung from her waist, including a book-shaped pincushion, embroidery scissors, a matchbook, a little journal with a pencil in the binding, a penknife for letters, and hairpins.

"You never know when you might find yourself with time to do a bit of embroidery or read a book."

"Perhaps you could sell the ones you make. The quilted style might be the way of the future."

"Maybe I will. Could be the way to make my fortune, though self-praise is no recommendation."

She was often talking about that, how she could make her fortune by publishing the secret recipe to her amazing cookies or writing a book on how to use washing soda to clean everything or by selling embroidered handbags. And why not when anyone else could publish an ad for "pink pills for pale people" or the latest remedies for "period problems"?

It wasn't like Marian had been born into a well-off family. Her own father had worked for the Phoenix Sawmill, and her grandfather had merely invested his hard-earned savings well in the railway opportunities that had sprung up overnight with the mining boom in Idaho. The Great Northern had expanded steadily and grandly to the point that now they were talking of building their own depot.

Not that Marian cared about such things, but the family lawyer had seemed to find it important to ensure Marian understood exactly where her money was working, how much she could count on earning each month in interest, and how much she'd have to pay from her inheritance to cover the death dues and funeral arrangements.

But the interest wouldn't be enough for Marian to live on, even if she'd inherited the house free and clear.

"Someday I'll make my fortune..." Now, it would be up to Marian.

* * *

"Good evening, my rose," Bernard said, his bulky frame leaning over to give his wife a loving kiss where she sat at the dinner table, waiting for him with Mr. Prescot. "I am terribly sorry, Mr. Prescot, but I'm afraid I won't be joining you both for dinner this evening, after all."

"Is everything all right?" the plump, partially mustached man asked him.

"I'm afraid I can't say much, but there's been another theft, and that's currently where I've been focusing my time and energy. The other detectives have requested I attend to this rather late call." *Requested* was putting it nicely, but as the newest detective, he didn't have much say in the matter.

"Did I hear Miss Gillen is ill?" Bernard asked Roslyn, taking her hand with concern.

"Yes, love, but do not worry over me. You certainly have plenty more important matters to attend to."

"More important than my wife? I should think not."

"Nonsense, the great detective has a case!"

Bernard grunted. "Nothing too worrisome for me."

He tried not to let the disappointment through in his voice. There'd been rumors circling the station that morning that cutbacks might be taking effect later in the year, and Bernard didn't want to be the "last in, first out," as was bound to happen if he didn't prove his worth.

Roslyn could apparently read the discouragement in his shoulders, however, for she asked if the chief mightn't have set him onto this case for a reason.

"Chief Witherspoon has enough on his plate what with the new mayor after his job and he's not even sworn in yet. He's doing his best to support the detective department but what we need is a sergeant of detectives."

"Like you?"

"I only just joined the detective ranks, Roslyn. I still have to earn my star, as far as the men are concerned."

He rubbed his mustache in an attempt to hide the grimace on his face as he recalled today's prank. He'd walked in this morning to find Detective Martin Burns standing at his desk, his arms crossed. Burns was a gentleman detective, his face clean-shaven, his hands smooth, with a penchant for high collars, flowered cravats, and smooth, black lapels on impeccable waistcoats—the very definition of a dandy. His arching eyebrows gave him a look of constant interest and attention, which led witnesses to want to tell him more—a quite helpful attribute in a detective.

"Are you done with the paperwork for the captain yet?" he'd asked, without even a good morning.

Bernard, who was a good foot taller than Burns, had simply nodded and sat down to find what he needed, realizing he still needed to sign the papers before handing them over. But when Bernard reached for his fountain pen, he'd discovered it'd been loosened so it dripped mercilessly on his paperwork, forcing him to redo it all.

Burns had simply snickered and said he'd be back later for the papers.

It made Bernard's cheeks warm in anger just to think of it.

"Besides," he said, allowing his thoughts to settle back on his wife, "I prefer the mystery to the management. How has your day been, Mr. Prescot?"

"Interesting. I visited a Miss Gladys Mitchell this morning about a clock and the possibility of her patronizing some of my work."

Bernard's bushy eyebrows rose in surprise. "I was just on my way to speak with Miss Mitchell myself. She had a thief break in last night."

Prescot's face flushed red. "Well, knock me over with a fetter! What a coincidence!"

"Indeed...," Bernard muttered. He didn't believe in coincidences. His father had always told him such a thing didn't exist when it came to police work. And Sherlock didn't believe in them, either.

"Don't go reading too much into it, love." Roslyn spoke softly, drawing his attention back to her face, rather than frowning at their boarder. "You know how the rich folk are. They'd rather not let on they're in trouble until they absolutely must."

Bernard grunted. "Perhaps."

"Why don't you take Thomas with you? I'm sure your brother would appreciate the chance to stretch his legs."

"And his mouth," Bernard muttered.

* * *

Thomas Carew was the spitting image of his twin brother, Bernard, though about three inches shorter—something the older brother by two minutes never let him forget—and twenty pounds thinner—something Thomas never let Bernard forget in return. He kept his face clean-shaven to avoid further comparison with his brother, and by this simple action seemed to chase most of the "twin questions" from the minds of those around him. Often people asked if his brother was Detective Carew, but hardly ever was he asked if his *twin* was Detective Carew.

He was surprised to see the twin himself clomping across the police station and up to his desk at that moment, his heavier frame—"It's all muscle," Bernard claimed—dropping onto his heels over and over again as he crossed the wooden floor.

"It's a wonder your head doesn't pop off your neck with the strain you put on it every day walking like that," Thomas declared, his face still focused on the paperwork in front of him. "Didn't you go home for some of Mrs. Hill's 'delicious' cooking?" He grimaced. He was glad he'd had lots of paperwork to keep him home from dinner tonight. He'd eat almost anything, but the current cook's food, if you could call it that, left his stomach oddly *hungrier* when finished.

"We've got a case," Bernard said, avoiding the gibe.

"And you need me to solve it?"

Bernard grunted.

"You're so eloquent, brother."

"That's Detective Carew in the station."

"Yes, sir, right you are, sir." Thomas stood with a half-salute and then stood at mock attention awaiting orders.

"Give it up already. It's just another burglary. I thought you might like to join me on the case. It's been awhile since we've worked together."

"Yes, sir. Three months, sixteen days, ten hours, and forty-two minutes to be exact, sir." Thomas's face broke into a grin. "Of course, you know this'll cost you."

"The way I see it, *you'll* owe *me* for dragging your sorry behind around with me and getting you out of desk work."

"Yes, sir, thank you, sir." Thomas grabbed his helmet before his brother could change his mind and headed for the exit.

They walked up Howard to Riverside and caught the North Monroe to Cannon Hill streetcar. It was the same line they took into town every day, only this time they continued to travel south to the city limits at 29th, and disembarked at the top of the South Hill. Bernard led the way down to the great iron gates that marked an otherwise unmarked private drive amongst towering pine and maple trees. Although this house might be considered "out of town" at the moment, it was apparent from Spokane's exponential growth that it wouldn't be long before this secluded house would have to allow for neighbors.

But however many houses clustered nearby, it would never get lost amongst them. The Brobdingnagian house—for it certainly belonged in Gulliver's land of giants—of Miss Gladys Mitchell greeted them at precisely seven forty-five. Thomas liked to pull out the magnificent Elgin pocket watch his father had left him whenever he could, keeping it pristine and in working order, mostly to remind Bernard that he'd been the one to receive the gift.

"Seven forty-five," he said with a punctuating click as he closed the gold cover.

Bernard grunted. He was doing that a lot more often lately. Thomas wondered if he mightn't be coming down with something. Like catchitory or swamp fever or something.

A butler in full regalia opened the door, looking like a servant from overseas. His face was tense, but it seemed, oddly, to relax upon seeing the two of them, rather than vice versa as was the more common reaction.

"Good evening," Bernard said, removing his derby. "I'm Detective Carew and this is Officer Carew. Miss Mitchell—"

"Thank you for coming so quickly," the butler interrupted. "Please, follow me."

Bernard glanced back at Thomas. It was clear he thought the butler was acting strangely, too. Maybe *he* was the burglar? But then, why relax upon seeing them rather than getting agitated?

It became stranger still when the butler led them through the house, past a grand staircase, three pocket doors, down the servant stairs, through a kitchen where Thomas was momentarily overwhelmed by the best smell in the world—bacon—and out the back door, down a small slope, past an ornamental garden, a vegetable garden, a shed with chickens, and a stable, and yet the butler *still* kept moving at a steady, if not quick, pace out across the lawn.

"Is Miss Mitchell in the stable?" Thomas finally asked.

"No, sir," came the curt reply.

He'd known it was no use asking. Butlers never said anything unless absolutely necessary. He'd read that somewhere in a book once.

They'd walked another mile and a half, it seemed, before he realized they were coming to the back edge of the property.

Against the backdrop of the forest he could see a rectangular stone building, which had been hidden from view until now by a gentle rise in the yard. Gray smoke plumes wafted out of a brick chimney, but something other than wood was burning. He couldn't quite place it. Perhaps oil or rubber? Maybe metal, seeing as outside the building he saw the pieces of an old carriage, extra wheels and rims, and long sheets of flattened steel leaning against the stone.

As he stepped through the wide doorway and noted the anvil beside the brick forge, he wondered what someone like Miss Mitchell was doing out here in a blacksmith's shop.

Then he had his answer.

She was wearing a light yellow silk thing that would've caused her legs to grab his attention first, had her head not been some two feet away from her body, still in shock, the mouth and eyes wide open in an eternal scream.

* * *

"Well, you don't see a body like that every day," Thomas said.

Bernard grunted. "Are you seriously trying to make light of a murdered woman?"

"That forge is casting enough light, I should think."

Bernard glanced at the brilliant coals still heaped up and glowing in the forge. The heat was so intense in the little shop he was already sweating and he wondered if the body mightn't burn merely by adjacency.

"Who found the body?" Bernard knelt beside the late Miss Mitchell. The odor of death didn't quite cover the scent of roses that must have once been a perfume but now, mixed with the smell of blood, made him wonder if he'd ever enjoy the scent again. Thankfully, his wife preferred lavender.

"Mr. Matsumoto, sir," the butler answered from the doorway. "He's the Japanese blacksmith who works in this shop. Miss Mitchell was supporting him as a patroness."

"What's a Japanese blacksmith doing in Spokane?" muttered Thomas, squatting alongside Bernard. "And why would he need a patroness?"

"Find out what you can from the butler while I take a look around," Bernard said quietly. "Head back to the house and call for the coroner and the wagon. And call off any other detectives being sent to investigate. Tell them I've got it." Bernard's heart beat a little faster at that thought. "Then begin rounding up the staff to collect statements. Send the blacksmith to me. I want to speak to him here."

Thomas nodded and rose again, pulling out a pencil and pad before leading the butler back outside.

Like a headless Snow White, the body was peacefully positioned parallel to the forge, alongside an anvil: the arms lay to either side, the feet stretched directly out, as though the killer had carefully placed the body before removing the head. A sign of respect?

Her clothes appeared to be intact, even though they belonged in an Asian play rather than a blacksmith's workshop, and her walking boots were still on each foot. Bernard gently picked up her hands to check the fingernails—there was no skin beneath them, so she hadn't attempted to fend off the attacker. She must have been drugged to have been lain out so placidly before the butchering began.

Yet the removal of the head led his thoughts in the direction of revenge. Images of the French guillotine rose before him as he took in the startling pool of dried red blood spread beneath the corpse, mostly soaked into the dirt, and the darker red spray that had spattered over nearby equipment.

His first impression of the place was that it was quite messy. In addition to the blood spray, ash and soot covered the brick forge. This was an almost entirely enclosed space, like a bread oven, complete with a hood and chimney over the top to keep the heat contained. Sand filled the work area, a poker left stuck in the warm sand beside the still-hot embers in a large pit where the heating of metal could be done. The hand-crank bellows were on one side, beside an enormous barrel full of coal, both of which he knew were required to feed the fire. At the other end was a long slack tub full of water for cooling the heated metal—its dirtiness indicating the blacksmith had had a busy day.

But when Bernard turned away from the forge, he realized it seemed to be a very organized shop outside of the radius of the murder. Dozens of hammers, tongs, chisels, and mandrels—and those were just the tools he could name—hung in their respective places on the walls nearby. It was clear this Matsumoto knew it was best to have a place for everything and everything in its place.

Bernard decided he'd better start at the entrance and see if there was anything else worth noting. He returned to the door and circled the room, first finding the leather blacksmith's apron that hung by the door—surprisingly clean of blood spatters. No coat hung by the door, though. He looked back at the dead woman. Her clothing was much too thin for the walk from the house to the workshop in these early April days. She did have walking boots. But no coat.

He wondered what had brought Gladys Mitchell out to the blacksmith's shop in the first place. Had she simply been out for a stroll, only to be met by a crazed thief—for he suddenly recalled they'd originally come here to inquire about a burglar—who went after her with a hatchet? Again, though, she wouldn't have taken it lying down, which meant premeditation. A thoroughly disturbing proposition.

The anvil and vise beside the body were what had clued him in to the work normally done in the shop. A man who worked with iron and steel, "the black metals," was not an uncommon sight so long as there were horse-drawn carriages in the world, but to have one just for her personal use tucked at the back of a vast property like it had something to hide? And Japanese? That was something worth noting.

Other than its location so far out of town, however, it appeared to be a normal blacksmith's shop. When he was a kid, Bernard had been fascinated by the blacksmiths' work whenever he and his dad stopped in. He remembered sitting and watching the men, creating so much more than horseshoes out of simple pieces of metal. His father had told him blacksmiths were engineers and artisans, not just toolmakers; that once upon a time they'd been called upon to act as dentists, doctors, undertakers, surgeons, and veterinarians, in addition to their normal duties. The job of a blacksmith was not as simple as it seemed, requiring a great deal of intelligence with numbers and business, leading to many holding the office of magistrate or warden.

He wondered if it was the same in Japan.

This particular blacksmith seemed to be working on weapons of some sort. Handles and barrels of guns lay on a table in different shapes and sizes. They didn't look like anything he'd ever held, personally, but perhaps this explained why the shop was situated so far out of town? If someone started shooting guns downtown there'd be more than a few problems. And yet, he glanced at the body by the forge, the murderer hadn't used a gun. There *was* a strange lack of bullets to go with the gun pieces, so perhaps that was why he'd opted for a hatchet.

Or maybe it had been a sword. Along the wall hung three ornate Japanese swords of different lengths, with intricate swirls and designs denoting mountains and horses and warriors on the black scabbards. They were breathtaking in their beauty. Bernard hesitated before shaking his head clear and taking them down, one by one, slowly removing the spotless lengths of steel from their sheaths with a smooth *sheek*.

No blood on the blades. For some reason this made Bernard happy. Perhaps to know such beauty hadn't been marred by murder.

After replacing the swords reverently back on the wall, Bernard moved to the next table where he found an assortment of gongs, chimes, tuning forks, and—was that a phonograph? Why would a blacksmith have a phonograph?

Well, that was about everything inside. Time to take a look outside.

Bernard stepped out into the refreshingly cool evening air and circled the building. Wild roses grew around the doorway, reminding him of the incongruous odor when he'd knelt beside the body.

By the waning light of the sun he found a hatchet wedged beside a wood stack. The blade was too shiny and clean for something used to chop on a regular basis. The wood handle didn't appear to have too much to tell until he noticed a bit of something red and sticky within a groove where the axe-head met the shoulder. The murder weapon had not been too cleverly hidden—unless hiding it in plain sight counted—but there had been some attempts at cleaning it. And yet, the area around the forge had been left a mess.

Bernard grunted. The clues were starting to fall into place. As Sherlock Holmes would say, "There is nothing like first-hand evidence."

* * *

"So tell me, was Miss Mitchell in the habit of hiding men in the back of her property?"

The butler, named Jennings Thomas had learned, walked with purposeful strides back toward the main house, Thomas in tow.

"Mr. Matsumoto lives in a guest room at the house. He only does his work back here."

"I see."

"Miss Mitchell was a woman of great sophistication and intelligence. Her relationship with Mr. Matsumoto was purely that of a patroness." The butler was speaking rather firmly, almost too firmly, Thomas thought.

"And what, exactly, was she patronizing?"

"Inventions."

"What sort of inventions?"

"I suppose blacksmith inventions," Jennings said with a shrug. "All I know is he was provided meals and lodging in order to have time and space to work on these 'inventions.'"

"And you have no guesses as to what they were?"

"I cannot begin to think what a Japanese sword-maker," he said with a sneer, "would have to offer Miss Mitchell."

"Perhaps it wasn't his swords Miss Mitchell was interested in."

The butler stopped, turned to Thomas, and glared in a manner only highly trained butlers could pull off.

"I would appreciate it if you would do your job to the best of your abilities and catch the killer of my employer. Sir."

"I take it you were fond of Miss Mitchell."

The butler's mouth twitched. "If being fond of a job that is somewhat rare in this small town counts, then, yes, I was fond of my employer."

"I see," Thomas said, writing lots of scribbles down in his memorandum book as though the man had said something important.

"We were all fond of her," the butler continued.

"And how many are 'we'?"

"There are four live-in staff here: myself, a cook, a groundskeeper/chauffeur, and a maid."

"*Just* four? Jiminy."

"In Great Britain, three times as many staff would be required to run a house of this size, sir."

"Well, I'm thankful to live in the great state of Washington, thank you kindly."

"With whom would you like to speak first?"

Thomas tapped his pencil against his cheek and noted the sun setting in the west. "Probably just be taking statements tonight. Where would be the best place for everyone to gather?"

"The kitchen, sir."

Thomas's stomach growled with pleasure—the scent of that perfect bacon had followed him all the way to the workshop.

Jennings turned on his heel and continued his march toward the house. "I wouldn't be surprised if Mrs. Curry has dinner on the table already."

* * *

Bernard studied the compact Asian before him. He'd half-expected the man to appear in a traditional kimono, but he looked like any other blacksmith in a simple shirt and pants. The only thing missing was a tie, but he probably didn't wear one because of his work.

"Officer Carew sent you my way?" he asked.

The Japanese man bowed his head slightly.

"I'm Detective Carew. You must be Mr. Matsumoto. I'm afraid I need to ask you a few questions, and it's getting dark outside, so we'll have to make do in here," Bernard said, explaining why they stood just in front of the forge and the corpse. Someone had to stay with the body until the coroner arrived, and he wanted to see how this man, whose workspace had just been used for murder, reacted.

"The butler said you found the body."

The Japanese blacksmith seemed to be staring fixedly at the corpse before the forge. The sight apparently didn't upset him.

"When was that?" Bernard asked.

"I am afraid I do not know," replied Matsumoto. "I do not wear a timepiece. I am only aware of time when I am working."

"And you weren't working when you found the body?"

"No. I had just returned from a walk."

"A walk? And you left the forge coals burning?" Bernard waved toward the fire.

Matsumoto's eyes drifted toward Bernard's face but settled on his left ear. "Naturally. The light of the forge can never be snuffed completely. It is a blacksmith belief I have carried with me from Japan."

"I see. So you were coming from the house at the time?"

"No. I have found fresh air expands my senses in numerous ways that facilitate the growing of new ideas."

The Japanese man spoke surprisingly good and careful English.

"After meeting Mr. Prescot, I felt a need to ponder his part in my future endeavors."

"Mr. Prescot?" His own boarder?

"Archibald Prescot." Matsumoto said clearly.

Apparently, this was the same person. But hadn't Prescot said he went to Miss Mitchell's house this morning? What was his involvement with this inventor? Wasn't he in Spokane working on the Great Northern Depot?

"So the last time you saw Miss Mitchell alive was at this meeting?"

"She was not in attendance," said Matsumoto, his voice a low rumble. "She came to the workshop earlier in the day—again, I cannot tell you for certain, but it was before noon—and requested my presence to meet another inventor at three o'clock, so I went up to the house around that time."

"So she wasn't expected?"

"No," Matsumoto answered, his gaze returning to the fire, or perhaps the body, Bernard couldn't tell which.

"But you were there definitely at three o'clock?"

"Yes, Detective," said Matsumoto. "I heard the grandfather clock chime three o'clock upon Mr. Prescot's entrance."

"And when was this meeting over?"

"Before four o'clock, as I left before hearing the clock chime the hour again."

"And you didn't go straight back to the workshop?"

"I went for a walk in the woods, as I said."

"Why not return sooner?"

Matsumoto's mouth twitched as his gaze returned to Bernard's ear. "When one begins pondering it is quite a simple thing to lose track of the time."

Bernard grunted. "And you didn't see Miss Mitchell in the woods while you were walking?"

"No, but I did hear someone."

"Oh?"

"I had just decided I ought to return to the workshop before dinner when I heard someone running from the direction of the workshop toward the house."

"What time exactly?"

Matsumoto's lip twitched. "As I said before, Detective, I do not keep track of time when I am not working. When I am at my forge, time is of the utmost importance. But when I am not..." He shrugged. "Time is inconsequential."

Bernard disagreed wholeheartedly with that statement. Time was of every importance to him and his work. "What about eating? Surely the cook prefers you attend her meals on time."

"Mrs. Curry makes allowances for my idiosyncrasies."

Bernard decided to move on for the moment, but made a note to ask the cook what she felt about such "idiosyncrasies." He knew for a fact that his household cook was irritated nightly by his or Thomas's inability to warn her ahead of time whether they'd be at a meal or not. But such was the life of policemen.

"And this person in the woods," Bernard continued his questioning. "Who was it?"

"I do not know, Detective. He or she was moving swiftly, that is all I can tell you." He paused and seemed to be considering whether to continue or not. "And perhaps was wearing some sort of coat, as I could hear it rubbing against their legs as they ran. I assume it was someone hurrying back for dinner."

"Do the other staff often go for walks just before dinner?"

"I thought it might have been Miss Mitchell, but..." He waved toward the body beside the forge. "Mr. Jennings kindly informed me it is her body I smelled upon returning to my workshop."

"Mr. Jennings?"

"The butler."

"You did not recognize her yourself upon finding her?" Although her head had been separated from her body, her face was quite easily seen by the light of the forge.

The Japanese man cocked his head slightly to the left, and the firelight glanced off his dark eyes.

"When it comes to things seen, I require others' eyes. I am blind, Detective."

Bernard practically choked on his surprise. He studied the man's face closer, looking for a sign. He wondered if the butler had left out this important bit of information on purpose, just to see him sweat—if so, he had missed his opportunity to witness Bernard's reaction. And the chance to explain why he'd said Mr. Matsumoto had found the body.

"Seems to me this means you *didn't* find the body alone, Mr. Matsumoto. That it was Mr. Jennings, in fact. Unless you tripped over her."

"No, Detective," said Matsumoto firmly. "As I said, I was still on the edge of the woods when I realized I must return to the workshop with caution, for something smelled amiss."

Bernard scrutinized his face for a moment longer, but Matsumoto's blank eyes simply studied him back in an unnerving stare.

"Was Jennings nearby then? To inform you the body was Miss Mitchell's?"

"No. I walked to the house and informed Mr. Jennings that I required his assistance at the workshop."

"And he came immediately?"

Matsumoto blinked. "No. He told me if I needed help I should ask Mr. Sigmund, as he was assigned to help me when I required it."

Bernard nodded. He wasn't surprised to hear that not everyone in the household approved of Miss Mitchell's choice in boarders.

"But eventually, I take it, he did come?"

"Yes, upon learning no one knew where Mr. Sigmund was at the moment, and I made clear the urgency of the matter."

"What did you say exactly?"

"'Someone is dead in my workshop. I do not know who.'"

Bernard imagined that set the butler on his way rather rapidly.

"So then Jennings came."

Matsumoto nodded. "He returned with me, and said, 'My God, it's Miss Mitchell,' and then returned to the house, where I assume he telephoned for the police."

Bernard nodded. That would have to do for now. He would have to rely on Thomas to get the others' statements for tonight. Then they'd see if they all lined up.

Officer Lawson's knock on the door signaled the arrival of the coroner and the paddy wagon, so Bernard thanked Matsumoto, asked him not to touch anything in the workshop until he could return tomorrow, and said that'd be all for the night. Bernard followed him out as he shuffled off, shaking his head as he realized that, to the blind man, there was no added difficulty finding his way in the evening darkness.

* * *

Eleanor couldn't stop crying. She'd been crying ever since that policeman had finally finished asking her questions and allowed her to return home for the evening. She couldn't understand it. She had not thought she was so enamored of her employer as to waste time and energy crying over her death.

She needed to clean something. It was her usual response to any emotion. Had to scrub it out before it weakened her too much. She was a strong woman. Others might look at her and see someone as quiet and as meek as a mouse, someone who needed protecting, but she could hold her own. She'd had to all her life.

Her husband thought her odd because she could spend all day cleaning another woman's house, only to return and clean her own home from top to bottom, as well.

He didn't understand. It was her way of coping with everyday life. Usually she could take her mind off of anything by cleaning. Even him.

And so she'd excused herself and rushed home to cry alone in the empty apartment above the carriage house where no one could belittle her or witness her tears.

But the cleaning wasn't clearing her mind. Instead, she kept thinking through her last conversation with Miss Mitchell, which she'd just relived while making her statement to the policeman.

She'd been just finishing cleaning the dining room after lunch, about to join Mrs. Curry in their usual teatime, when Miss Mitchell had come gliding down the stairs from her study and thrust a fat envelope into her hands.

"Post this as soon as possible," she'd said, brushing past like a woman on a mission. But then she'd turned as though remembering something. "And be sure the front parlor is prepared for receiving guests. Mr. Matsumoto will be hosting a new inventor, Mr. Prescot, at three o'clock."

Eleanor had recognized the name from the morning, when she'd been asked to send a message to him *before* calling the police about the burglary, but knew better than to say anything. She'd simply bobbed a curtsy and said quietly, "Yes, ma'am. Will you be joining them?"

"What?" she'd flared, turning on Eleanor angrily before taking a deep breath, apologizing for her brusque manner, and asking again, kindly, "What did you say? I'm sorry, I didn't hear you."

Eleanor had tried to wipe the shock from her face. Miss Mitchell may not have been the best employer, but she'd never spoken to her so. "I merely wondered if you'd be joining them, miss."

"No. I'm going for a walk. Please make sure that letter gets mailed off immediately."

And that had been it. She'd turned and walked off, thrusting her arms into her overcoat as she went, the grandfather clock in the hall chiming that annoyingly loud three-quarter hour. That had been the last time she'd ever seen Miss Mitchell's glamorous, piled chocolate-colored hair.

She hadn't known she'd been walking...to her death...

No, must distract. Only one thing for it: to clean.

Eleanor began by cleaning out the fireplace of all its ash and cinders, wiping down the mantelpiece so there wasn't the slightest bit of black or gray about. Then she went to the bedroom, clearing the bookshelves and trunks, chests of drawers of shoes and stockings, pulling out clothes from the wardrobe and hanging them back up again—

What was this? Hair? On Mr. Sigmund's jacket? And not just any hair: hair the color of chocolate.

She glanced at the vanity mirror, taking in her thin, tired hair the color of corn. Not chocolate.

She stopped feeling sad.

* * *

Archie studied the mantel clock before him. The movements clicked methodically, the beat rhythmically providing a baseline for his actions. A balance cock connected a movement plate to a pivoting wheel, while a cadrature lay just behind the dial, near the front plate, transmitting the rotation of the movement to the clock hands. Each part important. Each part doing what it was designed to do.

What about his purpose? What part did he have to play in this new enterprise? How could he become a purposeful cog in a wheel that was pushing him to give up the security he had found in his workaday life?

He'd been quite happy in his clock shop in Connecticut, working for the Seth Thomas company, building up a nice savings for his own home someday, perhaps even a family. And then the gears of life had started turning, in some ways, a little too fast.

Before he knew it, he was on a train heading almost as far away as he could go without leaving the United States. Traveling out to the "wild west," though he'd found the west much more tame and personable than he'd originally imagined.

He smiled as an image of stray curls and green eyes came to him.

Then again, he *had* met a real blacksmith—though unlike any he'd ever read about.

And Mr. Matsumoto was interested in manipulating sound just as he was.

Archie's gaze shifted from his experimental clock to his sketchbooks and notebooks, all full of the plans and diagrams necessary to bring his clock tower into existence. If he was going to pursue this little side job, he'd need to make sure he was still giving the required time and energy to the Great Northern's depot. More than that, he had big ideas for the clock tower itself.

What had started as just another job in Connecticut was quickly becoming something more significant. He now knew he was designing a clock that would be intrinsically valuable to the city and its people. For the man working within its radius, the hourly peal would be something to set his pocket watch to. A woman cooking a meal for her family could time the baking to its dulcet knell. It would be the landmark everyone remembered after they visited, and the sound of the bell chiming out the hour would be a sound recalled to mind as something unique to the city. A calling card of sorts, which reverberated through memory until one couldn't do anything but return to the city of its origin to hear those melodious bells once more...

The question was *how* would he make the clock so spectacular? It wasn't like he could make the chimes lull people to sleep—just think of the mess that would create downtown.

With one last twist, he set the mantel clock to play, placing it on his desk and sitting back to admire his work. The soft tinkling melody rang out as the steel comb rotated against the pinned barrel, the sound of chimes filling his ears. He listened carefully to determine if it was playing properly.

He thought he heard the Carew brothers returning downstairs as one final thought drifted through his mind before sleep overtook him: what a delightful, stimulating day...

* * *

"Well, that was one excellent meal, I must say," said Thomas, patting his belly grandly and plopping himself onto the leather Chesterfield.

"It certainly sounds like you made yourself at home," grumbled Bernard from his desk in the corner.

Thomas couldn't help it that they'd shown up just before dinner and *someone* was going to have to eat it and he just *happened* to be there taking statements and Mrs. Curry wouldn't *hear* of him sitting in her kitchen without food... Bernard could've come up to the house instead of hanging around with the body. He was just grumpy because he'd been stuck with a cold, dry meat pie once they finally made it back to their house. Because they'd found the body, it was their duty to ensure it was delivered to the coroner's for examination the next day before heading home. It was now almost eleven o'clock at night, though you wouldn't have thought it given the electrical arc lights sprinkled about downtown.

"Hey, I can't help the perks of the job." Thomas shrugged with a grin.

"You mean of a murder?"

"Don't be so dismal. There's a silver lining to every cloud—and every body so it happens."

Thomas tossed his helmet on a nearby armchair. It landed neatly upon the head of a carved bear cub climbing up the armrest, and his navy blue officer's coat soon followed. Then he pulled out his tobacco pouch and settled himself on the Chesterfield for a good smoke and a think alongside his twin. If Bernard didn't sleep, Thomas wouldn't sleep either. Couldn't let that big brain of his beat him to the punch of solving the mystery—again.

After all, he'd beaten him so often he'd been promoted to detective while Thomas was still patrolman. Stuck filling out paperwork and walking the beat instead of following the scent of an audacious murderer.

"What do you think a single woman like that was doing with a male boarder?" Thomas asked before taking a long draw on his pipe.

"I don't think anything. We've got to have facts before we start making guesses."

"Right-ho, Sherlock, me boy. Shall I grab your old violin for you?"

Bernard grunted.

"At least Watson sometimes gets more than a grunt in reply."

"You don't have to sit up with me, you know."

"Someone's got to play Watson to your Holmes."

Whether he realized it or not, Thomas knew Bernard greatly appreciated being compared to Holmes. He could tell by the way his shoulders straightened just a tad. And the lack of a grunt as a response.

Bernard stood up and moved to stand before the giant front window, staring out at the dark street, striking his contemplative pose.

"Fact number one: she was butchered," Thomas said around his pipe.

Bernard grunted. "That's one way of putting it. There was a surprising amount of blood."

"Yeah, that was a rather large pool beneath her, but I guess when you're beheaded the blood has to go somewhere."

"But there was also spray," Bernard said, turning to face

Thomas and waving his hands like an Italian. "I'd think there'd be less blood spray with a beheading."

"Did Coroner Baker tell you that?"

"No, thank you, I thought of it myself."

"One too many detective novels, if you ask me...," muttered Thomas.

Bernard didn't seem to hear him. "And yet the only tool with blood on it was the hatchet outside—and that had been cleaned."

"I'm sure that means something."

"Yes, but I'm not sure *what* as yet." Bernard ran a finger over his mustache, playing up the thoughtful pose a bit too much, in Thomas's opinion. "Let's look through the statements you took."

Bernard returned to the desk, turning up the Argand oil lamp, while Thomas stood to retrieve his notepad from his coat pocket.

He handed it to Bernard and returned to his seat, leaving him to flip through the pages, reading the shorthand they'd concocted together as schoolboys, providing them with a secret language for communication that had continued to this day.

Thomas pulled off his shoes and threw his legs up on the Chesterfield. He puffed lightly, attempting a ring or two but finding, as usual, he just didn't have the tongue muscles for such an effect.

Bernard wasn't going to be pleased with the little he'd gotten tonight. The servants had seemed distracted, barely picking at their own food while Thomas helped himself to the Turkish soup, perfectly cooked pork loin, french-fried potatoes with bacon, apple fritters, and beet greens, all finished with a delicious caramel custard and café noir. That Mrs. Curry certainly knew her way around a kitchen.

Bernard grunted.

"What?" Thomas asked.

"The butler verified that Prescot and the blacksmith met at three o'clock. I was surprised to hear it the first time when Matsumoto told me."

"Yeah, apparently the same Prescot we've got living under our very roof. It's gonna be an entertaining breakfast..."

"We mustn't jump to conclusions."

"I know, I know. I'm just saying, 'So, I hear you met with a murderer yesterday' is going to make for a great opening line."

"We don't know who murdered her yet."

"You're right. Better to ask, 'So, kill anyone lately?'"

Bernard turned and glared at Thomas in a way he usually reserved for miscreants.

"Never mind." Bernard always took things too seriously. Maybe that was why he was the detective. If so, maybe Thomas was better off *not* being a detective.

"It's possible he went over in the morning to fix a clock and *that's* when she discovered she'd been burglarized," murmured Bernard.

"He was at the house in the morning?"

"Yes."

"Why would he go all the way out there twice in one day?" Thomas asked.

"And why didn't he mention it? I don't know. Something to ask him."

"You know...perhaps she wanted to confront him first, thinking he was the thief? And when he found out she knew the truth, he came back and killed her?"

"Have you *seen* Archie Prescot?"

"Well, yes, but still. Anyone can lift a hatchet."

"But it takes a cold-blooded murderer to drug her first..."

"Drugs? No way you Sherlock-ed that one out just by looking at her."

"For your information, I believe she was sedated or knocked out in some way before she was beheaded, based on the manner in which her body was laid out before the forge."

Thomas puffed in reply. "All right. I'll give you that one. So what about Prescot?"

"I'll have to speak to him about it all tomorrow."

"Sounds like I'd better do it. Open mind and all that?"

Bernard grunted.

"I'll take that for an assent. Thanks for the vote of confidence." And Thomas puffed a perfect ring without thinking.

* * *

Bernard turned back to Thomas's neatly listed statements from each of the staff and then turned the final page to find he'd already collated their movements by time. Thomas may have had his mouth full of mashed potatoes and gravy but the kid was organized, he had to give him that.

3:00: Jennings was serving tea to inventors Matsumoto and Prescot in front parlor; Curry was having tea with Mrs. Sigmund in kitchen.

4:00: Jennings was cleaning tea things; Curry was cooking; Mrs. Sigmund returned to chores after not finding her husband for tea.

5:00: Jennings was preparing the wine and silver for dinner; Curry was cooking; Mrs. Sigmund was cleaning the dining room.

6:00: Jennings was setting the table for dinner; Curry was cooking; Mrs. Sigmund was feeding the chickens.

7:00: Jennings went in search of Mrs. Sigmund to tell her he couldn't find Miss Mitchell for dinner; Curry was putting on the "finishing flourishes"; Mrs. Sigmund was found by the potting shed.

7:15: Matsumoto approached Jennings and Mrs. Sigmund outside the potting shed and announced someone was dead in the workshop.

7:30: Jennings followed Matsumoto back to workshop, then rushed back past Mrs. Sigmund to call the police.

7:45: We arrive.

*Note: Someone telephoned the police about the theft around 6:00. Who?

*Note: Groundskeeper and chauffeur?

"Why did you ask them for their movements from three o'clock on?" Bernard asked.

"When I asked who had seen Miss Mitchell last it was Mrs. Sigmund, the maid; she saw Miss Mitchell leaving for a walk at a quarter to three. She noticed because the grandfather clock in the hall was chiming the three-quarter hour and she thought it odd she wasn't joining the inventors for tea in the front parlor at three o'clock. Apparently, no one else saw Miss Mitchell after that until Matsumoto found her around a quarter after seven."

Bernard nodded slowly. At least he finally had some definite times to work with. She'd been murdered sometime between three o'clock and a quarter past seven. That was a pretty wide space of time, and many of the staff had been busy with "chores" alone. As far as he could tell, any one of them might have slunk off to do the deed, clean up, and then come back to their duties.

Though it was much more likely the blind blacksmith had just taken his time after returning from his meeting with Prescot, and then pretended not to know who the body was in his workshop. Being blind had its positives, after all.

Bernard laid Thomas's list beside his own memorandum book where he'd written down the movements of Matsumoto. If Matsumoto was telling the truth, however, and the murder had happened just before his arrival, then where had Miss Mitchell been walking before she ended up at the workshop? Had she gone to the workshop of her own accord? What if she'd been led there at gunpoint by the thief? And why?

He kept coming back to the location. It must be important in and of itself. Why had the murder happened there, at that time, while Matsumoto just happened to be gone? What if he'd returned straight from his meeting with Prescot rather than going for a walk in the woods?

"I wish we could verify that Matsumoto took a walk in the woods after his meeting," Bernard said aloud. "But it seems the only person who might corroborate his statement is the person he heard fleeing from the direction of the workshop."

"If we knew who that was, we'd most likely know our murderer, as well."

Bernard grunted.

Thomas puffed. "You know, he might have made up the mysterious figure in the overcoat."

"True," Bernard admitted. "Needless to say, looking closely at everyone's movements from three o'clock on was a good call on your part."

"You're welcome," said Thomas.

"What's this note about a groundskeeper and a chauffeur with a question mark?" Bernard pointed to it in the memorandum book.

"There's four staff," said Thomas, another smoke puff escaping his mouth as he counted them off on his fingers. "The butler, Mr. Jennings; the cook, Mrs. Curry; the maid, Mrs. Sigmund; and the groundskeeper and chauffeur, Mr. Sigmund."

"So the groundskeeper and chauffeur are the same person?"

"Yes, the husband of the maid."

"You don't have his movements listed, or a statement."

"Haven't seen him yet. Only one I haven't tracked down. He'd left to run an errand downtown for Miss Mitchell, it seems, and hadn't yet returned."

"Hadn't returned? When did he leave?"

"No one said."

"What was he doing?"

"No one said."

"Not even his wife?"

"She was too busy with her own chores, she said, to mind her husband's every move."

So they had one missing member of staff.

"Odd that they were married in the first place. Don't married servants usually have to leave? I mean, I didn't think they'd still live in?" Bernard asked, as though Thomas would know.

"I'm not up on the latest manor staff manual," Thomas quipped.

Bernard stopped himself from grunting again.

"I suppose Miss Mitchell just didn't have an issue with it." Thomas shrugged.

Bernard grunted. That was the last time he'd send Thomas for statements on an empty stomach.

Two

Tuesday, April 16, 1901

Spokane, Washington

The Red Rogue was having a good night, or was it morning by now? Two houses down had provided some fine pieces of silver that were producing a pleasing jingling inside the burgundy overcoat, but most exciting was the matching set of miniature bronze girandole candlesticks with etchings of waterfalls cascading down to the base.

Now, the thief might have entered this next house in the same manner Red had entered last night's house, through the firewood door. But variety was the spice of life, and doing the same thing over and over, well, where was the fun in that?

Instead, Red ran gloved hands along one of the brick walls of the chosen house, getting a feel for the pattern of mortared cracks and flat surfaces. Once Red knew the pattern, the thief climbed up the sheer side of the gable wall and swung up over the eaves to make a home on the rooftop's shingles for a moment, just long enough to fling a small pebble from this lower rooftop up to the rooftop garden of the neighboring house.

The pebble flew through the air and hit with a soft *ping* off a metal guardrail surrounding the garden, then rambled and rolled across the floor of the garden, down the slight slope to the gutter where it careened downward with a *bink, bonk, bunk* until it came to the drainpipe at the end of the rut and completed its descent with a *thwump*.

The night was silent once again. Red prepared to leap expertly from the current rooftop to the neighboring one, now that the general layout of the garden above had been discovered by sound. First, Red carefully crawled in the experienced manner of one acquainted with rooftop pressure points, up along the valley rafter to the intersection with the upper ridge. There, the thief slowly stood, noting the angle of the slant to either side of the verge, the length from the ridge to the gutter, the length from end to end, and figuring the height of the house itself in comparison to the house beyond. Having spent a few years now upon rooftops, the figures and numbers came as naturally as an estimation of the number of people in a room.

Then, with a perfectly executed running leap, the Red Rogue bounded from one rooftop to the next, grasped the eaves of the neighboring house, swung up over the edge, crawled up to the ridge of the roof, and up and over the metal guardrail of the roof garden to its "inaccessible" unlocked door.

With a swift pull, the door was open and the thief was within.

* * *

It had been a long, restless night. Eleanor got up at five o'clock and fed the chickens first, opening the doors to their coop so they could wander the yard pecking bugs, gravel, grain, and other grit for their bellies. Then she watered the gardens. She did it out of habit—the plants and animals didn't know or care that Miss Mitchell was no longer with them.

Although this was technically Mr. Sigmund's job, she'd added it to her morning routine after she realized he'd never "find the time." These days it seemed he couldn't "find the time" to do most things—except run errands downtown for Miss Mitchell. Funny how Eleanor never heard the mistress request anything from the Tenderloin District next to City Hall, though that was where he was most often reported to be seen.

She sighed and rinsed her hands in the spigot by the potting shed, watching as the grime melted off into the soil at her feet. It was a pity everything in life wasn't so easy to clean up.

She turned the water off and made her way to the kitchen, prepared to do the cook's bidding, but instead found the older woman seated at the broad kitchen table, sipping a cup of steaming tea. Mrs. Curry's chestnut-brown curls were streaked with gray, framing her round face and hazel eyes as she stared off into the middle distance.

"Good morning, Mrs. Curry," she called out as she entered, startling the woman out of her thoughtful morning trance.

"Oh, good heavens! You surprised me, Eleanor, dear. Must've gotten swept away with my thoughts." She dropped her hand from her chest and took a sip of tea. "Not sure what will come of us now Miss Mitchell is gone."

"Dead, Mrs. Curry. She's dead," Eleanor said shortly, thinking of chocolate hair strands left where they didn't belong. "It's time to move on."

Mrs. Curry lifted her cup slowly and took another sip, studying Eleanor. "Yes, dear, as you say, I suppose. But where to? And may we? With the police about asking questions and wanting interviews?"

"They've already talked with us." Eleanor dismissed the police from her mind with a wave of her hand. "Perhaps we should begin by flipping through the wanted ads."

"You're certainly eager to get going."

Eleanor sighed. "I just don't see the point in hanging about when there's nothing to be done about it now. She's dead. There's no heir. If I don't find another job soon, there'll be no supper on the table."

"What about Mr. Sigmund?"

Eleanor finally sat down across from Mrs. Curry with a *plop*, avoiding her eyes.

"I haven't seen him since yesterday."

"He didn't come home last night at all?"

"No. And seeing as we both tied our lives to one woman, and that one woman is dead, I don't see how remaining here will do either of us any good."

Eleanor kept her hands busy grabbing a cup to pour herself some tea.

"I'm certain he'll find a new job quickly, dear, and then perhaps you can finally stop working yourself to the bone and start a family."

Eleanor almost scoffed in reply. Perhaps the cook didn't realize Eleanor was well over child-bearing age. She'd often been mistaken for someone younger because of her small form. Then again, Mrs. Curry was probably just trying to be kind.

"Perhaps," said Eleanor, sweeping over the issue and taking a sip of tea. It was too hot for her current mood.

Mrs. Curry sighed. "She didn't deserve such a way to go."

Chocolate strands. Eleanor's blue eyes flashed.

"Do you think it was the thief of the night before, perhaps?" Mrs. Curry posited. "Returned to finish his business and got caught by Miss Mitchell?"

"I doubt it."

"Why Miss Mitchell was in that workshop in the first place, I'll never know."

"Do you have the paper, Mrs. Curry?" Eleanor said curtly.

"What? Oh, yes, I believe I set it down...over there." She pointed to where it lay on a bowl filled with apples, as there was no clear counter space.

"It'll turn out all right, Eleanor," she said, reaching out to pat her hand comfortingly. "You'll see. You've still got your Mr. Sigmund."

Eleanor took the paper, thanked Mrs. Curry, and went back to the potting shed where she spent the next hour forcing herself to slowly piece letters together into words when really she couldn't even see straight.

* * *

Marian lay in the soft, downy cloud that was the feather bed her grandmother had made for her so long ago. She remembered watching her hand-sew the ticking for the mattresses—two to ensure a restful night's sleep, which every good homemaker knew was of the utmost necessity.

Nain had let her join her on her visits to the surrounding farms to buy the feathers. Once home, she had joyfully helped stuff the feathers into the ticking, bundle by bundle, leaping about the room to collect the strays as they wafted about on air currents. The currents were invisible to the eye but crafty enough to keep the feathers out of reach of an outstretched child's hand. Oh, how they'd laughed together then.

There were so many happy memories like that one to focus on. So why did the upsetting arguments and unsolved quarrels keep surfacing instead?

The sun hadn't risen, and yet she'd awakened this morning, tears streaming from sleeping eyes as she pulled herself from a nightmare laced in a memory of a recurring—and now so silly—disagreement over whether the dishes from dinner should be cleaned by the one who cooked the meal or the one who enjoyed the meal.

In the nightmare, she'd been washing the stack of cups and pots and plates, but every time she turned back to grab another item, the pile had doubled. Her grandmother had entered and found her miserably scrubbing the hundredth plate but instead of offering to help, had turned into a wolf, snarling at her ferociously and threatening to swallow her and the dirty mound of dishes whole if she didn't clean every last one of them.

Her hands shook as she raised them to wipe the tears from

her cheeks and pulled the heavy quilts over her head, attempting to block the dark house and all its memories, good and bad, from consuming her.

* * *

Bernard had to meet with the coroner first thing, which gave him the perfect excuse to miss running into Mr. Prescot at the breakfast table. A quick peck on the cheek for Roslyn as he grabbed a muffin for the road and he was off to the offices of Dr. Nathan M. Baker in the Hyde Block. It had been too dark the evening before for the coroner to offer any sort of helpful information, and so he'd made Bernard wait.

The Presbyterian Minnesotan was a little man who made up for his stature with his knowledge. Although he'd only been coroner since '98, his medical acumen was unsurpassed, making him someone Bernard had admired from afar, but never had the opportunity to work with. Till now.

Bernard tipped his hat to the doctor as he entered, but in response all he got was a reedy, "Detective Carew. Here to take a look at the Mitchell woman?"

Dr. Baker's bald head gleamed in the new electric light of the morgue. His tiny ears had no purpose given they weren't holding up the pince-nez perched upon his long, pointed nose above his thick mustache.

"I'll get straight to the point. It appears this woman was dead before she was beheaded."

Bernard did a second take.

"Yes, you heard right." Dr. Baker led him to the long white table with the silhouette of a woman beneath a heavy white sheet. He pulled this back to reveal the head of Miss Mitchell, more accurately placed above her neck than it had been the last time Bernard had seen it. It allowed Bernard to notice how attractive she was—had been. Her brown hair framed a heart-shaped face with curved cheeks and bow lips. A most striking beauty.

"I admit, I suspected she'd been sedated—since her body was laid out so complacently—before having her head removed," said Bernard.

"That's because she was dead already. Strangled. Look at these marks."

Bernard leaned down to see where the doctor had cleaned up the severed area. Sure enough, to either side of the ragged wound were dark blue and purple splotches befitting the grasp of a man with large, strong hands.

"Strangled," Bernard grunted. "And *then* beheaded..." He let his mind mull over this for a moment. "This shines a whole new light on the situation."

"I should think so."

"But...why both? It doesn't make sense."

"That, Detective, is *your* problem now."

* * *

Thomas sat in the parlor before a fidgety Archibald Prescot. In deference to his sister-in-law's womanly sensibilities, he hadn't broached the subject of murder in the manner he'd concocted the evening before, no matter how Bernard grunted. But now they were alone and he could try to surprise the portly fellow into a confession.

"So, we haven't had much of a chance to talk, you and I," Thomas began, resting his right ankle across his left leg in an air of relaxation. "You're here to build a clock for the Great Northern Depot, right?"

"Yes." Prescot stopped fidgeting and puffed out his chest in pride of work completed only in his head. "I am, I mean," he pushed his glasses up his nose, "I've actually been helping the contractors with the clock tower design from Connecticut since the beginning. I'm here now to make final sketches before they begin building, then I'll return next year along with the clock to help with the installation."

"Don't they usually just mail-order one these days? Send it across country by train?"

"I wouldn't know." Prescot shrugged. "This is my first tower clock."

Thomas nodded. "Just saw a nice little article about it in *The Spokesman* the other day. Said it'll be the 'finest depot building west of St. Paul.'"

"I certainly hope my part will be memorable."

"Hm," Thomas murmured, taking a page from his brother's lines. "Heard you also have a nice little side hobby going with clocks—even met with Miss Mitchell yesterday?"

"That's right," Prescot said slowly, raising an eyebrow wonderingly.

Well, here he went: "Gladys Mitchell was found murdered last night."

"Murdered!" Prescot repeated, his brown eyes bugging out behind his glasses. He wasn't fidgeting now. In fact, his entire body had gone stiff as a board, his hands gripping the bear-shaped armrests of the chair in which he sat.

"Murdered," Thomas repeated, for emphasis, keeping his posture relaxed but his keen eye focused on the suspect. "Her head was severed from her body."

Prescot's mouth opened and closed. "But...I..." He sighed, closed his eyes and shook his head. "Well, knock me over with a fetter."

It was Thomas's turn to be confused. He placed both feet flat on the floor. "Excuse me?"

"Just an expression."

"Yes. But I'm pretty sure it's 'knock me over with a *feather*.'"

Prescot looked at him. "No, it isn't."

"Yes, it is."

"It can't be. You can't knock someone over with a feather. You might *blow* someone over *like* a feather. But you couldn't knock them out."

"Yes, it—oh, good grief." Thomas shook his head. Some people's education. He pulled out his memorandum book and pencil. "The point is: you were at Miss Mitchell's house *twice* yesterday, in the morning and afternoon."

"Yes, that's right." Again Prescot sighed, this time leaning back in his chair, removing his thick glasses, and rubbing his eyes as he rested the back of his head against the antimacassar. "But I didn't kill her."

"So you say. Please account for your actions."

Prescot returned his glasses and looked at Thomas, straightening up. "Gladly." As he spoke, his hands waved wildly, like the tail end of a happy dog. "The first time I met with Miss Mitchell yesterday we were discussing an invention she was testing for me. The meeting ended when she declared she'd like to support me and my work as my patroness. She invited me to meet with the other inventor she patronized that afternoon at three o'clock."

"And why do you think Miss Mitchell requested your presence *before* telephoning the police when she'd been burglarized the night before? Perhaps she thought you knew something about it?"

Prescot went pink. "Well, I, um, my invention, that is, had been an idea for a sort of new alarm mantel clock in order to catch a thief."

"An 'alarm mantel clock'? How could a *clock* catch a thief?"

Prescot shrugged. "It's difficult to explain."

"Fine. And when it *didn't* work, Miss Mitchell was so impressed she wanted to talk to you immediately about becoming your patroness?"

"Not exactly..." But he stuttered into silence and didn't seem to be able to explain it any other way.

"Let's move on for the moment." Thomas waved away the silence. "So after the morning meeting you stuck around?"

"No, I left and returned."

"Where did you go?"

"I...I went to Montrose Park." Prescot blushed again.

"Alone?"

"Yes." Still pink.

"That is, Miss Mitchell did not accompany you?"

"No!" Prescot burst, his face a bright red color now.

Thomas nodded and scribbled for awhile in his memorandum

book. Once he raised his head, Prescot's face was back to a normal color but he had a silly smile on his face. The man was definitely hiding something. Perhaps a certain level of familiarity with the dead woman?

"How familiar were you with Miss Mitchell?"

"I'd just met her, if that's what you mean?"

"I mean, she's a single woman with one male inventor already boarding with her. Why didn't you board there, as well?"

"Well, I haven't...hadn't been asked yet." Again the energy seemed to slip out of him.

"So when did you first meet her?"

"We traveled west together from Buffalo. Purely by coincidence!" he added forcefully, putting one hand out as though to stop Thomas's thoughts from going down the track they were already headed. "We just talked about my ideas and she said she'd test one out for me once we got to Spokane."

"Right. The broken alarm clock of the first meeting."

Prescot nodded.

"And the second meeting?"

"That wasn't with Miss Mitchell. It was with Mr. Matsumoto. We met at three o'clock in the front parlor—the one covered corner to corner in Japanese parachute...paraphrase..."

"I believe the word you're looking for is 'paraphernalia.'"

"God bless you."

Thomas grunted before he could stop himself. He was turning into Bernard after all.

"As I was saying, Mr. Matsumoto and I met there for about an hour. We finished sometime around four."

"Did Miss Mitchell join you later?"

"No."

"Really? Why wouldn't the patroness attend the introduction between her two inventors?"

"I...don't know. I hadn't thought it odd until now."

"She didn't come in at all while you were meeting?"

"No."

"So the last time you saw Miss Mitchell was in the morning about the clock?"

"That's right."

"And where did you go after the second meeting?"

"I headed home for dinner—where your brother saw me, in fact," he pointed out emphatically.

Thomas didn't react. "So Mr. Matsumoto was with you in the house from three o'clock to four?"

"Yes."

"And at four o'clock you came straight back here?"

"Yes."

"Did you see anyone on the road? Miss Mitchell, for instance?"

"No." Prescot shook his head. "But I took the streetcar and it had been a long day, so I honestly didn't see much of anyone."

A long day. It certainly had been. For murderers and detectives. Bernard had been right: Prescot certainly didn't look like the type to kill someone who'd just offered to pay for his hobby. But then again, the flush of pink in his cherubic face had suggested there might be more passion hidden in the depths of his bespectacled being than one might first be led to believe.

* * *

The black daisy eyes were staring at Marian again this morning, but she was having difficulty finding it within herself to go out again after that nightmare, even though yesterday had turned out well.

"Lightning never strikes the same place twice," she told the chair, using an old favorite of her Nain's against her. "Just because yesterday I made a new friend, who's to say I'd have the same experience today?"

Laugh and the world laughs with you, weep and you weep alone.

"Touché."

For the first time, it occurred to Marian that perhaps her grandmother had repeated those proverbs for this very reason: so even when she was gone, Marian would still have her.

"Oh, Nain," she sighed, "you're still here." She laughed at the daisy pattern. "Or at least your chair is. Once again, I'm being propelled out the door by a chair. Dear me, what *will* become of me?"

Just then, there was a knock at the door.

Marian started from her chair, then stopped and checked herself. If it was one of Nain's friends come to call, she'd need to show the proper decorum to match the black mourning dress and jewelry she'd donned this morning after forcing herself from the bed. She glanced in the small mirror by the door, tucking that habitual stray curl behind her ear. But when she finally opened the door, she was not prepared for who was there.

"Eleanor?!" she cried out.

Time had passed cruelly upon the countenance of this old friend. She took in the tousled blonde hair that was the very definition of "towheaded," the small, pointed nose, rosy cheeks, pale lips, and heart-shaped face. Her eyes were the palest blue and were set close together above her nose. Worry lines streaked her forehead, aging her more than her forty-some years. While Marian liked to think she'd maintained her youthful body while living in the hilly city of Seattle—though her calves had grown to unprecedented proportions—Eleanor looked tired and weary, like life had not been kind to her in the years since they'd played in and around Nain's house. This did not diminish Marian's absolute joy in seeing her again, however.

"Marian!" the woman on her doorstep cried out in return, and the two embraced as though not a day had passed, all decorum and age forgotten.

* * *

Bernard was bone-tired and his day was only just getting started. He had barely slept, so intent was he on lining up his questions for the following day. This was his first, and maybe last, chance to prove to the other detectives, and to the chief, that he had what it took to remain Detective Carew. It had just been his luck that one of the many burglary calls had turned into a murder. Not so lucky for the victim, of course...

His mind returned to the body under the sheet and Dr. Baker's diagnosis.

Bernard realized now he had just two questions, which he thought was pretty good considering the news that the victim had been killed *twice* in two different ways.

One: Was she strangled and beheaded by two different people?

Or two: One person?

The distinction felt important to Bernard.

If she was strangled and beheaded by two different people, the two men who "discovered" the body in the workshop—the blacksmith and also the butler who'd identified the body—certainly sprang to mind. Or perhaps the burglar was in fact two people who had returned?

If she was strangled and beheaded by one person then the question was: Why? Had strangling her not been enough? Or had the murderer intended to behead her all along but strangled her to make it easier?

Both actions felt incredibly personal. Whoever had done this had held a very deep reason for doing such violence to Miss Mitchell. There was one reason that immediately leapt to the forefront of his mind: lust. Lust for her to be his and she refused, or lust for her to be only his and she'd cheated on him with another man.

Then something new occurred to him: What if the killer had beheaded her to *hide* the strangulation? Then he was looking for a very clever killer. Someone who hadn't just killed her out of passion, but with malice aforethought. But why would someone try to hide a strangulation? What would the strangulation tell him that the killer didn't want him to know?

He supposed the fact she was strangled did narrow his suspects a bit.

His thoughts drifted through the household. Matsumoto was small in stature and blind, but even so he'd heard stories of samurai warriors and knew the man shouldn't be discounted. He'd seen the butler, Jennings, had the height and strength to strangle. And the mysterious missing groundskeeper/chauffeur; perhaps he'd returned. And then there was the burglar...

How did Sherlock do it? How did he start with so many possibilities and narrow it down till all that was left was the truth?

Look at the details. The little things the other detectives would miss. If they had taken this case, all of those suspects would be at the station right now giving statements, and some of them would be beaten into changing them. In fact, he highly doubted whether the other detectives would have looked any further than the Japanese inventor. But Bernard was not the other detectives. He was no Lestrade. He was going to bring a new kind of detecting to the force.

Bernard hopped aboard the streetcar gliding up the South Hill, his thoughts and questions rearranging themselves as he rode through Cannon's Addition and disembarked to walk the final length to the late Miss Mitchell's home.

He stopped at the end of the long drive and took in the lay of the land. The house was one of those new Cutter mansions built way out in the country, but not so far out telephone lines and electrical wires couldn't connect to the house in a spiderweb of trouble. There were even lines connecting to the carriage house to the west, no doubt so the mistress could call for a carriage, or perhaps even an automobile. It looked like the upper floor of the carriage house had also been transformed into staff housing.

He'd need to verify where each staff member lived. Since Miss Mitchell was a single woman, it was already odd for her to be accommodating a male boarder, but also to have employed two male workers, never mind that one of them was married, well, it was against all propriety no matter what century they were in.

As he approached the house, he decided he'd start by getting answers from whoever opened the door, assuming it'd be the butler, Jennings.

He was not disappointed. He removed his hat and coat and handed them to Jennings to hang, watching the butler's towering frame and sturdy build as he placed them on hooks in a closet beside other overcoats. Then Jennings led Bernard to the front parlor.

Bernard had never been in such a house, and found himself wondering where Miss Mitchell got the money to decorate to such an extreme. It was clear Miss Mitchell held something of an interest in Japanese art, but he was at a loss for words to describe such a room.

The butler waited patiently for him to complete his study and explain his purpose. He was dressed in a sharp new suit, his shoes polished to a high shine. His dark blonde hair was slicked back and parted down the middle in the standard practice, his face unlined and clean-shaven, providing a clear view of his rather prodigious nose and stern mouth. He stood straight as a telephone pole, his hands behind his back, his chin pointed out and up in a manner of superiority. This man did not suffer from a lack of confidence in himself.

"I'd like to speak with each of the staff in turn today, and I can begin with you. Mr. Jennings, yes?"

"Yes, sir," the man replied with a slight bow of the head. "I did give a statement to the other policeman yesterday."

"I understand. But you forget we originally came about a theft. I'd like to hear more about that, if you don't mind."

"You will need to speak with Mrs. Sigmund. I was asked to

telephone the police to attend to the matter, but I am not as well-acquainted with the circumstances nor the pieces that were removed, although I do know they were items taken from this room."

"No one heard anything that night? Or noticed anything missing?"

"No, sir. Only Mrs. Sigmund noticed the missing items."

"Mrs. Sigmund is the maid?"

"Yes, sir."

"May I speak with her now, then?"

"I'm afraid she went out this morning. I am not certain when she intends to return, as we are all unsure about our duties at the moment."

"Naturally." Bernard nodded. "Has Mr. Sigmund returned?"

The butler scoffed. "Not that I am aware of."

"Is that odd?"

The butler glared toward the dragon bench. "It is not uncommon for the chauffeur to be sent on an errand of which none of us has any knowledge, except Miss Mitchell."

"Hm," Bernard murmured. The butler didn't care for Mr. Sigmund, it would seem. "How long has he been the chauffeur?"

"I believe that he has always been the driver, sir, as well as the groundskeeper. Only recently has he been given the title of 'chauffeur' rather than 'driver,' with the arrival of the automobile."

"I see." Bernard took a seat on the dragon bench which Jennings was still studying, in an attempt to force the butler to meet his eyes. The butler seemed to understand, but only let their eyes meet for a moment before pointing his chin aloft once again and continuing to talk to the masks on the wall. "What can you tell me about him?"

Again that small scoff escaped the man, like he was holding an excess of air in his puffed-up chest.

"He shouldn't still be here, sir."

"What do you mean by that?"

"I mean," his eyes connected with Bernard's, "that a man who is that cruel toward his wife has no place driving a woman of standing like Miss Mitchell."

Bernard grunted at the butler's ferocity. "I see. Would you kindly elaborate?"

The butler's eyes shifted again and he held his breath before sighing, "No."

Bernard's eyes widened. "Why not?"

"Mrs. Sigmund does not deserve her name dragged through the mud."

"I would like to remind you I am trying to solve a murder, and Mr. Sigmund is currently missing. I need to know everything I can about the man before I find him and question him."

Jennings looked at the masks again.

"Do you and Mrs. Sigmund have an understanding?"

The butler was visibly shaken.

"Never!" he spat, his demeanor collapsing. "I would never. Mrs. Sigmund is a beautiful person who deserves happiness. That is all."

"Right. And yourself?"

"Myself?"

"How long have you been here as butler?"

The banality of the question seemed to throw Jennings off for a moment.

"Six months," he finally answered.

"So you have not been here long."

"No, sir."

It may not seem like a long time, but Bernard felt that six months was long enough to cultivate a "knight in shining armor" image.

"May I just say, you seem highly trained for someone in Spokane. You speak as though you've worked in the finer houses of Seattle, if not abroad."

The butler had regained his composure. "I have, sir." He did not expound on this information, but neither did Bernard really care at this juncture. He and Thomas could locate all the staff references once he arrived.

"And the cook? How long has she been here?"

"She, too, was here before I started. The Sigmunds started here as a couple, I believe, about the same time."

"And when was that?"

"I do not know, sir. You will have to ask Mrs. Sigmund or Mrs. Curry."

"And the living arrangements? Does everyone live-in?"

"Yes, sir."

He should have held off asking Jennings about his relationship with Mrs. Sigmund. The butler seemed intent on answering in terse statements after that little confrontation. "And where might that be?"

"The Sigmunds live above the carriage house, Mrs. Curry lives in a room near the kitchen downstairs, and I have a room on the third floor."

"And where is Mr. Matsumoto's room?"

"On the second floor of the house."

"And Miss Mitchell's room was also on that floor?"

"Yes, sir."

That would have made it easier for her to "speak" with Matsumoto about his work privately.

"And her study?"

"Connected to her bedroom."

What a maze of a house. Of course his first murder had to be the country-house detective story with too many suspects and odd complications.

"Would you take me to her study, please?"

The butler deigned to meet Bernard's eyes. "Will that be necessary, sir?"

"Is there a problem?"

The butler looked away again, but this time down his long aquiline nose rather than above it. "I only wondered, sir, since she was murdered in the workshop?"

"Yes, but she lived in this house. It will be necessary to discover more about her life to answer the questions of her death."

Jennings nodded. "I see, sir. But I'm afraid I don't have the key, sir. Mrs. Sigmund is the only one with access."

Bernard's eyes narrowed. How convenient.

"Perhaps we should check the door, just in case it is unlocked."

Jennings shifted his weight restlessly but then seemed to realize he had no excuse to deny him this, at least.

He turned and led the way out of the parlor and up the grand staircase to the second floor. Turning at the top of the stairs, he led the way to a door at the end of the hall. Jennings gave the handle a small shake, then turned quickly. "It appears to be locked, sir."

Bernard reached forward and checked the door himself, unwilling to take him at his word. "Is this room always locked?"

"Yes, sir, as Miss Mitchell's private affairs are within."

"And only Mrs. Sigmund has a key?"

"Yes, sir."

"I see, thank you, Jennings. And you said her study is connected to her bedroom?"

"Yes, sir." Jennings pointed to the next door down the hall.

"And that is always kept locked as well?"

"Yes, sir."

He continued walking farther down the hall, forcing Jennings to follow. "What's down there?"

At the end of the hall was a dumbwaiter between two more doors.

"This door leads to the servants' stair that goes through the entire house from the basement to the third floor," Jennings explained, opening the farther door lined in a lighter-paneled wood, as though marking it for the servants' use. It was only upon noticing this that Bernard realized the rest of the floor was paneled in a darker wood. "The master staircase only leads from the first floor to the second, though there is a stair beneath it that leads to the basement."

Then the butler turned and opened the second door, which opened on a bathroom. "This bathroom is for Miss Mitchell's private use. The servants' one is downstairs next to Mrs. Curry's room."

"That must make it rather inconvenient for you," Bernard said, recalling Jennings bunked on the third floor.

The butler shook his head. "It's still less inconvenient than having to use an outhouse."

Bernard grunted in agreement.

"And those two doors?" He pointed to the other side of the grand staircase.

"One of them leads to Mr. Matsumoto's room, and the other would have been used for any guests or other boarders at Miss Mitchell's discretion."

Bernard nodded.

"Will that be all, sir?"

Now would be the perfect time for harder questions, but Bernard couldn't think how to shake the truth out of the man just yet.

"Yes, thank you. I assume Mrs. Curry can still be found in the kitchen?"

For the first time the butler's face cracked into what might have been a smile as he looked up at the ceiling. "Mrs. Curry will leave that kitchen only once ovens clean themselves."

* * *

Marian couldn't stop smiling, pleased beyond words to be reconnecting with a dear friend.

"I read in the paper that you had returned," Eleanor explained.

"In the paper? Whatever are my personal affairs doing in *The*

Spokesman-Review?" Marian asked, placing a pot of water to boil on the range.

"Oh, you know how it is. When there's little news, they like to place small 'brevities' about the goings-on of the locals. It said you'd returned to close up your grandmother's house. They published your grandmother's passing, too. I was terribly sorry to hear of it. She was such a dear. I'll always be grateful to her for taking me in and giving me a job when I needed it most."

Marian nodded sadly, her fingers running over the bog oak necklace she'd picked out that morning. "I know Nain always appreciated how clean you kept the place, and me." She smiled fondly. Although Eleanor may have been paid for her work as a housemaid, she'd been more of a nanny or governess to Marian than anything. She realized that unlike most girls, she'd been blessed with three mothers: the one she'd lost and couldn't remember, the grandmother who'd raised her, and the one she'd seen as more of an adult playmate than anything. She twisted the ring on her right pinky as she realized Eleanor was the only mother she had left, and she'd never thought to see her again.

"Close up the house...yes, I suppose that's why I'm here. I haven't the heart to close it yet, though. I fear I may drift back into Spokane society yet, especially if good friends like you are still here." Even as she said the words she knew it was true that Eleanor may be just what the doctor ordered. She led Eleanor to join her on the Chesterfield by the fire, across from the chair that whispered to her, *It is a poor heart that never rejoices.* Nothing like renewing an old friendship to remind oneself of the beauty of living. "I suppose I'm glad after all that *The Spokesman* found my return newsworthy."

"I admit, I was actually searching the classifieds, for you see, I find myself newly out of work."

"I'm so sorry to hear it. You haven't a family to support, do you?" Hungry young ones clutching at Eleanor's knees would have explained the tiredness that marred her face.

"No. My husband and I were never blessed in that way. But perhaps that's for the better." Eleanor rubbed a hand subconsciously over her upper arm. Marian couldn't see anything there but the long, brown sleeve of her shirtwaist, but the gesture implied something she hoped she was misinterpreting.

"And what does your husband do?"

"He and I both used to work for Miss Gladys Mitchell. I worked as a maid and Mr. Sigmund has been groundskeeper and driver until last month, when Miss Mitchell got one of those electric automobiles and he became 'chauffeur.'"

But Marian had been distracted by the name "Sigmund." An image of ginger curls and a sinister sneer swept before her.

"Not Cecil Sigmund?"

"The very same. Have you met?" Something flashed across Eleanor's face and disappeared just as the kettle boiled in the kitchen.

Marian stood as she explained about her run-in downtown the day before. "What are the chances?" she proclaimed as she went to prepare the tea things.

"Indeed," she heard Eleanor mutter from the other room.

Marian placed the tea leaf blend in the pot and poured the boiling water over it, then placed it on a tray amongst the matching tea set and carried it all carefully into the parlor.

"We'll let this steep for just a minute and then it'll be ready," she said.

But Eleanor seemed stuck on the subject of Mr. Sigmund. "You said he was down by City Hall?"

"Um, farther south: I was looking for my favorite restaurant on Washington. I'm afraid I was a bit distracted. It was my first time leaving the house since I've returned and I was surprised by the noise of downtown. It was almost as bad as Seattle. One lump or two? Cream? Lemon?"

"Just lemon, please," Eleanor said, watching Marian pour the tea through a silver strainer into her cup. When Marian was finished, she handed the cup to her along with a lemon slice. Eleanor squeezed the lemon firmly into the tea and then began sipping it slowly, methodically, her gaze distant.

"But you said you're recently out of work?" Marian took her own cup and tried to change the subject. "What happened with Miss Mitchell, if I may ask?"

"Oh, it's actually quite horrible. She was murdered."

"Murdered!" Marian's cup came down with a louder *clink* than she'd intended.

"Murdered. Just last night. Or afternoon. Or something. It's all been quite a whirl."

"I'm sure." Marian was deeply curious and shocked, but strove to be sensitive as well. "We don't need to speak of it, if you don't want to."

But Eleanor had come to life with this urgent news, and now seemed eager. "On the contrary. If it doesn't make you too uncomfortable, talking through it might clear my head a bit." She set her tea down. "You see, yesterday was strange right from the start, seeing as we were robbed the night before—"

"Robbed *and* murdered? What are the chances?" Marian couldn't help but interject.

"Yes, exactly. What *are* the chances? And yet the police have yet to ask about the thief. So far, they've just been interested in us, the staff, and where we all were at the time. The impudent officer who questioned us last night had the gall to invite himself to dinner. None of us had an appetite, naturally, but he packed his face while we all sullenly gave him statements.

"But back to the theft, it was stranger still because Miss Mitchell asked me to send for a Mr. Prescot to come look at some clock *before* having the butler call the police! Rich people, you'll find, are uniquely eccentric."

Marian felt a tingle pass over her when she realized once again Eleanor had mentioned someone she'd met only yesterday. No matter how large a city Spokane became, it would always be a small town where you couldn't step off the front porch without running into an old friend.

Marian gave a polite chuckle. "Yes, I—"

"Miss Mitchell was the queen of eccentricities, however," Eleanor forged ahead, "as she collected inventors like vases. Mr. Prescot was just the latest in a long line of them. We currently have one boarding with us who works in a little shop at the back of the property: a Japanese fellow."

Eleanor paused just long enough for Marian to ask, "What could he be doing that would interest a woman of Miss Mitchell's standing?"

"I ask myself the same question. All I know is, that's where she...the body...was found." Eleanor's face went white and she became extremely interested in studying her teacup and saucer, picking them up again and sipping quietly, the excitement drained out of her in one quick flood.

Marian let the silence lengthen as she considered her friend's story. Overlooking the morbidity of it, she found herself strangely fascinated by the riddle of it all. "So do you think the inventor did it?"

Eleanor sighed and nodded. "I suppose it all comes of encouraging foreigners and eccentrics." She held her cup without drinking. "Mr. Sigmund and I should never have both taken work at the same house. It had seemed like such a good idea at the time. We were newly married, with no money of our own, and Mr. Sigmund was so determined to make his way up in the world, and I had read too many novels set in great British manor houses..."

Marian suddenly realized her friend was quietly crying. She reached out a comforting hand.

"But just think. If it hadn't happened this way, if you hadn't been looking for work in the paper this morning, you might never have crossed paths with *me* again." She smiled and squeezed Eleanor's hand. "And I am ever so glad it did happen."

* * *

Eleanor looked up at her dear friend. She'd meant to come this morning to comfort Marian—the one who had actually lost someone she loved—and was finding herself consoled instead.

Her eyes fell on the black-beaded jewelry around Marian's throat that gave way to a dark, crepe dress. She'd never seen Marian in black before, knew she made a point of avoiding the color, feeling it was too grim and morbid, not to mention rather uncomplimentary on a woman with that Scots-Irish pale skin. The pain and sadness clearly etched on her face spread across her entire small, thin frame. Yet, somehow, Marian managed to make grief look graceful.

"Thank you," Eleanor said softly, pulling her hand away in the guise of lifting her cup to take a sip.

Her hand was shaking. She set her cup and saucer down and took a deep breath to steady herself, pulling out a handkerchief.

"I don't know what's come over me. One would think as the only maid in such a large house I'd be glad to have a reason to try something new. But part of me actually enjoyed the strenuous work that let me beat out my frustrations. Perhaps a scullery maid might have come in the next wave of hires. Though in my experience, young maids tend to always be breaking down in tears and running off to their rooms with a 'headache.' It would have been *my* job to break her in and, in the end, when you want something done right, you just have to do it yourself."

Marian smiled across from her, but Eleanor knew Marian had no idea what hard work was like. She'd grown up in this charming house with a loving family, albeit not her own parents, and yet she'd always been shown love. Eleanor, well, she'd had to work from the time she could hold a pail to feed the chickens. Her father had been cursed with four daughters on a working farm, which meant a hard life and no gratitude for the long, difficult labor, just food on the table when they earned it. She wasn't one to shrink from hard work. Perhaps that was why she'd taught herself to find joy in the little things, like a freshly scrubbed floor, or dusting the decorative items in the front parlor.

She took in Marian's complex entanglement of auburn curls, which framed a round face that had somehow grown into a young woman's since she'd last seen it. It was difficult not to sink back into fond memories of times gone by.

Marian's intelligent young eyes had watched her every move back then, even offering to help when she could. It had been a wonderful situation after her old life with her first husband had come to an end, leaving her floundering and searching for a new life, a new start. Mrs. Kenyon was so different from her current—or rather, late—mistress. She'd insisted on doing all the cooking herself in the house, and many a time, Eleanor had been invited to join the family for meals. She'd been treated as a member of the family, rather than a servant. So very different from Miss Mitchell, who seemed determined to adhere to a strict class structure—probably because she was new money, not old, and so felt it necessary to make that line more clearly defined.

Miss Mitchell. Just yesterday morning she'd been scrubbing the floors when she'd heard, "Eleanor?"

And there she was, queen of the castle.

"Yes, ma'am." She'd stood stiffly and bobbed, her knees creaking, the dirty rag in her hand plopping into the bucket at her feet.

"I'll be writing some letters in the study in a moment. Please ensure the desk is fully stocked with ink and paper *this* time."

She'd glided past without making eye contact, her yellow silk kimono-bloomer costume—of her own invention—making a statement about women's rights or some such nonsense. The bloomers were completely nonsensical and all about the risqué manner in which she showed off her ankles and defined legs to the world, while the kimono tunic top was thanks to a current fascination with everything Japanese—from her decor to an inventor to her clothing. As she'd followed the yellow tidal wave of womanhood up the stairs, she'd wondered what the woman was thinking.

Eleanor knew now what she was thinking. Miss Mitchell thought she could use her feminine wiles to turn men's heads and give her what she wanted—be that a plate of oysters or the vote. She was one of those women who, if she set her mind to it, could have anything, or any*one*, she desired.

Eleanor tugged her sleeve down over her wrist and the tender bruise that had revealed itself there this morning. Then she took a deep breath, releasing her memories of yesterday out her fingertips and forcing her hands to become still before taking up her cup again.

* * *

Bernard found Mrs. Curry with her head in the oven.

He cleared his throat as he entered and she pulled a rather red, plump face out, followed by a pan of fluffy brown rolls. Bernard was hard-pressed to think of anything that smelled quite so comforting as freshly baked bread.

Beneath the cook's graying brown curls, sparkling hazel eyes greeted him in a manner that seemed eager to please.

"Pardon me, Mrs. Curry. Detective Carew. I'm afraid I need to ask you some questions."

"Naturally! Let me just stir the stew for luncheon, then I'll get us a pot of tea for while we talk."

She set the rolls down and lifted the lid on the large pot on the stove. Bernard's second-favorite smell in the world greeted his nose and he smiled like a young man who's come home from college. Now he understood Thomas's reason for staying to dinner the previous night.

"I'd love a cup, thank you." He sat at the broad, worn wooden table, marked with the numerous cuts of knives and the burn marks of many a hot pot. Other than the *clinks* and *clanks* of Mrs. Curry moving about with purpose, the room was pleasantly still at the moment, and exuded a warmth that beckoned relaxation.

It wasn't long before Mrs. Curry joined him at the table with a tea set. He took the proffered cup and saucer after the tea was poured black the way he liked it. He smelled the bitter scent before sipping it politely and nodding his enjoyment to the gracious woman across from him.

"So, what do you want to know?" Mrs. Curry asked, pouring herself a cup with cream and two sugars.

"Well, perhaps we should begin with your statement from yesterday. Would you mind repeating it?"

"Not at all, considering all I did was cook all afternoon. I never left the kitchen. I was here all day, just as I am every day."

"You never stepped outside?"

"I rarely do. It's difficult to remember when exactly I might have done so yesterday."

Bernard took another sip. "Did anyone pass through your kitchen in the afternoon?"

"Well, yes, almost everyone at one point or another. How late were you thinking?"

"Let's say starting from quarter to three."

"At a quarter till I would have been finishing the cleaning from lunch with the help of Eleanor and Mr. Jennings. I like to clean and then take a short tea break at three. Generally the other staff join me."

"The *entire* staff?"

"Yes, normally, but yesterday Mr. Jennings was serving tea in the front parlor and Mr. Sigmund did not join us, either, though that often happens if he's assisting Mr. Matsumoto or driving Miss Mitchell somewhere. But Mrs. Sigmund didn't think he was doing either of those things so she went to find out if he wanted us to keep a cup aside for him."

"Did she find him?"

"I don't know for certain, but I don't think so, as his cup was still sitting on the sideboard even after the murder was discovered and reported."

"Had Mr. Sigmund been around earlier that day?"

"I'm afraid I don't usually know the whereabouts of everyone else in the house except at meals and tea time." She looked genuinely sorry for the lack of information and Bernard gave her an encouraging smile. "Mrs. Sigmund keeps me company when she can, but most days Miss Mitchell had a list for her that stretched to Seattle and back, and she'd often lend a hand in the garden—I think mostly for the fresh air after all that cleaning."

Bernard grunted. He wondered when Mrs. Sigmund found time to sleep when it sounded like she was carrying the entire household on her back. "What about when Jennings was preparing for dinner? Wouldn't he need to come down for food and the like?"

"Yes. He begins preparing for dinner quite early. Sometimes five o'clock."

"And when is dinner served?"

"Not till eight o'clock." Mrs. Curry leaned forward, her fingers still wrapped around her cup as she added conspiratorially, "I think he likes to take his time taste-testing the wine to pair with the meal, if you understand what I mean."

"Ah." Bernard nodded. He wondered what else the butler might be up to in that time. "Speaking of dinner time, was Mr. Matsumoto often absent from meals?"

"Yes, but I think he gets lost in his work sometimes. I don't mind. My late husband was like that. He'd often get so busy with work he'd forget I was at home waiting for him." She set down her teacup. "I always leave a plate warm for Mr. Matsumoto in the oven for when he does turn up eventually. Sometimes I send Mr. Sigmund out to fetch him, if he's here, but not frequently."

"Why not?"

She played with her empty cup, considering her words. "I don't think Mr. Sigmund enjoys being helpful, in general, but especially with Mr. Matsumoto. It's unfortunate Miss Mitchell insisted Mr. Sigmund be the one to assist Mr. Matsumoto when the inventor needed it, but I suppose there's really no one else available."

"I see. And does Mr. Matsumoto ever join you for tea?"

"Oh, no, which surprises me, as I assumed tea was an important meal for the Japanese, but come to think of it, I don't know that he's ever been properly invited. As a boarder, it's difficult to know exactly where one should place him. He eats his meals, when he does attend, upstairs with Miss Mitchell, but I've often thought he'd prefer to join us down here."

Bernard nodded.

"And how long does tea usually last?"

"I generally have to get dinner started, so I like to have tea cleared by four o'clock. Yesterday, Mr. Jennings cleared the upstairs tea after four, however, so I was running a little behind."

"You do all the cleaning yourself?"

"Mrs. Sigmund assists with the dishes when she can, but yesterday I did not see her after tea until she came to deliver the news with Mr. Jennings."

Bernard nodded. "May I ask for your reaction to the news?"

"I was so shocked I honestly didn't know what to think. No, that's a lie." She set her teacup down. "All I could think was, 'What am I supposed to do with this pork loin?'" She shook her head. "I should have felt more. A cook and her mistress often become intimate on a different level than other staff because we spend hours together each week planning the menu, especially whenever we took on boarders and she wanted to try more exotic dishes like chop suey."

"How long had you been her cook?"

"I came on when she built this house three years ago. She was so young. I think this was her first time running a house on her own. Especially of this size. No wonder she filled it with people. She's one of those what you call 'new money' types, so I don't think she rightly knew what to spend it all on."

New money. There were plenty of those. It had started when the wealthy mine owners didn't want to raise their families around the riots and destruction occurring near the mines in Idaho and Montana, and so, rather than address the issues the unions raised, they'd come to Spokane, hired people like Kirtland Cutter to build them mansions on the Hill, and had settled in with their new wealth. He assumed Miss Mitchell had also made her money investing in the mines or the railroads, like most people.

"Would you happen to know what business Miss Mitchell was in to make her money?"

"I'm afraid I don't know, but I can say it seemed she'd come into more around the time Mr. Jennings joined us." Mrs. Curry set down her cup and stood. "And now, Detective, I'm afraid I must get back to my work. It'll just be Irish stew, I fear, but I do hope you'll join us for our midday meal."

"I would be honored, Mrs. Curry," said Bernard, suddenly as happy as a child.

* * *

"Ah, smells like childhood," Thomas said as he walked through the door, removing his helmet and rubbing his belly. "No, it smells *better*." Something about the twinkling eyes of Mrs. Curry made her look like a fairy godmother out of one of those fairy tales. He took in the broad, smiling face and found he had a winning smile to offer in return.

"Well, you both must stay, naturally," said Mrs. Curry with a blush. "Luncheon is at one."

Thomas winked at Bernard, who grunted. No doubt he'd hoped to enjoy a meal without Thomas to make them even, but there was no way Thomas was going to miss out on another delicious homemade masterpiece. He'd made his way up the Hill as quickly as possible just for that reason.

"Thank you," Bernard said to Mrs. Curry, and grabbed Thomas's elbow to lead him out of the kitchen and back to the front hall. Bernard straightened his stiff collar and tie once they were alone. "So, how did your interview go with Mr. Prescot this morning?"

Thomas filled him in. "He's a bit soft around the edges, and a bit odd," he summed up.

"But in the end he does have hands big enough to do the deed, especially now we know she was strangled and not just hatcheted."

"We know what?" Thomas whipped around from hanging up his helmet in the front hall.

"Dr. Baker just told me this morning."

Thomas shivered. "Every time I hear that man's name, I think of the story that went around at the time of the Great Fire."

"I don't recall anything connecting Dr. Baker with the Great Fire," Bernard said with a frown.

"No, not Dr. Baker, 'the Baker.'"

Bernard continued looking at Thomas like he'd just said he was considering becoming a ballet dancer. "Lots of blame was thrown around at that time. People were scared and upset."

"Yeah, but this one was really weird. Rumor had it that the one dead man was actually discovered in an oven."

"An oven?" Bernard repeated.

"Yeah, like a range."

"That's not possible. You can't fit a body in a range."

"I know. It was rumored that the bones were all in a jumble,

as though the man had been chopped into pieces before being...well, baked."

Bernard shook his head. "That is almost the craziest thing I've
ever heard."

Thomas shrugged. "It's just a theory."

"I'm almost positive the papers reported that the one death
was someone who jumped from a hotel window."

Thomas leaned in. "That's what the papers *reported*. Why
would they tell the truth?" Thomas clapped Bernard on the
shoulder and straightened. "I can't help thinking of it when Miss
Mitchell was first strangled. I mean, why else would the killer
strangle her and then cut her head off? Maybe he was going
to chop up the whole body and throw her in the blacksmith's
forge?"

"But it was only her head that was removed."

"Yeah, but what if the killer was interrupted?"

Bernard furrowed his brow. "Like by a blind inventor?"

"Yeah."

Bernard shook his head. "We can't jump to conclusions. Especially crazy ones. I'm trying to remain unbiased."

"I understand, Holmes, I understand. Just throwing out the
crazy theories of Watson to help jog that masterful brain of
yours."

Bernard grunted.

It was Thomas's turn to shake his head. "Strangled, huh? That
does change things a bit."

Bernard went on to repeat what he'd learned from Jennings
and Mrs. Curry.

"So, who's next?" Thomas asked, pulling out his notepad.

"Mrs. Sigmund. I need to ask someone about the theft, and it seems she's the one to ask, but she's been out all morning. I also want to find out if her husband ever returned home last night, and if not, if she knows where he might be hiding."

"Perhaps the Mrs. went to look for him this morning?"

"It's possible. We need to search the house, especially the study upstairs. Given Jennings's discomfiture every time the study was mentioned this morning, I have a feeling that room is going to take some time. We'll need to find the staff records so we can check their references and backgrounds, and I'd like to find her account books. And a will would be helpful, too."

"Got it: references, accounts, will. Given we have less than an hour until luncheon, shall we save the study for later?"

"Always thinking with your stomach," grumbled Bernard.

Thomas eyed Bernard's growing gut and then at his own smaller stomach. Just wait till he had some of Mrs. Curry's cooking. He wouldn't be grumbling then.

"But I also don't have the keys to the study yet—Mrs. Sigmund has them, too," Bernard admitted. "So let's start in the basement and work our way up."

"Why the basement? There's nothing there but the kitchen—which we've already seen and will see again—and Mrs. Curry's bedroom."

"I don't recall Watson ever being this argumentative with Sherlock."

Thomas put up his hands in surrender. "You're the boss, Detective."

They returned back down the stairs, this time turning to the left instead of the right in order to check out the two utility rooms there. Within was everything one would expect to find in a basement, from the furnace to the stacks of cordwood to the spiderwebs that stuck to Thomas's face.

"*Pthe, pthe*," he said, trying to spit out any spiders that might have come along for the ride. "Have you seen enough yet?" He shivered.

"Why don't you start checking all the wood for hiding spots?"

"You're kidding me, right?" Thomas stared open-mouthed at the small mounds of wood covering one side of the room up to the ceiling.

"Yes," Bernard chuckled, "for now."

Thomas didn't appreciate the humor.

Bernard grabbed the dirty key hanging on a hook next to a locked door and tried it in the lock. It turned.

"One key down," he said, leaning forward into a long shaft that led up to a small iron door, just large enough to allow in a cord of wood. "Wood chute," he said, his shoulders admitting even he couldn't find anything interesting about that. Then he suddenly leaned forward and picked something up between his fingers.

"Don't tell me you found a clue," said Thomas, shaking his head. If he had, there'd be no living with him after this.

Bernard chuckled again. "Yes, yes I did. What do you make of this?"

Thomas leaned forward and took a closer look. It was a bit of red fabric, dark burgundy in color.

He shrugged. "So the groundskeeper got his sleeve caught on a cord of wood as he slid it down."

"Or," Bernard said triumphantly, "I just found the entrance of our burglar."

Thomas looked again at the fabric. "Every thief I've heard of wore black. Not red."

Bernard put the piece of fabric in his small vest pocket usually reserved for coins.

"I guess this time we've got a red rogue instead of a black bandit."

"Give it up, Bernard. It's my role to make cheesy jokes."

Bernard closed the door at the end of the chute and locked it, returning the key to its hook. They continued their tour of the basement and then went back up the stairs to the front of the house, stopping in the grand foyer to decide which direction they should head next.

To either side were pocket doors that were left open during the day, allowing them to stand in one place and see into both the front parlor or receiving room and also into the living room or music room, or whatever rooms in large homes were called. They took a step into the music room and walked through to the library.

The library was an entirely enclosed, private place with no windows or doors, just three walls covered in what appeared to be first edition books. Thomas nudged Bernard and nodded toward a book on display: Anna Katharine Green's *The Leavenworth Case*, a detective story that was said to have inspired the great Conan Doyle himself.

Thomas knew he wasn't the only one who'd love to get his hands on a copy of Jules Verne's *Around the World in Eighty Days* or Wilkie Collins's *The Moonstone*, or was that Victor Hugo's *Les*

Misérables? It was almost impossible to find that one in French in America. Mother had raised her boys to appreciate good literature. He could practically hear Bernard next to him longing to plop down in that expensive-looking leather armchair with any one of these books and just lose himself for a couple of hours.

Thomas continued to walk around the room admiring the collection. *The Scarlet Letter* by Nathaniel Hawthorne was beside, surprisingly, only one of Edgar Allan Poe's collections, *Tales*. But of course, an entire shelf was devoted to Dickens's work, from *The Pickwick Papers* to *Edwin Drood*, a rather terrible attempt at a detective story, Thomas had always thought—feeling nothing had been lost by the fact Dickens hadn't finished it before he died.

"This would've been a great room for a murder," he said. "I bet the place is soundproof with all these shelves of books. Why would the killer choose the workshop instead?"

"What makes you think the murderer had a choice in location?"

Thomas shrugged. "Why would Miss Mitchell be at the workshop unless the killer drew her there for his purposes?"

"She is patroness to an inventor who works there."

Thomas nodded. "Yes, but she doesn't strike me as the type to visit often when she can learn everything she needs at meals with him."

Bernard grunted. Thomas was beginning to think Bernard's grunts were signs Thomas wasn't too far off on his guesses.

"Let's move on," he said, turning on his heel and walking back into the music room.

Thomas had decided to call it "the music room" in his own

head, rather than "the living room" because of the magnificent piano in the corner near the front window. The sunlight streamed between the curtains and caressed the top of it, as though God himself wanted Thomas to sit and play. He could tell from the look on Bernard's face, however, that now was not the time to dabble in his more classical notions—especially since he'd never actually taken lessons and could only play scales at a moderate pace.

The brothers took one look around the room and then continued across the foyer and into a receiving room that was so Japanese in decor Thomas felt he'd stepped overseas, though somehow he doubted a real Japanese parlor would be quite so cluttered.

Bernard glanced around the room once and grunted. "How could anyone notice that something went missing in this house? No wonder it takes so long for the rich to care enough to call the police."

Thomas nodded in agreement. "Mrs. Sigmund certainly hasn't a lack of things to clean in this place."

Bernard pointed at the empty space on the mantel of the fireplace. "Prescot told you he was here about a mantel clock?"

"Yes, an 'alarm mantel clock,' he said. Think that was where it used to be?"

"Must be. Unless the burglar stole something from there. But my money's on Prescot. Bet he took it home to fix. We'll have to ask him tonight."

Thomas pulled out his memorandum book and wrote it down.

Bernard led the way out and down the hall, past the majestic staircase, and into the dining room, where they found Jennings setting the table for luncheon.

He turned and nodded his head in a slight bow as they entered. "Mrs. Curry informs me you'll be dining with us once again. Would you like to be seated with our boarder or with the staff?"

"We get an option?" Thomas asked.

Jennings's lips twitched but remained in a firm line.

"We're perfectly fine being seated with the staff, Jennings. Please don't go to any extra effort on our account," said Bernard.

Thomas's shoulders slumped. He'd hoped they'd be able to eat like the upper-crust for once, but, as usual, Bernard had to be all humble and such.

Jennings bowed slightly in answer and returned to setting. Bernard remained standing in the doorway, watching his slow and careful movements as he placed plates upon plates and forks beside forks and glasses beside glasses. All Thomas could think about was that someone had to clean all those extra utensils—and this was just a setting for *one* man.

"So, this is what you were doing when Miss Mitchell was killed?" Bernard asked suddenly.

Jennings flinched and straightened. "I don't know, sir. When was she killed?"

Nice deflection.

"We don't know for certain when exactly the murder occurred. Could've been anytime before seven fifteen."

"I already told you my duties from three o'clock on," Jennings said, glancing at Thomas.

"Yes," Thomas answered. "Does it really take you two whole hours every night to set the dining room for two people?"

Jennings stiffened. "You have no idea how varied and time-consuming a butler's duties can be."

"You're right," said Thomas politely, "I don't. That's why I'm asking you."

"It depends on the evening, but generally, yes, it can take two hours to prepare the wine, the serving silver, and set the table for dinner."

Thomas stifled an open scoff. He bet "preparing the wine" could take *hours* if done properly.

The butler continued, "Miss Mitchell liked to entertain."

"Was she planning to entertain last night?" Bernard asked.

Jennings glanced at the table. "No."

"So there were no special preparations to be made?"

The butler stared at the flowery centerpiece. "No."

"And was the meal an overly complicated one?"

Jennings glanced at Thomas, perhaps thinking even he could answer that question since he had partaken below stairs. Thomas had to stop himself from licking his lips at the memory.

"No."

"Then were you doing anything out of the ordinary last night?"

Jennings straightened again and looked straight at Bernard. "Yes," he declared firmly, as though just remembering he did have an excuse. "Yes, I recalled I hadn't yet telephoned the police about the theft discovered that morning. I had forgotten until I walked past the telephone in the hall and remembered. As you know, I called around six o'clock, as I'm sure they told you at the station."

Well, that was one possible explanation for the late phone call. And that meant Jennings was most likely not out at the workshop beheading his mistress and building up a fire to bake her. Thomas imagined that sort of thing took a little time.

"Yes, and Miss Mitchell was not seen from three on. Verifying your location at six o'clock does not clear you from suspicion," Bernard said.

"Well, from three o'clock to four I was serving tea to those *inventors*," Jennings said, his lip curling.

"What do you have against those men?" Bernard asked.

After a quick breath the butler replied, "Nothing," his eyes returning to the table.

Bernard twitched his mustache.

"We'll see about that," he said, leaving the comment hanging as he turned on his heel and walked through the serving door into the small butler's pantry. There were cabinets full of silver and a dumbwaiter in the corner.

Thomas opened the door to the dumbwaiter and looked up and down the narrow shaft, then followed Bernard down the servants' stairs to the basement. There they found Mrs. Curry setting the table. She looked up expectantly and bade them take a seat. Thomas could tell Bernard was not quite ready to stop in their tour of the house, but it would never do to be inattentive to a cook of Mrs. Curry's standing.

Mrs. Curry ladled out the delectable-smelling Irish stew and set their bowls before them. All thoughts of murder and mayhem were driven from his mind and he let himself sink into

a delightful rest accompanied by warm soup and a dinner roll
slathered in creamy butter.

* * *

Archie threw a stone into the roaring Spokane River, which
passed through downtown like Moses passing through the Red
Sea, dividing Spokane cleanly into its north and south districts.
Along the south side of the river sat the industrial Havermale
Island, across which ran the Great Northern Railroad. On the
southern side of that island, rising above the still waters of the
south channel, was the place where he was to craft his masterpiece as an addition to the depot.

G.A. Johnson and Son of Chicago were familiar with the
building of railway depots—it was one of the firm's special-
ties—and hoped to complete the first floor by August 1. They'd
had to change some of their plans along the way due to the expense of materials, but in the end, they all knew the people of
Spokane would be quite proud of their modern depot.

The depot would be 316 feet in length and 56 feet wide,
formed from a mottled gray-pressed brick and trimmed in sandstone, with a red roof of clay tiles with terra cotta trimmings.
Inside, the first floor would be of mosaic tile, the other two of
maple, the interior finished with oak, the wainscoting of cream-
colored enameled brick with marble bases, and high ceilings
marked by brick archways. There would be two entrances: one
leading to the women's waiting room, which would lead to the
restaurant, and another into a men's waiting room connected
to a smoking room. The most up-to-date bathrooms and con-
veniences would be found in each, from marble drinking foun-

tains to bronze and polished stone fixtures. No expense would be spared in providing first-class elegance and luxury, ensuring that Spokane would provide a first impression of pure amazement.

Archie's clock tower itself would stand an awe-inspiring 155 feet high. Each of the four clock faces would be nine feet in diameter with yard-long hands stretching toward roman numerals; it would be setting the record as the largest clock in the Pacific Northwest. But this was only the beginning. The heart of the clock was still waiting to be brought forth, out of Archie's head and into mechanical reality, a clock that must stand the test of time, proving that Spokane was a town firmly looking forward to the future.

Archie now stood on the Monroe Street Bridge, southwest of the island from which his clock tower would rise. He'd found he much preferred the beat of the river over the clanging rail yard as a backdrop for his thoughts. The *clip-clop* of horses' hooves pulling carriages down Monroe was barely audible over the thundering rush of the Spokane Falls. He drew on his sketchpad quickly and decisively, letting the pace of the falls determine his strokes, and not the agitated thoughts swirling through his mind—though the speed of each was about the same.

Why was he so darn unlucky?

Yesterday, his life had been roses. A patroness for his sound theory work, a lovely garden walk with a charming young lady, and an intriguing meeting with a brilliant mind.

Then *bang*. Or *whack* more like.

He grimaced at the mental image. He was thankful that when he met Matsumoto at the workshop this afternoon the body of Miss Mitchell would no longer be present, but his stomach twinged at the thought there might still be...evidence about.

How could they suspect him? Look at him. Did he look like a murderer? He was quailing at just the *thought* of blood.

"We meet again," came a rosy voice behind him.

He turned and all of his worries were swept up in one warm, friendly, parasoled smile. It took him a moment to find his voice amidst all his happiness.

"Hello, Miss Kenyon. Whatever are you doing here?"

"Oh, I like to walk out and about. Clear my head a bit. And the falls always seem to do the trick nicely. When the rose garden feels too far a venture, of course." Her voice rippled like soft silk. He couldn't help but smile when she talked.

"I'm glad you happened across this way."

"Me, too. What endeavor are you working on at the moment?" she asked kindly, coming up alongside him and peering at his sketches from beneath her slanting black hat. "The clock tower, I see. I like the way it draws the eye upward, to the heavens. Like a cathedral."

"I like to think of it as the clock tower from *Cinderella* by Perrault: 'She thought that it was no later than eleven when she counted the clock striking twelve.' It was one of my favorites as a child."

"Mine, too!" Miss Kenyon interjected. "I never much cared for the Grimm version with all the slicing off of feet parts and eyes pecked out by pigeons."

"I agree. Perrault's Cinderella offered the stepsisters forgiveness and even married them off to noblemen. A much better morale for the tale, I think." They shared a smile before he continued. "I hope my clock tower will remind all passersby and new arrivals to Spokane that here is a town where anything can happen. There's so much potential lying in wait in these buildings."

"In the people more than in the buildings, I should think. But as I'm a photographer, I suppose I do see what you mean."

"What do you photograph?"

"Anything and everything, but mostly houses and buildings lately. People want to chronicle their achievements, and these days a person's house can tell you a lot about how far a person has come up in the world."

"Especially in Spokane, where it seems there's quite a lot of development occurring."

"Indeed. I've been in Seattle these past five years, however, where there's just as much advancement."

"Where in Seattle?" Archie asked, as though he was familiar with the city beyond its notoriety for rainy weather.

"I studied with a photographer whose studio was just off the wharf. The smell of fish takes me right back." She wrinkled her nose beautifully.

Archie smiled. "What brought you to Spokane from Seattle, if I might ask?"

Her face darkened and she turned her attention from him to the river, studying the falls before answering.

"My grandmother passed away about a week ago."

"My sincere apologies," said Archie, removing his hat for a moment and bowing his head. "I should have—," he began, looking at her black hat again but stopping when he saw her face. "I'm sorry. I can see she was quite dear to you."

"Thank you."

They stood there in the roar of the falls, together, subdued. He couldn't think what else to say. He'd never lost someone he actually cared about. His mother had died of influenza when he was twelve, and his father had died ten years ago—a cruel, harsh man who had become steadily so absorbed by his mechanical work that he hadn't time for his son. At least before he'd died he'd instilled in Archie's hands the ability to follow his precise, clockwork movements, providing him with the skills he now used every day. So perhaps he should have felt more when he died, but he didn't.

"I am glad to be back," Miss Kenyon said beside him. "I had forgotten how lovely Spokane can be in the spring. The whole city seems to be coming alive. The construction is a bit noisy, but here, beside the falls, it's so wonderful how it drowns everything else out..." She closed her eyes and sighed. "It seems I find myself unable to escape the draw of Spokane no matter how hard I try." She opened her eyes again and smiled at him.

Archie's heart picked up speed.

"So what do you think of our little town?" Miss Kenyon asked, the playful silken lilt back in her tone.

"To be honest, it's much more..." He searched for the word.

"Civilized? Cultured?"

He laughed. "Precisely." Archie returned his homburg to his curly head. "When I first heard I'd be coming out to Spokane, I expected the 'wild west' like in the newspaper stories. Instead, I was greeted by a place of surprising sophistication and elegance to rival any city out east. The fashions are consistent, there's even some first-class theater so I hear, and the technology is not far behind, though I haven't seen a telephone box since my arrival and only one automobile..."

"Yes, there's more of all that in Seattle, though I don't understand the draw toward technology that's so loud and noisy." She stopped like she'd said something offensive. "I'm sorry. I didn't mean—I mean, I'm very glad to hear there'll be a clock tower downtown. It's the noise of the trains that I can't abide. And I imagine a world full of automobiles would only be similarly dreadful."

"There's no need to apologize. I agree! That's why I'm attempting to make chimes that won't be obnoxious or noisome."

"Thank you. As a citizen of this town, I am most grateful to you." She sighed. "I hadn't realized Spokane's worth, honestly, until I traveled west. Between here and Olympia are a number of small towns trying to build themselves into the next Seattle, and finding it's a combination of location and luck."

"Isn't most of life?" Archie said.

"Very true, sir, very true." She nodded, her wide-brimmed hat shielding and revealing her striking green eyes.

"Have you ever been out east?" he asked.

"Unfortunately, no. But perhaps now, in this time of change in my life, I might have the chance to travel and find my own place."

"You have no ties to Spokane? No other family?"

"All that was left of my family was found in my grandmother. With her passing, I am free. As free as I always wished to be. And yet, now, I find myself wishing to stay in the comfort of the known. It's like...well, it's like too much freedom. I went west to discover myself, to find what I could be without my grandmother, but it seems all I found was how much I needed her. And I found it too late." She looked down at her hands, turning the ring on her right pinky. "She had such small hands," she mumbled.

Archie looked at the simple gold band. He wanted to compliment her hands, but felt that would be too forward. Instead, he tapped his pencil against his sketchpad and searched for something to say.

"I find myself wondering at my freedom in this job. I thought I'd enjoy the ability to explore my own side projects while I worked on the clock tower, but instead, I keep coming up against dead ends—in some ways literally." He grimaced. "It's all very discouraging." He sighed. "But nothing worth doing gets done fast."

"You sound like my grandmother," Miss Kenyon said, the delight in her voice filling her smile.

"Originally I was to return to Connecticut at the end of the summer, but I find myself considering staying here." Archie busied himself putting his sketchpad and pencils away in his satchel. "Spokane has all the magnetism of a load line."

Miss Kenyon gave a small tinkling laugh and nodded in agreement before asking inquisitively, "Have you thought of recording the river for your other idea?"

"A good thought," he said politely, though he had actually done so already.

She turned to look at the falls. "The Spokane has a profound rhythm at its heart; I should imagine vibrations from the sound could move mountains."

He chuckled. "May I say, Miss Kenyon, what a delight it is to speak with you once again."

"You most certainly may," she said with a smile, her green eyes dancing as they turned back to him.

His stomach twinged again, but for quite a different reason this time.

* * *

Eleanor returned from her refreshing visit with Marian to find Mrs. Curry cleaning her kitchen, as was her habit after luncheon, before tea, and before moving on to begin the whole process again for dinner.

"There you are, dear. Where did you sneak off to this morning?" the cook asked, plunging a flannel rag into a gallon of hot water and borax before vigorously scrubbing one of the countertops.

Eleanor blushed. "I'm sorry I rushed off like that. I saw in the paper that a friend of mine was back in town, and what with the current state of the house, I needed a moment without the thought of murderers hanging over my head."

Mrs. Curry smiled. "Of course, dear. I only wondered if you had found a new situation so soon."

"Oh, no. Not yet."

"I must warn you: the police are back and about. They specifically want to talk to you about the theft."

Eleanor nodded. Of course they would. She sighed.

She watched as Mrs. Curry continued to scrub. She wasn't too surprised to see her doing so even after losing the mistress of the house, figuring that, like herself, Mrs. Curry found something rejuvenating in the action. But she also knew better than to offer to help. Only Mrs. Curry could clean her kitchen. If Eleanor had done some part of it—even rubbing emery paper over the steel handles of the range—Mrs. Curry would only have done it again once she'd left.

Eleanor could be trusted with the dishes, however, so it was there she headed now, rolling up her sleeves. There was a small gathering of simple glasses and a stack of plain white china plates and bowls from the downstairs table, and nothing from the upstairs table, which meant the inventor had not deigned to come to the house for luncheon...again. Even with the loss of the mistress, it just felt like such a slight to Mrs. Curry for him not to attend a meal she'd been working on all morning.

She sighed and grabbed a large wooden bowl from beneath the sink—the china and glasses were less likely to chip or break in such a bowl—and filled it with warm water and just a little washing soda. Then she grabbed a clean dishcloth and began the process of taking each dirty piece gently in hand, starting with the glasses, washing them in the soapy water, rinsing them in the sink under hot water, and placing them to dry on a cloth on the other side of the sink. The process was organized and methodical, the way she preferred life. After the glasses came the sauce dishes, followed by the silver, then the china dishes and empty plates, scraping the food into the refuse bucket before washing them fully, refreshing the hot water and washing soda often to remove the grease cleanly and easily.

Both women were silent in their work, letting the previous day's events wash away in the simple routines of cleanliness. Or attempting to wash them away. What was she going to do without Miss Mitchell? What job could she hope to find where she would have the calming motherly presence of someone like Mrs. Curry? All she knew was cleaning, and although it was a job that would always be necessary, she was a creature of habit, and did not look with anticipation on any sort of change, much less change that had come so drastically. So suddenly...

After the dishes, Eleanor rinsed the large copper pot in which a stew had cooked, sifting a very fine layer of ash over the bottom to scour the copper clean. Then came the smaller items: ladles and cooking utensils and silverware—

Eleanor squeaked when she felt a hand gently touch her shoulder.

"Only me, dear," said Mrs. Curry, turning Eleanor at the shoulder and gripping her in a reassuring hug.

Eleanor hadn't even realized she was crying again until she felt her wet face against Mrs. Curry's apron. It seemed her emotions had come full circle. So far she'd gone from crying to anger to excitement and back to crying in less than a day. Was this what grief felt like? It suddenly occurred to her that she'd never had cause to experience it before, so perhaps this was how some people reacted.

"It'll be all right, dear, you'll see. The only way through life is to expect the unexpected." Mrs. Curry gave her a soft pat on the back like a child.

She really was behaving like a child.

"Has Mr. Sigmund returned?" the cook asked quietly into Eleanor's hair.

Eleanor's corn-colored hair. Not chocolate. She straightened and wiped her tears.

"No," she said shortly. "I'm sorry. I just need to rest." She left the remaining dirty water, not even bothering to flush the sink clean with boiling water and washing soda, and walked back to her rooms alone.

* * *

Archie had come by way of the main house, where he'd been directed by Jennings to head as far back as he could go toward the woods, in order to find the blacksmith's workshop.

As he came over a rise and finally saw the low stone building, there was a sudden high-pitched tone followed by the shattering of glass.

"What—!" He stopped in his tracks, his eyes darting about frantically for the source of the sound, looking for Matsumoto's gun.

"Mr. Prescot, I assume?" came Matsumoto's voice. Archie approached the Japanese man, who stood outside next to a table with a thin horn set up before a tuning fork, which was pointed at a wine glass stem on another table a good twenty feet away. At the base of this table lay a pile of shattered pieces from what appeared to have once been other wine glasses.

"What are you doing?" asked Archie.

"If you would be so kind as to take this wine glass and set it on the far table for me, I will show you."

Archie took the glass from his hand and did as he said, carefully brushing the stem of the previous glass down to join the others. Then he returned to Matsumoto's side.

The blind man took the tuning fork and knocked it against the edge of the table, setting it back on its stand before the thin horn. He moved something up and down the base of the fork until suddenly the glass on the other table exploded into pieces.

Archie's head jerked toward the other table. He'd been watching Matsumoto, not the empty wine glass, but now there was nothing left but the stem.

"It works!" he cried.

Matsumoto smiled. "Yes, it does. But one still requires a table..."

"*Still?* That was fantastic!" Archie said, exuberant over the experiment. "But how did you get the tuning fork's tone to match the resonance of the glass and make it shatter?"

"Ah, you noticed. I have been working on using gutta-percha to create a modifier, which can be used to adjust the tuning fork's frequency once it has been struck. This will find the correct resonance to cause an effect. Every glass is different, so sometimes the tone does not need much adjusting and other times it does."

"Gutta-percha? Like what's used for telegraph cable insulation?" Archie's mind flashed to his conversation not so long ago with a young lady about exactly such a thing.

"Yes."

"How about that," he muttered.

He was suddenly very envious of the time and money this man had to develop and test such experiments when Archie was still having to work a normal job to pay the rent. His gut started to plummet again at the realization he'd been so close to joining him, only to have his patroness ripped away, like an umbrella in a mighty wind. There was no way this man had killed Miss

Mitchell, Archie decided. What reason could he possibly have for wanting the woman providing all this for him to be dead?

"All right," he said, adjusting his satchel across his shoulder as he considered its contents and the man before him, "let's forget for just a moment that our patroness has been murdered and you may be the murderer."

"Continue." Matsumoto waved his hand dismissively, his eyes focused on Archie's forehead.

"Let's talk physics." Archie pushed his glasses up his nose. "Sound may move in waves, but it doesn't actually have weight or mass, something that can push a gear into motion."

"Yes, I have been unable to determine the answer to that riddle as yet."

"Well," Archie took a deep breath, here goes, "what if you passed the sound through water? Wouldn't it vibrate the water, and water, which does have mass, might push a gear?"

Matsumoto's gaze moved to Archie's ear.

"That could work," the Japanese man said.

Archie realized he'd been holding his breath and let it out in a great *woosh*. No going back now. In one swift, impulsive sentence he'd given away his Big Idea. He hoped it was worth it. And that he hadn't just given it to a murderer.

He heard his pocket watch chime two o'clock—a brief staccato double-beat.

"What was that?" Matsumoto asked.

"Oh, just my pocket watch." Archie pulled it out and popped it open. Then he flipped it over to the side only he ever looked at, the side that led to the heart of the watch, which only the creator should ever behold. He handed it to Matsumoto, who held it reverently, like a precious jewel, running his fingers over the inner workings, an appreciative smile crinkling his eyes.

"I must admit, I have not spent much time studying clock-works. Too much of the work cannot be felt or heard but must be seen. Can you tell me what I am feeling?"

"The jewels and movements are quite standard, but what I've done is found a way to have a variety of chime patterns on one pinned barrel, so that I can have a different song play for each hour as it sounds, rather than just the standard count wheel sounding off the hour."

"That sounds like very delicate work. It is certainly no small thing you have created," said Matsumoto, handing the watch back. "The clock in the front parlor. It also plays a unique sound, yes?"

"Yes, I attempted to create a series of chimes that would lull someone to sleep, but...it didn't work." Archie's shoulders drooped. "Miss Mitchell was robbed the night before her murder and I wonder...if it was actually the thief who murdered her? If so, I worry that I'm partially responsible..."

"You are not the thief, are you?"

Archie smiled. "No, I'm much too busy to have time to go out and steal from other people. I just feel reprehensible because I made a clock that should have caught the thief the first time. If it had worked, the thief would be in jail now, and maybe, perhaps, Miss Mitchell would still be our patroness."

"We would not have needed Miss Mitchell for much longer," said Matsumoto.

"What do you mean?"

"We have a barrel that can funnel sound in a specified direction, a way of adjusting a tuning fork's tone to a particular resonance. You may have just brought the final piece to the experiment with the water, and you already have the capability of miniaturizing sound." Matsumoto smiled. "Seems to me we have everything we need."

"Except a patroness," Thomas Carew said, appearing over the hill with his brother at his side.

At the sight of his housemates, Archie's stomach flipped. Their conversation had just taken a very interesting turn toward the future, but with the arrival of the police, it'd be back to murdered patronesses.

Thomas's long strides brought him up beside Matsumoto as Bernard Carew joined him.

"You didn't make it up for luncheon." Bernard's voice growled like a bear's. Archie was intimidated already and started to sweat. "We wondered what was keeping you."

* * *

"You missed quite the stew," said Thomas, rubbing a hand over his belly.

"I will be sure to apologize to Mrs. Curry later," said Matsumoto. "I often miss luncheon, however, since sometimes my work keeps me too busy to pause for meals."

"My work would never keep me from such cooking," said Thomas, shaking his head in dismay.

"We've come to ask you some questions," said Bernard. "This is Officer Carew, Mr. Matsumoto. My brother will speak with you while Mr. Prescot and I step over here."

Thomas was eager to see this blacksmith for himself again.

The night before, when he'd sent Matsumoto to Bernard at the workshop, he hadn't noticed his blindness.

"Mr. Matsumoto—," Thomas began, but stopped quickly when he looked at the man's dark eyes. "I'm sorry, but are you really blind?" Thomas had never been one to mince words.

"You want to know how I can move so easily."

"Well, yes, it's quite difficult to imagine a blind man capable of blacksmithing."

"Yes, I suppose it might be. Though to me, I cannot imagine any other way."

Thomas pointed at the sword that hung from Matsumoto's belt in a beautiful scabbard worthy of ancient Japan, opposite an oddly shaped gun that looked more like something from Colorado. "If Bernard hadn't specifically said no one should touch the forge, I'd ask you to make me a sword right now so I could watch you work."

"And I would have been happy to do so for you, but I understand the need for us not to disturb the crime scene."

"'Crime scene.' I like that. May I use that one?"

"Be my guest."

The blind man smiled and Thomas smiled back. He liked this fellow. "Perhaps you could simply tell me a bit more about your process."

"I do not do things much differently than any other blacksmith. I am just more aware of my surroundings. One of the most important aspects of blacksmithing is maintaining awareness of the heat of the fire, as this affects the metal in different ways. Because I am blind, I listen to the roar of the flames and am able to hear the change in the heat. I have even been told that because I listen, rather than look, I often hear the change more accurately than a blacksmith with sight."

Thomas wondered who had told him that, but guessed that pretty much any blacksmith who had crossed his path would want to test Matsumoto's skills against his own. "So what do you make with your forge? Swords? Horseshoes?"

"I make my own tools, since the work I am doing is not what most blacksmiths are doing."

"And what work is that?"

Matsumoto's eyes studied Thomas's ear. "As a blind man, I have had to find new ways of understanding my surroundings. As a young boy, I developed the ability to 'see' through the use of clicks with my tongue." Matsumoto made a series of short, quick chirps that sounded like he was calling to a horse. "It may sound odd to your ears, but to me, they can tell me the nearest object, and sometimes even what that object is."

Thomas raised one eyebrow.

"Yes, I know it sounds unbelievable, but I have been able to teach others to do the same, even the seeing, if they close their eyes and focus on their hearing rather than trusting their sight. With my inventions, I hope to share this ability with the whole world."

"And this ability helps you to see around your workshop?"

Matsumoto nodded. "I keep my items in specific locations so I can always find them, and I can 'see' my workspace quite clearly in my mind, having walked it and worked it end to end for two years."

"You've been here for two years?"

"Yes."

"And Miss Mitchell...she was...?"

"My patroness. Nothing more. She was a patron of the arts. A woman with great devotion to the expansion of new ideas."

"Rather a young woman to have such an inclination, don't you think?"

"The young often have the most open mind in regards to the future."

Thomas had to agree there. "So for two years she's been your patroness?"

"Yes. I was given this research area, as well as room and board, and I have endeavored to live up to the patronage upon which my very subsistence relies."

"Have you had any success with your...inventions?"

"Success does not lie in creation but awareness. My research has made me aware of many things on many levels. Creation may follow in time."

"I see. So you have nothing physically to prove what you do all day every day in this secluded corner of the property?"

"I do not see how it should matter much."

"You don't, eh? It doesn't bother you that the body of Miss Mitchell was found in your workshop?"

"As I was not here at the time, no, it does not 'bother' me, as you say."

The man was smooth. Too smooth. Time to ruffle some feathers.

"We discovered Miss Mitchell was strangled before she was beheaded."

Matsumoto chuckled softly. "You think *I* strangled her?" He held up his small hands. They were crisscrossed with scars from years of working with molten metal blindly. Frankly, Thomas was surprised the man still had all his fingers.

"Samurais, I have read, are great warriors."

Matsumoto waved a hand down his everyday shirt and pants and shook his head. "I am no samurai."

Thomas pointed again to the sword and gun hanging at his side. "Wearing a weapon so prominently might indicate otherwise around here."

Matsumoto pulled the short sword so swiftly from its black scabbard that Thomas didn't even have time to flinch. He held it out to Thomas across open palms, bowing over the sword so low that Thomas could not see his eyes, but only the shiny black hair on the back of his head. Thomas almost took a step back, the action was so quick, and yet so deferential.

Gently, he took hold of the black-iron guard and held the sword up. Matsumoto rose slowly, his blind eyes somehow seeming to watch the blade as it glinted in the sunlight.

"This was the last blade I made with my father before leaving Japan. It is a *wakisashi*, and it is only half of a samurai's *daisho*."

"And the other half?" Thomas asked quietly, mimicking Matsumoto's softer voice.

"A *katana*, a four-foot-long blade."

"Is that gun your *katana* then?"

Matsumoto pulled out the gun and ran his fingers over it. "The *katana* is the soul of the warrior. If I was a samurai without a *katana*, then I would have no soul. But as I said, I am only a blind inventor, not a samurai."

"Or your soul has been traded for science and technology."

Matsumoto's steel eyes looked toward Thomas's and the silence spread between them, thick like a heavy blanket.

"Bernard told me you have three other swords in the workshop," Thomas said, daring to break the muffling stillness. "Are there any others we should be aware of?"

Matsumoto shook his head slowly. "No."

He returned the gun to his belt, and Thomas offered the *wakisashi* to him, bowing over the blade as he returned it to the blind man.

"So tell me more about your work here. In fact, let's take a little tour of the 'scene of the crime,' as you called it." Thomas didn't think Bernard would mind, so long as they didn't touch anything. But as soon as they entered, he realized this was going to be mighty difficult, since the only way Matsumoto could tell him if anything was out of place was by touching it.

Without *moving* anything then.

"I'd like you to walk around the workshop with me and tell me if you notice anything different," said Thomas.

Matsumoto didn't question him or suggest he check with Bernard first, which Thomas appreciated.

Thomas walked directly behind Matsumoto as he began at the doorway and felt along to the left, touching the leather apron hanging on its hook first. He continued around, touching the items on the table with the phonograph, then on to the swords on the wall—three as Bernard had said. Then around to the coal barrel, which was about half full.

Matsumoto frowned as he felt the top of the coals collected there, then felt along the inside of the barrel to the top, and back again.

"Something wrong?" Thomas asked.

"There are less coals here than there were when I closed the shop before going to meet with Mr. Prescot yesterday."

"Are you certain?"

"Quite. I always ensure I have enough fuel before beginning any work. Running out half way through a project would be most detrimental."

"All right, I'll make a note of it." He pulled out his memorandum book and added it to his notes. "Anything else? Oh! Watch your step there!" Thomas reached out and took Matsumoto by the elbow, helping him narrowly avoid stepping on the large dried blood spot that marked where the body had been. "I wouldn't recommend touching anymore things right there," Thomas said, leading Matsumoto back around to the other side of the anvil. "It's quite messy just there."

"I keep my forge spotless, Officer Carew, so you can know that any signs of mess are from the murderer, not me."

Thomas felt some doubt about this as he took in the ash and soot that covered the forge hood and work area. How could a blind man keep something like that clean? But there *was* a lone poker lying next to the forge.

"Did you leave any tools out before you left?"

"No," Matsumoto said firmly. "What is it?"

But Thomas was reticent to share, worried Bernard would think he was giving the show away to a suspect. "Nothing. I was just checking."

* * *

Bernard walked with Prescot over to the edge of the woods, leaving Thomas to have his turn with the blind blacksmith.

Prescot shuffled up to Bernard hesitantly, his already round shoulders hunched forward in trepidation, his hands clutching the strap of his ever-present satchel as it slung across his wide chest. He let go long enough to push his thick glasses up his nose as he said, "Good to see you, Mr. Carew. Sorry I missed you at breakfast this morning."

Bernard wasn't looking forward to this. He knew it was going to be difficult for him to question someone he'd invited to live in his home with his family. So naturally, he postponed the inevitable by asking Prescot to tell him more about his work on the clock tower.

After the twelfth pinned barrel combination description, Bernard gave up.

He decided he was going to do this quick, like slicing an envelope with a letter opener. The clockmaker would never see it coming.

"So this morning I went by the coroner's. He revealed some fascinating information: Miss Mitchell was strangled before she was beheaded."

Prescot's face paled. "Dear God."

"Indeed." Time to ratchet things up a bit and hit the nail on the head—see if he got a reaction. "I think this leads us nicely to another rather interesting thought: she must have known her attacker. To be strangled by someone standing in front of you usually implies you know and trust—or trusted up to that moment—the person with his hands on your throat." He aimed a knowing look at Prescot.

"I barely knew her!" The man's cheeks reddened and he put up his hands defensively. Large hands. Certainly big enough to strangle a small neck.

"So you say. But perhaps she had been your patroness long before yesterday, and instead it was only yesterday you learned she'd had the gall to secret away another rival inventor. That might make a man angry, perhaps even a bit mad."

Prescot's eyes were bugging out quite emphatically at this suggestion, his face draining of color by the second.

"Let's take a little walk into the workshop," said Bernard, taking Prescot by the arm and forcing him to follow past where Matsumoto and Thomas were just exiting.

But as they entered the workshop and walked around the anvil to the large red spot of what had been a pool of blood, Prescot fainted neatly into a crumpled heap on the floor.

"I'm gonna guess he's not our murderer," said Thomas succinctly, joining him in the doorway.

"No, I would guess not."

Thank God for that.

* * *

When Archie came to, he was more than a little embarrassed.

Thomas helped him to his feet and led him discreetly toward the main house, Bernard ordering him to sit and drink some water while Thomas called a carriage to take him home.

"Bernard means well," said Thomas quietly as they walked back across the open yard. "He's got to suspect everyone, perhaps *especially* those who are boarding with him. Can you imagine his embarrassment if he'd discovered he'd taken in a murderer?"

Archie nodded but kept his thoughts to himself. He might have only just arrived a few days ago, but he felt living with the Carews he'd earned a little more than being barked at like a dog and then thrown toward blood—he gulped—to see how he reacted.

He adjusted his satchel, took a deep breath of spring air, and tried to think about something else. He tried not to think of the still faint scent of roses that had overwhelmed him when he'd entered the workshop. It had really been that scent memory *and* the sight of...her...blood that had made him queasy. The last time he'd smelled those roses she'd been offering to make his dreams come true...

As they approached the house, Archie saw the butler casually smoking outside the kitchen door without any of the standard composure and dignity one would normally associate with a butler. He reminded Archie of the conmen that would stand on street corners in Boston, jumping on unsuspecting, timid people as they walked past.

"Is that the killer?" He motioned toward Archie, who leapt in surprise. What was it about himself that made him appear menacing this afternoon?

"I doubt it," said Thomas. "Unless he chopped off her head blindfolded to avoid the sight of blood." He clapped Archie on the shoulder as though they were best friends, nearly knocking him over with the surprise of it. "Steady there, old man," he said with a loud laugh.

Archie frowned.

"The thief then?" the butler asked around his cigarette.

Archie was about to answer when Thomas interrupted. "He's in the clear, which is more than I can say for you, Mr. Jennings."

"Me, huh?" the man said, taking a quick breath in through his large Roman nose. "Which one am I looking good for? Killing or thieving?"

"Not sure yet," Thomas said with a shrug.

Thomas was rather easygoing for a policeman, Archie thought, especially in comparison to his brother.

"Didn't know butlers were allowed to smoke," Thomas went on. "Thought they were above all that."

"Perhaps when we're employed," said Jennings, pausing to puff a smoke ring, "but without a mistress of the house, I fear my time is being wasted waiting for you to release us to find new situations."

"She was just murdered yesterday!" Archie exclaimed.

Jennings shrugged. "Man's got to make a living." He removed the cigarette long enough to state, "There's more to life than waiting around for the next big thing. Sometimes you have to just take life by the throat and make it give you what you want. No one else is going to help you. You have to help yourself."

Well, there went all the ideas Archie'd ever held true about the firm loyalty of butlers.

"You sound like a man who's not afraid to get his hands dirty. And here I thought butlers cleaned up messes, rather than making them," said Thomas.

Jennings looked at him coolly, holding smoke in his mouth before puffing it out like a dragon.

"You still have Mr. Matsumoto," Thomas pointed out.

"Again, without a mistress of the house, I'm uncertain where exactly he falls in my duties. Seeing as he didn't find it necessary to attend luncheon today, even though I still went to the effort of setting the table, I find him steadily slipping from my notice." He sucked on his cigarette till the end burned red.

Archie could tell the butler was upset about something—his voice had lost its sonorous pomposity—but for some reason he didn't think it was the inventor's behavior that bothered him so much.

"Perhaps you've already got a side job to keep you busy?" Thomas said.

Jennings looked at him and puffed.

"Perhaps you found you could steal from your mistress quite easily from under her nose, and when she caught you, you reacted before you could think through the repercussions."

"Butlers don't behead their employers."

"I always thought butlers didn't smoke, either, and see where we are now."

Jennings's eyes narrowed.

"No need to jump on Jennings so harshly, young man," cut in Mrs. Curry's voice. "We're all a bit stiff today, wondering what tomorrow might bring."

* * *

Mrs. Curry's interruption did exactly what she most likely intended by drawing Thomas's attention away from the butler. Of course, it helped that she was holding a plate of freshly baked—was that lemon he smelled?—muffins.

He had to stop himself from smacking his lips before saying,

"So I hear. Is it really so difficult to find work in a growing city like Spokane?"

"You'd be surprised," said Mrs. Curry, turning to head back into the kitchen. "No use standing around outside. Why don't you come in and join us for our tea?"

Thomas went to pull out his father's pocket watch when he heard a delicate three note chime from Prescot's vest pocket.

"What was that?" he asked.

Prescot smiled and pulled out his watch. "My pocket watch. It's three o'clock on the dot."

"I see. Perfect time for a spot of tea, then." Thomas turned back to the cook. "We'd love to join you, Mrs. Curry, thank you." Thomas removed his helmet and followed the cook into her domain. Already seated at the large oak table was the maid, looking even more haggard and care-worn than she had yesterday evening.

"Afternoon, Mrs. Sigmund," Thomas said, with a tip of his head.

The woman merely nodded her head in return, continuing to sip at the teacup held within pale, white fingers.

He took a seat at the table and Prescot sat beside him. Jennings entered behind them, picked up a cup, and stood in the corner, as though trying to avoid further questioning. Mrs. Curry retook her seat before a half-full cup beside Mrs. Sigmund, placing the plate of muffins in the center of the table.

"So," Thomas began, "any sign of your husband, Mrs. Sigmund? Just cream, please," he said in response to the proffered additives, helping himself to a muffin—yes, definitely lemon but with a sprinkling of rosemary. He was beginning to wonder if Mrs. Curry had been his mother in another life.

"No, sir," the maid said softly, avoiding his eyes.

"I see. And you still maintain you don't know where he's snuck off to?" Lemon crumbles fell from his lips. He used his fingertip to pick them up again, emphatic he wouldn't be letting one morsel go to waste.

Sad blue eyes rose and met his. "I don't know where he is." The eyes shifted.

"When did you see him last?"

"Yesterday afternoon," she said firmly, pulling her sleeve down over her wrist.

"I wonder if you would mind giving me a tour of your humble abode later, as I hear you live in a separate apartment above the carriage house? I'd like to see it."

The sad eyes focused back on her tea. "Yes, sir."

"Perhaps together we can discover where your husband has scurried off to."

"Yes, sir," she mumbled again.

He sighed as he finished his muffin and reached for a second one, bumping hands with Prescot as he did the same. Prescot shifted in his seat beside him and looked apologetic, but Thomas didn't see any problem with showing Mrs. Curry their gratitude for her skills, so he grabbed another one with an encouraging smile in the clockmaker's direction. "You know, we were originally called in for a burglary, rather than a murder, but so far, no one has been able to give us further information on the event. Instead, everyone has said you're the woman to talk to." He directed his attention back to the maid as he bit into a second warm burst of sweetened lemon. "Do you recall what was stolen? It's possible there's a connection."

"I doubt that. I cannot imagine why the thief would have been in the workshop, since the original items were stolen from the front parlor," Mrs. Sigmund voiced softly. "Four golden candlesticks, a Daguet box, a *noh* mask, and some sapphire jewelry. We have photographs of all the lost items because Miss Mitchell liked to keep a record of her collected pieces."

"That's helpful," said Thomas.

"I'll go get them for you," the quiet woman said, rising from the table.

The men half-rose as she did and then settled back to talk things over with Mrs. Curry, who leaned across the table and started speaking swiftly in a stage whisper as soon as Mrs. Sigmund closed the kitchen door.

"Poor thing. Tried to help me wash the dishes earlier and broke down in tears. She's lived a hard life, that one. Came here all rosy-cheeked and innocent and in love when they first started. Now look at her. In just three years she's become a truly middle-aged woman. All the fault of that husband of hers. Mr. Sigmund is not what one might call an attentive husband, if you get my meaning. He was often using his job as an excuse to run out on 'errands' for Miss Mitchell, disappearing for half a day with no one the wiser as to what exactly he was doing. Or claiming he was 'helping Mr. Matsumoto' when we all knew he was downtown again gambling. Or spending the other half of the day in that carriage house, tinkering away with this and that. And the garden!—have you seen it yet? It's incredible what Eleanor has accomplished. Yes, *Eleanor*, not her husband the groundskeeper. Not to mention how she feeds and cares for the chickens in between her normal duties. There used to be horses, too, when there was a carriage, but now, thank goodness, at least she has one less thing on her mind. I'm not surprised he's disappeared with all the hubbub. Probably didn't want to be caught out in one of his 'secret endeavors'—"

Mrs. Curry finally cut off as Mrs. Sigmund returned with the photographs.

"Thank you," said Thomas, taking the photographs as he rose. He couldn't help but also notice the bruise on her wrist that peeked out from beneath her shirt sleeve. Perhaps Mrs. Curry didn't know about everything going on with the Sigmunds after all. "Where did you say Miss Mitchell kept these?"

"I don't think I did, but they were in her study, filed in the top left drawer."

"Ah, yes, the study. As I recall, you're the only one with a key?"

"Yes."

She reached down and held up her chatelaine from where it hung at her waist, a wide assortment of keys and other necessaries jingling and jangling. "I have keys to every door in this house. In some ways, I'm more of a head housekeeper than a maid in this mansion. Not that Miss Mitchell ever seemed to notice the amount of work going in to keeping up her standard of living." Her voice was still quiet but there was such force behind it, Thomas was quite surprised.

"Now, Eleanor, you know she would've hired help in an instant if you'd ever once broached the topic with her," said Mrs. Curry, still seated and sipping tea nonchalantly.

"Would she? Really? Do you think she ever once noticed us? *You*, Mrs. Curry? Did she ever once come below-stairs to meet with you about dinner arrangements? Or take offense at the way Mr. Matsumoto never notified you when he was going to miss a meal? The only time she did notice you or me was when something went wrong!" she said, her voice finally raising to join the strength of her emotions. "But the men. Oh, men she noticed. Because she had to notice them. Had to notice her effect on them. Because so long as she had an effect on them, she could control them—"

"Stop, Eleanor." Mrs. Curry stood and whirled in one swift motion that silenced the maid. "That's enough. We shouldn't speak ill of the dead. Especially one so young and innocent in the ways of the world."

"*Innocent*?!" Mrs. Sigmund cried. "You think she was *innocent*?" She turned to Thomas. "I'll meet you at the carriage house, Officer Carew. I have something to show you that might help you form a more truthful opinion of Miss Mitchell." And with that, she flew out of the room like a valkyrie.

Thomas grabbed two more muffins for the road, stood, thanked Mrs. Curry for the tea, and excused himself and Prescot.

Outside the kitchen door, he asked Prescot if he still needed a carriage to take him home.

"No, thanks. I think I'll walk a little. Clear my head."

"Sure thing. Thanks for keeping me company through all that." Thomas nodded back toward the still-fresh tension of womanly tirade.

"I take it I've gone from suspect to assistant?" Prescot asked.

"Something like that. Have a nice walk home. Sure I'll be seeing you around." And placing his helmet back upon his head, he returned to the workshop to grab Bernard.

* * *

Bernard dismissed Mr. Matsumoto so he could be alone in the workshop with his thoughts. He walked to the forge, which was still smoldering. He irritatedly noticed that someone had moved the poker that had been in the sandpit last night. He thought he'd told Thomas and Mr. Matsumoto not to touch anything. He turned and surveyed the scene from that point of view, returning to that first moment when they'd discovered the dead woman.

Why had the murder happened here? It seemed there were only two possible reasons.

One: The murderer had found Miss Mitchell here and either because of her surprising him or vice versa, he'd strangled her.

Two: The murderer had brought or led Miss Mitchell here on purpose and an altercation had ensued leading to her strangulation.

If it was the first, then why had Miss Mitchell come out to the workshop? What had she been here to do if she knew her inventor was meeting at the house at three o'clock? And if she hadn't left the house to come straight to the workshop, where had she gone first?

If it was the second, then why had the murderer picked this location to draw Miss Mitchell to? The obvious reason was the variety of weapons available. His eyes perused again the wall of swords, hammers, tongs, and back to the forge. But none of them had been used, unless they'd been cleaned more thoroughly than the hatchet outside.

If it was this second choice, the natural next question was *how* had the murderer drawn Miss Mitchell out to the workshop? Had he written her a letter telling her to meet him there at three o'clock? But then *why*? The missing chauffeur sprang to mind. Perhaps they'd been having a rendezvous. But why here? Where would one—

He was glad he didn't have to finish that thought as Thomas's shadow blocked the sun in the doorway.

"Mrs. Sigmund would like to give us a tour of her home," he said.

"Oh would she?" Perfect timing.

"Perhaps I suggested it, but she didn't balk at the idea."

"Probably means there's nothing there for us to find."

"Oh, there's definitely something there to find. Mrs. Sigmund made that quite clear." He recounted her sudden switch from quiet mouse to agitated cat in the kitchen. "She's waiting for us now."

Bernard waved a hand and followed him out toward the house.

On the way, Thomas filled him in on his interviews with Mr. Matsumoto and the household. Seemed he was capable of gathering information after all. He glanced at the crumbs on Thomas's uniform. So long as muffins were involved.

"We need to collect more information on Mr. Sigmund, starting with this visit," said Bernard. "His lack of appearance this far into the investigation makes me wonder if he's either our murderer or our burglar on the run."

"Certainly fits the profile."

"I agree."

They met Mrs. Sigmund outside the carriage house, set back amongst sizable thorny rose bushes. They entered the carriage house from the front and she led them back, past a brand new automobile. Thomas was distracted for a moment by the shiny black carriage and electric engine until Bernard nudged him to keep moving. They passed through to the auto shop, which was strewn with a variety of tools—some on the ground, some on benches along the wall, some hanging in the oddest places.

So when they'd tiptoed around and over the mess and been led up narrow stairs to a small apartment door, Bernard was shocked to find the place was practically sparkling with cleanliness. Every wooden surface was clear of dust, the mantel and fireplace were white without a hint of soot, and the carpets were free of tracked dirt, mud, or other signs of spring. Obviously, Mrs. Sigmund was the type who brought her work home with her, so to speak.

"You have a lovely home," Thomas said politely.

As Mrs. Sigmund moved ahead of them, he hung back and tapped Bernard. "Did you notice the automobile?" Thomas asked softly.

"Very nice," Bernard muttered.

"No, I mean, if the automobile is in the carriage house, he's not 'running an errand and hasn't returned'—whoever heard of a chauffeur not enjoying the perks of the job?"

Bernard grunted. "We'll take a look when we leave. Good work."

As they entered the small parlor/living room Bernard strode toward an end table where he found a framed wedding photograph of two attractive—though no longer young—individuals.

The woman was short and slim, the man tall and well-built. They were seated together on a Chesterfield, about two feet apart, not touching, hands clasped in their laps, hers around a wedding bouquet. Her dress was white and simple, with a high collar of extensive lace; his suit was pin-striped, and his top hat was cocked at a jaunty angle that revealed thick, curly hair. Their faces were quite serious, as was typical of those who took the time to sit for a photograph, though Bernard had always prided himself that in his wedding photograph with Roslyn it couldn't be denied they were both bursting with joy.

"We'll have been married three years this October," a timid voice said coming up behind him.

He turned. Her face was wistful, lost in memories. The assertive side Thomas claimed to have seen in the kitchen seemed to have retreated for the moment.

"I'm sure he'll come home soon."

The woman sniffed. "It's not like him to be gone for so long. Usually when he...goes into town...he's back by dinner, in case Miss Mitchell needs him for an evening party or something."

Thomas's head lifted. "I couldn't help but notice the automobile we passed, Mrs. Sigmund. Does that indicate he did return?"

She stiffened. "Sometimes he would take the streetcar down if he intended to stay for more...personal errands."

"Mrs. Sigmund," Bernard began, trying to draw her eyes to his, but she kept them focused on the photograph. "I'm afraid I'm going to need you to answer some difficult questions."

Now the eyes lifted and he saw they were of the palest blue. And frightened.

"I don't know where he is," she said shakily, brushing her hair subconsciously behind her ear.

Was that a bruise yellowing there? Or just the light? Bernard thought he could tell the difference.

"Do you know what he usually did when he went 'into town'?"

She looked down again. Bernard waved a hand toward a chair and she sat. He sat across from her and Thomas remained standing, his notepad and pencil out.

She sighed deeply, which seemed to let out some of her pent-up tension. "Mr. Sigmund has many sins. One is gambling, I think. At least, I don't know how else he can afford the new suits, the liquor, the late nights out—"

"Unless he was a thief," offered Thomas.

Bernard kept his focus on the woman's face. She didn't seem surprised by this suggestion.

"Yes. Perhaps. I suppose. I've never noticed items missing from Miss Mitchell's house before, though."

"Perhaps he was gathering a final haul before killing her and making a run for it."

Mrs. Sigmund's eyes widened.

Bernard glared at Thomas. "We don't have any facts to suggest that's what happened."

Thomas shrugged.

Bernard turned back to Mrs. Sigmund. She'd been about to say something else before Thomas sidelined the conversation. "And the other sins?" he asked gently, his eye glancing to the bruise behind her ear.

But it wasn't that she admitted to.

A tear escaped from the corner of her eye. She glanced at the wedding photograph.

"I think he...no, I *know*...now...he was having an affair...with Gladys Mitchell."

* * *

It all poured out of her from there. Eleanor showed them the chocolate hair she'd discovered on his suit. Although it meant everything to her, it meant seemingly little to them.

"He may have been having an affair, you're right, but there are many other possible reasons for this," the larger of the two policemen said, rather patronizingly. "He was her driver, after all."

"I know what it means," she said firmly.

"Do you have any other proof? Letters? Exchanged trinkets?"

The evening before, she'd rifled through all of Mr. Sigmund's things for just such signs.

"No," she said curtly. "But that doesn't mean I'm wrong. A wife knows. This has happened before, you know."

"He's had affairs before? Or you've thought he was having an affair with Miss Mitchell before?"

"I mean, men say they love you, will always love you, but as soon as age begins to shadow your face, your body, they're off and running after the nearest young thing." Her voice was beginning to crack in anger.

"But at the workshop? I have a difficult time imagining Miss Mitchell and your husband meeting there. Of all the places to meet for an assignation, I don't think a dirty place like that would fit the style I've come to associate with Miss Mitchell."

Eleanor glared at the bearded detective. "Of course not. You never even met her, but you're still a man." She could feel the heat rising within her again, just like it had in the kitchen. "Men never could think ill of Miss Mitchell."

"Jennings did. Does," the bearded officer said quietly.

"What do you mean?"

"I mean," he said, meeting her glare, "that not *all* men are drawn into this web of lies you seem to think Miss Mitchell wove about herself. Jennings actually seems to think you deserve better than your husband, and I think, if given the chance, he'd do something about it."

She blinked. "Wait, you think Jennings might have killed Miss Mitchell because she was having an affair with my husband?"

This time the policeman blinked. "That wasn't quite what I was thinking, but yes, that would work."

She studied his face. "Jennings has never once defended me from my husband, even when he could have done. What makes you think he'd kill his employer to protect me?"

"Love is powerful," the bearded one said gruffly, picking up their wedding photograph again. "May I take this with me? We're going to need to write up a description for the paper to search for Mr. Sigmund. He's been gone too long to be innocent."

Finally something she agreed with.

* * *

Archie found himself back at Montrose Park, wending his way along the paths through the budding trees and plants reaching for spring. The satchel slung across his chest was getting to be as heavy as his cares, full of his dreams and hopes for a future that may never happen. He was pleased beyond all measure, therefore, when he saw the young lady who kept crossing his path seated on a bench beside Mirror Lake, on the end where the ducks liked to make their home. She was writing in a small journal, her brow slightly furrowed in a rather adorable fashion.

"Miss Kenyon!" he called out, waving. "Fancy meeting you here!"

"Why, hello, Mr. Prescot!" Miss Kenyon gave him a half-smile; she seemed to be pushing aside whatever had been preoccupying her thoughts as she wrote, closing the journal with the pencil in its binding and placing it back in her chatelaine purse.

"This is what I'd call a precipitous meeting." He smiled jovially at her as he approached.

Her mouth twitched and she started to laugh.

His smile faltered and he blushed slightly. "Did I say something wrong?" Perhaps "precipitous" was incorrect? He did seem to always have the wrong words coming out of his mouth when he was feeling flustered. He pushed his glasses up his nose.

"You just know how to make a girl feel at ease, is all. There's no minding the cares of this world when Mr. Prescot is in attendance. What brings you out so late in the day?"

"I was just on my way home from what seems to be turning into a sort of side job at the home of the late Miss Mitchell."

Her smile widened. "A friend of mine who works there was just saying you'd been to the house."

"Really?"

"Yes, Eleanor—Mrs. Sigmund now."

"Ah, yes, Mrs. Sigmund." Her angry outburst regarding Miss Mitchell could not easily be forgotten. "How did you know her before?"

"She came to work for my grandmother after the Great Fire. She was hired as a maid, but as she lived with us and had no family, she was also a sort of nanny for me. I was only eleven at the time." Miss Kenyon's pale face turned up in memory, a stray curl blowing against her cheek. "Eleanor told me a little about all the unfortunate affairs happening at the house these past few days. So tell me: does your 'side job' involve thievery or murder?" She smiled at him and her eyes twinkled, but he couldn't stop the blood draining from his face to his neck.

She seemed to notice immediately. "Oh, I'm terribly sorry. I only meant it in fun."

"No, not your fault at all...not at all." He avoided her eyes, removing his glasses to rub them on a handkerchief he pulled from his pocket.

"I merely meant have you taken up detecting, perhaps, in your spare time?"

"Oh!" He nodded, trying to shake the fear that even *she* seemed to think him capable of such atrocities. He replaced his glasses. "Oh, well, I suppose, for all intensive purposes, that is, in a manner of speaking, I suppose I may be finding myself in such a role." He was tripping over his words and making a mess of things. He tried to steer back on track. "It's all a bit disconcerting, to tell the truth. No one is being considered innocent. Not even me. I was actually a suspect for a time. But my consciousness is clear, and I think I've got the police to trust me," skimming over the real reason they seemed to have crossed him off the suspect list. "I'm currently boarding with the detective on the case, Detective Carew."

"Really? That's thrilling!"

"Yes. Perhaps. Now that he seems to trust me. But just yesterday,"—had it really only been yesterday?—"Miss Mitchell was going to be my patroness, and I was setting out to do some rather interesting work in sound theory with the other inventor boarding with her."

"How wonderful!"

"Again, perhaps. But now she's dead and the other inventor may have killed her, though I don't think so. To be honest, I'm quite lost. Even your friend's husband is suspected of being a murderer and a thief."

Miss Kenyon gasped, her eyes wide in dismay.

"I mean, he may be innocent!" Archie waved his hands to try to erase the statement. "I don't know. After all, I hope the inventor is innocent."

Miss Kenyon shook her head. "Do the police think the thief and murderer might be one and the same?"

"Well, someone stole from Miss Mitchell and someone also killed her. It seems too contagious for it not to be the same person."

Miss Kenyon stared at the ground. "Poor Eleanor."

"I'm so sorry, Miss Kenyon, I've said too much."

"No, no, not at all. I—I'm afraid I must be heading home." She stood, still avoiding his eyes.

"Yes, yes it is getting rather late. May I escort you home?"

"No, thank you, Mr. Prescot. I...think I should like some time to consider what you've said...and how I might help my friend."

"Of course." He tipped his hat. "I apologize again if I was inconsiderate—"

"No, please forgive me," she said, reaching out and taking his hand. His whole body stilled. "I am sure I will run into you again very soon, Mr. Prescot. Good night." She smiled and squeezed his hand and then turned to walk toward the streetcar stop.

"Good night," he called after her, cursing his mouth as he plopped down on the bench where she'd been sitting.

What a day. What a terrible, horrible day.

* * *

After enjoying yet another glorious meal at the hands of Mrs. Curry—he'd never known beefsteak pie could taste like that, much less alongside the best duchess soup, fried halibut, shredded potatoes, and hot tomatoes he'd ever had—Thomas joined Bernard in the long walk up the servants' stairs to the second floor so they could begin the arduous process of searching through the dead woman's study.

He groaned as Bernard unlocked and opened the study door.

"You're going to regret eating so much later tonight," said Bernard, completely missing the reason why Thomas was groaning.

"It's not my stomach, Bernard, it's my head. Look at that desk—it's almost as Brobdingnagian as this house! And the drawers beside it. And the bookshelves. This looks like a man's den, not a woman's study. Where are all the plants and paintings of plants?"

"And how would you know what a woman's study should look like?"

"I've courted women, Bernard. Just because I haven't found the love of my life like you doesn't mean a thing."

"You're getting older."

"So are you."

Bernard grunted and walked over to the desk. "Fine, why don't I take the desk and you search everything else. That door should lead to her bedroom, I think." He pointed toward the side door.

"It's locked," Thomas said, shaking the handle.

Bernard held out the keys. "Look for another ring of keys in there, too, would you? We have yet to find Miss Mitchell's personal set."

Thomas took the ring and unlocked the adjoining door. He stepped into the floral Japanesque room. "Found the plants," he said, letting himself in.

Full, green plants lined the windows, offering a fresh scent of, well, green to the room. He'd never been good with flowers so he didn't even try to classify them or the smells emanating from them. Similar smells could be found no doubt in the perfume bottles on the mirrored table covered with brushes and combs.

The bedside table drew his attention, however, as on top was a neatly stacked pile of drawings and sketches. He picked them up and was surprised to find they were diagrams of something scientific. He couldn't make heads or tails of it except for something that looked like a funnel, and something else that looked like a tuning fork. Whatever it was, it was hardly light bedtime reading.

* * *

Bernard tried to ignore the cloying smell of fake roses that emanated from the door now open onto the dead woman's bedroom. He sat down at the Japanesque ebony desk decorated with gold engravings and red cherry blossoms, and immediately found organized envelopes, sheets of lavender-scented paper, stamps, and pages headed with gold-embossed lettering "GJM."

As Mrs. Sigmund had told Thomas, there was a collection of photographs in the top left-hand drawer. All of them seemed to be of the items he'd noticed in the front parlor.

In the top right-hand drawer was a collection of fountain pens and a small journal. Bernard hesitated before opening it, but within he only found notations of the weather, and a few addresses in the back. She had a Mr. L.L. Westfall located in the Fernwell Building listed as her lawyer. Bernard would need to pay him a visit first thing tomorrow to find out about Miss Mitchell's will.

Jennings's references were something he particularly wanted to find, given the man's odd manner when they'd spoken earlier. Miss Mitchell was thankfully a very organized person, and had thoughtfully collected all the staff references in a drawer to the left. Bernard thumbed through them until he found a collection of reference letters Miss Mitchell had placed behind a piece of paper with *Reginald Jennings* written across it in a flowing script.

"Reginald" even sounded like a butler's name. He started reading. At first, nothing struck him about the letters. There were three and they all voiced high praise of the man, his manner, and his work ethic. But then he realized all three had used the words "high moral standards"—exactly those three words and in that exact order. It seemed odd to him that three completely different people would use that exact same phrase to describe one person.

He read the letters again. Nothing else felt out of place. He looked at the names of the authors of the letters.

He laughed.

Thomas returned from the bedroom with papers in his hands. "No keys in here. What?"

"I know why Jennings didn't want me in here."

Thomas waited for him to continue, actually quiet for once, but Bernard was having trouble controlling his smile in order to explain.

"His references—they're all written by people who I just happen to know died last year."

Thomas reached for the letters. "How could you possibly know that? No one reads the obituaries that closely."

"You do when you're a detective hunting for a thief who's been hitting funerals throughout town."

Thomas shrugged in acquiescence to Bernard's genius. It was another moment, however, before Thomas's grin matched Bernard's mirth.

"You mean to say, there's no way to confirm the letters," said Thomas.

"Exactly. He must be lying!" Bernard said enthusiastically. "I'll bet they're all false testimonies. I bet he's never even been a butler before in his life!"

* * *

Marian rocked in her rocking chair before the fireplace, *The Spokesman-Review* open on her lap, taking a leisurely read through the day's articles. She appreciated the suggested daily menu, but since she had yet to re-stock the pantry since her arrival and had mostly worked her way through what Nain had kept on-hand, she had no way to make clear soup, boiled white-fish, cream sauce, mashed potatoes, parsnip fritters, olive and egg salad, cheese crisps, chocolate pudding, and coffee as suggested for dinner. She'd most likely go out again, though she hated the idea of leaving the house now she was home. Perhaps she'd merely try her hand at the recipe included for apple salad instead.

The article in the women's column was mildly irritating, since the author's suggestion for women to claim the title of "society woman" relied solely upon her having "money—that is, more money than the rest of those who are in her set." At least the description of the pictured dress—"myrtle green cloth, trimmed with narrow bands of black taffeta on the cross"—sounded quite beautiful.

After that, however, she found herself skipping pages, looking for something encouraging, but instead her eye kept landing on things like "Mrs. F.F. Emery Lost Purse." The only positive news seemed to be that the street sprinkling had started as the "Dust Preventers Work Business Section and Browne's Addition." She did finish the short article entitled "To Greet the Chief" about the plans for President McKinley's visit to Spokane at the end of May, but then gave up on news.

She flipped to the classifieds. There her eye skimmed through the female help wanted; it was almost all housework, something she didn't want to do in her own home, much less someone else's. She smiled when she saw the ad for a watchmaker, and stopped at the listing for a "man and wife for small ranch near Spokane," her thoughts returning to her friend.

Poor Eleanor. She hoped what Mr. Prescot had said wasn't true. The woman had been through enough trials in life. She wondered what Eleanor and her husband would do now. That was, if her husband ever came back and proved he was innocent.

But even then, Marian knew her friend would never truly move on until they found the murderer. She recalled the wide variety of emotions her friend had cycled through just in the course of her brief retelling.

Maybe she could help Eleanor. Maybe by solving the riddle that was currently holding her life at a standstill, she could help her friend find the strength to move forward. With or without her husband. With that attitude, she decided to read the article in the evening paper, the *Spokane Chronicle*, about Miss Mitchell's murder.

It didn't take long to find. The murder was front-page news: "Gladys Mitchell Butchered on the Hill, Police and Body Stumped."

Marian gulped as she read the details Eleanor and Mr. Prescot had kindly left out. Miss Mitchell hadn't just been killed, she'd been beheaded *and* strangled—a recent discovery by the coroner which "shed new light on the kind of murderer they were dealing with." The article suggested that it was possible the murderer had reacted in a blind panic, but that strangulation usually meant the victim knew her killer, which led one to consider the men in Miss Mitchell's life. According to the article, there were only three at the house at the time of the murder: a Japanese boarder (whom Mr. Prescot had called an "inventor"), a butler, and Eleanor's husband, the chauffeur/groundskeeper, who was missing. Not to mention Eleanor had said Mr. Prescot had come in to look at a clock in the morning, and he himself had said he'd been spending a lot of time there recently.

Mr. Prescot was a big man. She recalled her first encounter with him and the startling, loud impression he'd made stomping out of the forest. But then again, his kind eyes behind his glasses, his "intensive purposes" and "precipitous" malapropisms, and the way he blushed whenever he said something to her in an attempt at humor were too endearing for him to be a murderer. Not that such reasoning would work before a jury, but it was enough for her.

Besides, Mr. Prescot had said himself the police had ruled him out, was even boarding with the detective. She smiled.

That left three other possible men, and perhaps more the paper hadn't listed.

She wondered what sort of "inventor" the boarder was, and why Mr. Prescot thought he was innocent. The butler had been guilty in one of Conan Doyle's Sherlock stories, though she couldn't recall which one at the moment.

Perhaps there was some intriguing background story there that wouldn't come to light until the end? Perhaps he was really Gladys Mitchell's father and had finally returned to claim his daughter, only to be secreted away under the guise of "butler" to avoid a scandal, and when it became too much for him, he'd strangled her in a fit of rage!

Dear me, child, sometimes your imagination does run away with you.

Marian laughed with the daisies. Only the voice of her dead grandmother speaking to her through a talking chair would attempt to dissuade her from her wild imaginings.

Truth is stranger than fiction.

The fire had practically died as she'd become lost in thought, and she rubbed her arms for warmth. Eleanor had rubbed her upper arm at one point, too, but it hadn't been the rub of one seeking heat. It had been the subconscious rubbing of a past injury. And later in the visit, Marian had noticed a deep, yellowed bruise peeking out from under Eleanor's hairline behind her ear.

She considered what they'd been discussing at the time of the arm rub.

Mr. Sigmund. Her husband.

"My husband and I were never blessed in that way. Perhaps that's for the better," she'd said, in response to Marian's question if she had children.

That bruise...

Miss Mitchell would've had bruising around her neck, too, indicating to the coroner that she'd been strangled before she lost her head.

And if a man could leave bruises on one woman...why not two?

* * *

"Where is that butler?" Thomas asked loudly as he and Bernard descended the main staircase. "I've got a thing or two to say to him before we leave."

Someone cleared her throat to his left and he realized Mrs. Sigmund was standing there, rubbing her hands together worriedly like a rabbit.

"Mrs. Sigmund? Is something the matter?" Bernard asked, walking heavily over to her.

"I—I'm afraid—"

Thomas wondered why *now* she seemed unable to call upon the fire that had given her words such heat twice today.

"I'm afraid...I think...Mr. Jennings is no longer with us."

"He's *dead*?!" Thomas shouted, his voice echoing off the foyer walls so that Mrs. Sigmund's eyes seemed to be bouncing about, trying to follow it as it flew.

"N-no. No. I merely meant, he seems to have left the house." She focused on her hands. "After what you said, I went looking for him, just to—well, ask him about it—and I can't seem to find him anywhere."

It didn't take long for Thomas and Bernard to search the house top to bottom only to realize the maid was right.

The fake butler had flown the coop.

"Mrs. Sigmund, while I have you," Bernard said, after they'd admitted they couldn't seem to locate another man in her life, "we were wondering if you'd know where Miss Mitchell would keep her keys?"

"Probably in her coat pocket."

"And where might I find her coat?"

"Well, the last time I saw Miss Mitchell she was pulling on her coat...so I'd imagine it'd be in the...workshop?"

Bernard frowned. "You're correct, but it wasn't there."

"I don't understand. She left with it on." She hurried to the front hall closet and opened the door, stepping inside to look at the row of hanging coats. She reached out and pulled down a trim brown driving coat, presenting it to Bernard and Thomas. "This is hers."

"The one you saw her wearing last?"

"Yes."

Bernard searched the pockets, pulling out a ring of keys and a pencil.

"I don't understand. How did her coat end up back here at the house?" Mrs. Sigmund asked.

Thomas nudged Bernard. "Mr. Matsumoto's mysterious running person had a coat on..."

"If he was telling the truth," Bernard murmured, picking up on Thomas's thought, "then it might have been the murderer covering themselves in Miss Mitchell's overcoat on the way back to the house to avoid recognition."

"But that means the murderer must be a member of this household."

"And two of those members are missing."

Three

Wednesday, April 17, 1901

Spokane, Washington

The Red Rogue launched off a wall to the east and up, over a garden fence, doing a somersault in the air to bring feet beneath, landing with a soft *thop* in the backyard of the next house on the block.

The thief didn't even slow. Instead, in a swift, easy movement, Red sprang from the ground to grasp the edge of a low second-floor balcony garden, swinging an agile body up before climbing nimbly over the ironwork, landing on cat's paws in a near-silent *whump* amongst the herbs.

Crouching, the thief tried the window. Locked tight. No matter—

The hairs on the back of the Red Rogue's neck prickled.

Someone was watching.

The thief could feel it, right to the tips of the red curls that hid beneath the driving cap.

A soft glint of moonlight caught something just inside the windowpane, beyond the sheer curtains: a pair of glasses on a nightstand.

And beyond them, a plump round face was looking right at Red, the eyebrows furrowed and the eyes squinting, hopefully unseeing, above the oddest attempt at a mustache ever seen in Spokane. The man reached for the thick glasses on the stand—but that was all Red saw before springing back over the ironwork and off the balcony ledge, landing on the ground with a soft *whump*, and sprinting off into the darkness.

*　*　*

Archie was in a land filled with bells. A city of bells. Where everything chimed and binged and bonged.

It was his city. The city he'd created with his bare hands.

A city of sounds. A city where every single thing ran on sound waves.

And he'd built it. He'd built it all.

The clock tower. Automobiles. Ranges. Call boxes on every corner. Everywhere he turned he heard another chime. There were loud ones and quiet ones. Long ones and short ones. Strong ones and weak ones. But every chime signified something working.

Something he'd created, *working*.

But then...the chimes warped. They became discordant. And

everything was crashing together into one terrible, horrible noise that became visible like a giant pool of blood, spreading, sinking, stinking across the whole city until everything would be swallowed up in the great, wet redness of it all.

He had to fix it. He had to fix it now before it was too late. But he couldn't breathe. It was suffocating him. Drowning him. He was going to die because of something he'd created—

Someone was knocking on the door to his bedroom and he was pulled forcibly out of his nightmare. The bedsheets had engulfed his face and he struggled to pull them away and breathe the sweet, cold air of morning. Finally, he was free.

He wiped away the cold sweat dripping from his face and took deep breaths.

The knock came again.

"Yes," he finally croaked out.

"It's Bernard, Mr. Prescot," came the reply.

What did that man want with him now? He'd already humiliated him before Matsumoto. He'd been avoiding Bernard ever since, which was made easier by the fact that the brothers hadn't come home for dinner again last night.

"I'm still sleeping," he said grumpily, forcing himself to take deep breaths to steady his heart.

The silence outside his door told him Bernard had gotten the intimation.

"Prescot, I'm sorry."

Maybe not.

"I apologize for speaking to you so rudely, like a common suspect. It was wrong of me. I could have at least given you the benefit of the doubt, having known you a little better than the average miscreant."

Archie sighed. There was only one thing to do.

He grabbed his glasses and stood, wrapping his dressing gown over his striped pajamas as Bernard continued, "I'm sorry I forced you into an uncomfortable situation."

Archie took another deep breath, pushed his glasses up his nose, and opened the door. Bernard stood there looking as shamefaced as a mutt caught with torn slippers in his mouth.

"It's all right, I suppose," said Archie with a sigh. "You were doing your job. Wouldn't expect any less of you."

"Thank you. I truly do apologize. I'm not that kind of detective. I know badgering suspects doesn't work. I don't know what came over me. I just really need to solve this case..."

"I know, and I want to help you in any way I can."

"Thanks. We caught a break last night, after you left. We found Miss Mitchell's coat in the hall closet."

"Her coat."

"Yes." Bernard seemed excited but Archie didn't understand why.

"Isn't that where her coat *should* have been?"

"No." Bernard's grin was so wide it was visible beneath his mustache. "That's just it. It *should* have been in the workshop with her body. But it wasn't. It was in the hall closet."

Perhaps Archie was just having a difficult time waking up, but he still didn't see the importance. "And that means...?"

"It means you're officially off the hook! It means the murderer was someone living in the house, and for some reason, they brought her coat back with them. Which means you couldn't have done it."

"Because I don't live there." Archie got it now. Bernard seemed quite happy about this discovery. "But why would the murderer bring her coat back?"

"He probably wore it, maybe to cover the blood on his clothes. The amount of splatter that was evident—"

But Archie wasn't listening anymore. He grimaced and was glad Bernard noticed and stopped his elaboration.

"The point is: you're no longer a suspect." Bernard slapped Archie on the shoulder in a friendly manner, nearly knocking him off his feet.

As different as the Carew twins were, they sure did a lot of things the same.

"By the way, did you happen to hear anything last night?" Bernard asked, turning from the top of the stair. "Only, Mrs. Carew said she woke in the middle of the night to the sound of something landing on the garden balcony outside your room, above her window. The woman has the sensitive hearing of a hunted rabbit and what with Miss Gillen giving her notice so suddenly, I think she's worried when I'm not home until late."

"Actually, I did, come to think of it. It was some time in the middle of the night and I woke to see someone on the ledge there. They were gone before I could get a good look with my glasses on." He gave a sheepish shrug. Such was the way of the blind. "All I saw was a figure in a dark red overcoat and boots leaping from the balcony with a soft squeak. Whoever it was was quite acrobatic."

"Dark red, huh?" Bernard scratched his chin. "So are you planning to come out to the house today? To work with Mr. Matsumoto?"

Archie stammered, surprised by the sudden switch in topic, which was probably why Bernard had done it. "I—well, I did hope to stop by later today. If that's all right?"

"Perfectly fine," Bernard said, though Archie felt like he cut himself off from saying, "if you want to be associated with a murderer." But Archie still didn't think the inventor capable. At least, he felt sure if he *did* murder someone, it'd be by accidentally shooting them with a sound bullet. "I'd like to have you there next time I talk with him," Bernard continued, "to help me understand the work you're doing together. I'm sure I'll see you there. I have a feeling I'll be spending a lot of time at that workshop until I can get this thing solved."

"Me, too," said Archie, and turned to get dressed for what was sure to be another thought-provoking day.

* * *

"Miss Mitchell, why won't you listen to me?" Eleanor asked.

She knew she was dreaming.

She knew because the Miss Mitchell that stood before her had a thick line around her neck and was bleeding onto her clean carpet.

"Please, go!" she shouted.

She did not want to have to clean blood out of the carpet. It was so difficult and time-consuming. If only Miss Mitchell would move into the kitchen where it could be wiped off the tiled floor.

But Miss Mitchell would not move. She just kept staring at Eleanor.

"I'm sorry," the dead form of Miss Mitchell said in a wispy, sad voice.

That wasn't how her voice had sounded in life. In life, she'd been sure of herself, of where she was going and who she needed to take her there.

But now, Miss Mitchell was just sad.

The ghost took a step toward Eleanor.

Eleanor started to cry. She was so tired. So tired of knowing the truth. So tired of not being able to do anything to stop it.

She was so tired...so tired...

She let the tears fall. One by one. Though she knew they'd do nothing to change the past.

"I'm so tired of the lies, Miss Mitchell," she said through her tears.

Miss Mitchell reached out to put a hand on Eleanor's shoulder.

A skeletal claw of a hand.

Reaching out, not to comfort her, but to kill her, to strangle her.

She screamed herself awake.

Her pillow was on top of her face, trying to suffocate her while she slept. Part of her wished it had.

* * *

Now that they knew the murderer was a member of the household, it seemed clear to Thomas it was between the two missing men: the adulterer who'd killed his mistress or the fake butler who'd wanted to protect his con.

The chase was on, the game was afoot, and all that. Nothing like a good chase. Got the blood boiling.

So naturally, Bernard wanted Thomas to do paperwork.

"We need to get the facts down in an orderly manner before it's too late," his brother the detective argued on the way to the station. "The chief will be wanting to know where we're at in the case and I'm not sold on Sigmund or Jennings as our murderer. We have no proof. Only that they're both missing and one of them was maybe having an affair with the dead woman while the other had something to hide. It doesn't all necessarily line up."

"It only makes sense."

"Not to me. There's still the inventor whose papers just happened to be on her bedside table, too, don't forget." Bernard continued his long strides. "Besides, there are many reasons why one of her hairs could have been found on Sigmund's jacket."

"Oh, sure. I've seen lots of drivers comforting their passengers," Thomas said, letting his words drip with sarcasm. "Why just the other day I was walking down Front Street and saw a lovely lady in red being comforted by her driver—oh, no, wait, that was in the Tenderloin District, so..."

Bernard just shook his head. "But why would he kill his mistress? Where's the motive? There's a connection there, I'll concede, but no motive."

"Maybe she tried to break it off with him? Perhaps after meeting Prescot that morning she'd changed her tune?"

Bernard gave his brother a look that said, *Enough jokes.*

"Fine. Jennings then. The man is shiftier than a tomcat in heels."

Bernard grunted, which was as close to a laugh as he was going to get.

"They're both missing, Bernard. To me, that pleads guilty."

"All right, but of what? Maybe Jennings has done a runner with the stolen goods and we'll find him in Seattle hawking them in a shop? Or maybe Sigmund's waiting to sober up after a bad night at Dutch Jake's gambling tables? Or maybe he will turn up with a completely excusable story about an errand he was running for Miss Mitchell?"

"Without the automobile?"

Bernard grunted. "I'll give you that one. So he hasn't gone far."

Now Thomas was giving him a look that said, *Just admit it. I'm right.*

Surprisingly, the look worked.

"All right, fine," said Bernard. "See what you can find out about both men's backgrounds while I pursue another angle."

"Right ho, g'uv!" Thomas gave him a short salute and marched toward his desk as they entered the first floor of City Hall.

* * *

Bernard approached the desk sergeant with sure, purposeful strides. Hollway was a small, thin man with a walrus mustache that stretched to his chin, and wide ears that seemed to be holding up his sergeant's cap. His eyes could flash in a manner that made even Bernard wary, thus his attempted bravado whilst passing through the man's domain.

"Morning, Hollway," he said with a tip of his derby. It had actually taken him a good month to get used to entering City Hall wearing a suit and derby rather than the navy blue uniform and helmet that had seen a lot of action on the streets of Spokane. Now he wouldn't go back for all the world, though, and thus was relieved to finally have a murder case land in his lap. The other detectives had tried to out-maneuver him by giving him only robberies, but he'd show them. There'd been a reason Captain Coverly had recommended him for detective, and here was his chance to prove it.

The grizzly bear in him wanted to growl, however, when he approached his desk only to find Detective Martin Burns standing there in his dandy suit, his smooth hands thumbing through *A Study in Scarlet*. His eyebrows arched even higher than usual as Bernard approached.

"Caught your killer yet, Carew?" Burns asked, emphasizing the alliteration with a grin.

"Only day three, Burns," Bernard said, hanging his hat on the back of his chair.

"Got any leads?"

"None I plan on sharing with you," Bernard said, surprising himself with the rudeness of his reply. He couldn't help but be reminded of the last time he'd found Burns standing at his desk.

"I'll leave you to it then," said Burns, putting his hands up defensively after returning the book to Bernard's desk.

Bernard checked his pens and desk drawers carefully before taking a seat. Nothing seemed out of place.

He sat down and quickly stood again, bending down to remove the straight pin that had been left perpendicular to his chair.

It was like he was back in school. He shook his head clear and sat down again, determined to solve this case and finally prove his worth within their ranks.

He hadn't wanted to admit it to Thomas just yet, but he was still curious about the burglar angle. Even though the coat in the closet seemed to indicate the murderer was someone in the house, he still felt like they were missing something pertaining to the thief's visit on the night before the murder. Maybe the coat had been returned by someone protecting the murderer or thief? Maybe there'd been something in the coat pockets they'd pulled out in the meantime?

There was also that bit of red fabric he'd found in the wood chute, which seemed to indicate the opposite of the coat: that someone had entered the house secretly, without the keys.

Then there was the red-coated burglar who'd attempted to hit his own house the night before—it was too tempting not to pursue that connection just a little.

If he found something worthwhile, *then* he'd tell Thomas.

He began by pulling out his notes from all the burglary cases he'd been assigned since becoming a detective in January. The burglaries were so varied it would be difficult to find any similarities.

His very first case had been one the detective before him had never followed up on from fall of the previous year. Bernard had thought it was just a prank being played on him by the other detectives, since the stolen property had merely been some clothing off a washing line. But Mrs. Edwards had made it very clear she didn't see anything funny about the loss. The reason for her annoyance had been made even more clear when Bernard discovered the other detective had failed to note that the thief had also helped himself to a few candlesticks on a side table by an open window. No wonder she'd been upset the police had never caught the thief.

Candlesticks. Wait. Bernard thought back over his long week. There *had* been a surprising number of candlesticks reported as stolen recently. He went through the pile, setting aside all burglaries that included at least one set of candlesticks. He ended up with quite a stack. And most of them within the last week. Interesting.

He thumbed through the smaller stack, looking at the objects stolen besides candlesticks. Within this pile he noted that nothing of substantial size had been taken, meaning the burglar was most likely concealing the goods about his person. He must have had a bag, or a coat with lots of pockets. Prescot had said the figure last night was wearing an overcoat—"a dark red overcoat." His mind flashed to his first case and Mrs. Edwards's missing clothing. Hadn't one of them been a burgundy overcoat? Could it really be one and the same?

He focused on the more recent burglaries and was surprised to note that all of these victims had reported a lack of apparent entry. None of the victims had woken to smashed windows or broken locks. Indeed, most of them hadn't even realized anything was missing until they went looking for a specific item of jewelry. Originally, in Miss Mitchell's case, he'd thought this fact meant that it was an inside job. But given the fabric in the wood chute and that he had found more than one theft with this description, he was starting to wonder if he was looking for one particular kind of burglar who was making himself at home in Spokane.

Now he was getting somewhere.

"Message," said Thomas, standing next to his desk with his arms crossed. He was tapping his foot.

Bernard furrowed his brow. "Have you been waiting awhile?"

"I've said, 'Message,' four times and you just kept reading."

"Sorry. Following a lead."

"Find something?"

"I thought I might have, but I suppose I'll have to come back to it." He sighed. "Who's the message from?"

"The lawyer. Says he'll meet with you any time today," Thomas read from the back of the card.

Bernard had dropped his card at the Fernwell Building on their way to City Hall that morning. He was glad to hear the lawyer was open to meeting with him. Hopefully, it boded well for the exchange of information.

"Want me to come with you?" Thomas asked as Bernard stood and returned his hat to his head.

"I'll take this one alone, thanks." Bernard grabbed Westfall's card from Thomas's hand and was gone before his brother could argue with him.

* * *

Eleanor was trying very hard to focus on her job, but the lack of sleep the previous night was making it incredibly difficult to care.

She plucked herself up and reminded herself she still had a job to do until she was released from service. Perhaps today would finally be the day the detectives closed the case and she could move on.

She thought she'd begin in her favorite room, the front parlor. With Miss Mitchell gone and her impending need to leave, she felt some reluctance to part with all the enchanting Japanesque art collected there. Perhaps she wouldn't even dust, but would simply spend time admiring the art before it disappeared into the collection of some worthy benefactor.

On her way, however, she peeked into the dining room. The table wasn't set for breakfast, which reminded her that Jennings had disappeared. The comments made by the two policemen in her apartment the day before skittered across her mind: "Jennings actually seems to think you deserve better than your husband, and I think, if given the chance, he'd do something about it."

Even though she'd declared that Jennings had never defended her against her husband, it hadn't been true. She'd come across them once outside the house, close to blows and red in the face, practically spitting in each other's eyes.

"Don't you dare threaten me, you pompous hornswoggler!" her husband had been sneering in a low, contemptuous growl, raising his leather driving gloves as though prepared to whip them across the butler's face. "You know what happens to people who try to stop me from having my way?"

"Yes, I do. I've seen your wife—" Jennings had noticed her then and suddenly all the fury in his face had left him like a popped balloon. All that had been left was pity.

"Leave him," he'd said, coming up and pulling on her elbow to lead her away.

She'd let him drag her to the chicken yard but there she'd shaken him off.

"Go. It's all right."

"But—he'll kill you someday. You know he will."

"You're forgetting, Mr. Jennings. I love my husband. He needs me. I can't leave him."

She'd seen then he truly didn't understand. No one did.

She didn't really understand it herself.

* * *

Marian had found it almost impossible to fall asleep the night before, concerned as she was for Eleanor.

She'd tried to put herself to sleep by reading her favorite book from childhood: *Maid Marian* by Thomas Love Peacock. Although her namesake was called by another name until halfway through the book, she'd always found encouragement within the humorous and exciting text.

One of her favorite quotes was in the very beginning: "Some of the women screamed, but none of them fainted; for fainting was not so much the fashion in those days, when the ladies breakfasted on brawn and ale at sunrise, as in our more refined age of green tea and muffins at noon."

She always laughed at that line, but her favorite part of the book came later when, "Hereupon, which in those days was usually the result of a meeting between any two persons anywhere, they proceeded to fight. The knight had in an uncommon degree both strength and skill; the forester had less strength, but not less skill than the knight, and showed such a mastery of his weapon as reduced the latter to great admiration. They had not fought many minutes by the forest clock, the sun; and had as yet done each other no worse injury than that the knight had wounded the forester's jerkin, and the forester had disabled the knight's plume; when they were interrupted by a voice from a thicket, exclaiming, 'Well fought, girl; well fought.'"

The first time she'd read the story, her surprise at the revelation that it had been Marian and not Robin fighting the knight had been the cause for many a tale of adventure reenacted about the house. It was something she'd carried in her heart into adulthood.

No matter how old the book might be, it would always warm her with its tales of derring-do and damsels who could defend themselves. It reminded her she lived in an age when women were being given more independence every day. To that end, she realized if she was going to stay in Spokane for an extended time, she'd need to find employment.

She'd fallen asleep thinking this and had awoken with a clear inspiration of what she needed to do. Perhaps she could find a place where she and Eleanor might work together, so no matter what became of her husband, they could start a new life together as friends.

And so, in the early morning hours, Marian found herself walking up the long drive to the mansion drenched in mystery. Somehow Mr. Sigmund had managed to obtain lily of the valley. The delicate, bell-like flowers seemed to tinkle in the young spring light. Ornamental hawthorn trees lined the drive, the small pink flowers just starting to bloom.

She breathed in the sweet-smelling air as she reached the doorstep and knocked hard on the stately front door.

No one answered. She knocked again, and when still no one answered, she stepped back to take a wider look at the house. The curtains were drawn across all the windows, as though the house were shutting itself off from the world in order to huddle up and grieve.

Or perhaps that was just what part of her wished she was doing right now.

She sighed and started back down the drive, but the cackling of chickens caused her to follow the noise around to the back of the house, where she found Eleanor standing amongst them, a bucket of feed in one gloved hand, the other sprinkling it all about. Marian walked up carefully, watching for little brown piles, unsure if chickens pooped.

"Good morning!" she called out.

Eleanor continued to sprinkle feed, her eyes vacantly focused on the ground before her. It was obvious she hadn't had a decent night's sleep since the murder.

"Good morning!" Marian said again, a little louder this time.

Finally, Eleanor looked up. Her eyes cleared as she saw Marian, and she smiled. "Good morning, Marian! What a nice surprise!"

"I admit, I've come with something of a purpose," she said when she reached where Eleanor stood. "I was wondering if you'd consider seeking employment with me?"

"Together?" Eleanor's smile grew wider. "You'd like to do that?"

"Yes, very much. I don't know anyone in Spokane, and since we've renewed our friendship and we both need jobs, I thought we might look together."

"I'm not sure what sort of situation would take on both a middle-aged woman and a sweet young thing like you, but I suppose it's worth trying." Eleanor's smile was such a cheering sight. "Mrs. Curry has the newspaper in the kitchen if you'd like to look at some wanteds with me."

"Yes, let's."

Eleanor hung the feed bucket outside the shed, along with the leather work gloves that had protected her hands.

Marian hooked her arm through Eleanor's as they walked back to the kitchen.

"I didn't know maid duties included the feeding of chickens," Marian said.

"I don't mind. It gets me outside. And I'm not really certain what my 'duties' should include for the moment anyway. My father was the type who didn't see the division of labor as a girl and boy divide. With four daughters, we had to make up for the lack of a son on the farm. I've done everything from grinding bone-meal grit for the chickens to chopping wood to scooping out the stables. It's the life of a farm girl."

Marian admired Eleanor's broad shoulders and knew the sleeves of her shirtwaist hid arms strengthened by a life of physical labor.

"You always did take on more than necessary," she said, squeezing Eleanor's arm and thinking of her childhood at the knee of this hard-working woman.

They'd reached the kitchen where they found the cook bustling about as though she were cooking for a household of ten.

"Mrs. Curry, I'd like you to meet Marian—Marian Kenyon, a dear friend of mine from younger days."

"It's lovely to meet you, dear. Would you be so kind as to hand me that towel behind you? Thank you. Kenyon. You're not related to Edith Kenyon are you?"

"She was my grandmother!" Marian couldn't help the thrill of jubilation that traveled through her.

"I knew her growing up," Mrs. Curry said cheerily, holding the towel over her hand and opening the iron oven door to check something that smelled splendid. Then she closed the door and turned around to continue chopping a plethora of vegetables. "When one is gifted with a Majestic range large enough to boast more than one oven, it is essential that the hottest one always be used for meat. Placing the meat at a high level of heat at the beginning is the only way to obtain that beautiful crisp outside, and a wonderfully juicy meat on the inside. Not even a dog likes a dry bone."

"Perhaps you might open a cooking school, Mrs. Curry?" Marian suggested. "Tips like that I would never have learned if my grandmother hadn't taught me, and I knew of plenty girls in Seattle that couldn't boil water, much less roast a leg of lamb."

"It's certainly a sad world we're coming to when it's customary to eat out more regularly than at home with one's own kith and kin," agreed Mrs. Curry.

"Might I help you?" Marian offered, feeling right at home in the comforting atmosphere of the kitchen.

"Thank you, dear. Those eggs need peeling and chopping." She pointed to the bowl of cooling boiled eggs and handed Marian an enormous knife.

Marian settled herself at the center prepping table and began working on the eggs.

"Who are you cooking for, Mrs. Curry?" Marian asked as Eleanor took a seat behind her at the large oak table surrounded by chairs, picking up the newspaper. It was good to see she could still take breaks now and then.

"Whoever has a stomach that needs filling. The animals are still hard at work and the garden is still producing and we still need to eat. Mr. Matsumoto is here, and who knows when those detectives might show up again. I do wish they'd get on with it and find the murderer before we lose anymore staff, and so we could know what the future might hold."

"'Nothing is certain but the unforeseen,'" said Marian before realizing she'd just quoted one of her Nain's proverbs.

"You sound just like Edith," Mrs. Curry said, looking up from her chopping with a smile.

Marian felt so happy she might burst.

"She would always spout these silly proverbs," Mrs. Curry said, "but you know, I find myself using them whilst about the kitchen."

"Such as?"

"Oh, you know: 'The way to a man's heart is through his stomach.' 'A watched pot never boils.' 'You can't make an omelet without breaking eggs.'"

Marian's smile grew.

"You must miss her something terrible," Mrs. Curry said, pausing and looking at Marian. "She was a good woman. Only met your grandfather once, but it was clear she loved him very much." She reached across the table and patted Marian's hand kindly.

"Thank you," said Marian. It looked like Spokane still had a great many good souls tucked between the hills.

* * *

Thomas was following his nose. And his nose was telling him that Lawson's wife, Millie, had sent him in with cinnamon rolls.

"Heya, Walt, how are you today?" he asked, stopping in front of his desk.

"The rolls are not for you, Thomas." Walter Lawson's deep voice resonated from a round face with a thin black mustache that, together with his charred cinnamon-colored skin, only made Thomas hungrier.

"What rolls?"

Lawson's head rose from focusing on his work, which lay beside a plate of beckoning treats.

"I was coming to ask you if you knew if Shannon was in," said Thomas. "Got a question for him."

"Right. I just brought him back in the wagon with another arrest. Sure he'll tell you all about it."

"Good to know." Thomas rocked back and forth on his heels for a moment before nonchalantly asking, "Could I steal a roll?"

Lawson rolled his eyes. "Fine," he said, but then snapped out a hand over them. "Just one," he said firmly.

"Of course," Thomas said with a grin, though he was a bit disappointed by the restriction. "Give your wife my gratitude."

He hurried back to his desk before Lawson could misunderstand his comment. The roll was a bit on the burnt side but it oozed with cinnamon and butter and—was that a hint of cloves? maybe nutmeg?—ah, the man didn't know a good cinnamon roll when it sat seeping into his desk.

A few superbly sticky minutes later and he was off to find Shannon.

"Carew! Just made me 12,000th arrest!"

"So I heard. Congratulations."

"I'll never forget me first arrest, made me second night on the force: a drunk printer was fightin' a telephone post." He guffawed and slapped his meaty thigh with his meaty hand. Although Officer William Shannon, a burly Irishman with a bushy mustache and a pair of piercing eyes, was often referred to in the newspapers as "one of the toughest officers on the force," everyone at the station knew he was actually as sweet as a soufflé, and about as puffed up. He was a good man, tough and fearless, but to the growing underworld of mobsters, Chinese triad, houses of ill repute, saloons, gamblers, and numerous thugs that populated Main and Front Streets he was "the Terror of the Tenderloin."

"You know I made 11,184 arrests in me first ten years?"

"Sorry to hear it's slowed down for you."

"What?"

"I said, have you heard of Cecil Sigmund?"

"Cecil Sigmund?" Shannon repeated with a snarl. "What do you want with that snake?"

"So you know him."

"Sure I do. Got a head of Irish red curls you don't forget easily."

Thomas showed Shannon the wedding photograph they'd borrowed from Mrs. Sigmund.

"Yes, that's him. Been thrown in the cells more than once for bein' drunk and disorderly."

Thomas nodded. "I thought you might've run into him in the Tenderloin. He's supposed to be a regular at the gaming dens, and perhaps at some of the other dens. Gone missing."

"Missin', eh? Last I saw him he was in Dutch Jake's place. Seemed flush. Maybe he skipped town 'fore losin' it again?"

"It's possible. If you do see him, let me know, will you? He's possibly a thief or a murderer, or both."

Shannon's bushy eyebrows rose at this. "Well, well. I'd heard the Carew brothers had gotten themselves a murder case. Would you like some pointers for when you finally do catch hold of Sigmund?"

"Sure." Thomas shrugged.

"It's real simple. You just slam 'im up against a building and let 'im know you mean business." Shannon pushed a thick finger at Thomas's chest. He could easily see Shannon shoving some sap against a brick wall with a force that would get a confession out of any man. No wonder he had so many arrests.

Thomas rubbed the spot where it felt like Shannon had left a bruise with just one finger. "Thanks. I'll keep that in mind."

He watched as Shannon marched off to pound some sense into something...or someone.

* * *

Eleanor flipped through the newspaper as Marian and Mrs. Curry talked and cooked together. She'd been glad to find upon coming to work for Miss Mitchell that, like for Marian's grandmother, she wouldn't be required to assist the cook beyond the cleaning of dishes. For some reason she'd always found she preferred the clean-up to the creativity required to produce edible dishes, especially for the upper-classes who seemed to be unsatisfied with a simple meat pie every meal. Thankfully, Mrs. Curry was a walking cookbook, with enough creativity to meet the needs even of a Japanese boarder, no matter how strange the dishes seemed to the average American stomach.

She wrinkled her nose recalling the last noodle dish Mrs. Curry had attempted for Mr. Matsumoto. It had included a rather tangy sauce she'd called "soy sauce," which had been obtained from Chinatown by special order. Eleanor was pretty sure most of that meal—whatever Mr. Matsumoto hadn't insisted on slurping down like a child—had ended up in the refuse bucket.

"Eleanor, would you be a dear and check on that roast for me?" Mrs. Curry's voice broke into her thoughts.

Eleanor stiffened but then forced herself to relax. She used the range's top portion all the time to boil water for cleaning; it was reaching into the oven's hot innards that put her on tenterhooks.

She stood and crossed to the range, grabbing a thick towel to protect her hand as she pulled the heavy iron door open. She reached in and pulled out the pan with the roast, as though she knew what to check to ensure it was cooking properly, then pushed the pan back in.

"Ouch!" Eleanor drew her arm back quickly from the oven.

Mrs. Curry sprang into action. She ran to the sideboard and cracked an egg into a separator, throwing the yolk into one bowl and the white into another, then grabbed the olive oil and mixed it with the egg white.

"If you apply this mixture quickly enough, no blister forms," said Mrs. Curry as she worked.

Taking a piece of clean linen from a drawer, she pushed the sleeve of Eleanor's shirtwaist back, rubbed a bit of the mixture onto Eleanor's forearm, then wrapped the linen about the burn. Her touch was gentle but efficient.

"What happened here?" Mrs. Curry asked quietly, pointing to the revealed bruise on her wrist.

"It's nothing," Eleanor said, pulling her sleeve back down over her wrapped arm.

Mrs. Curry said nothing more but turned to close the door to the oven.

"There's nothing worse than a burn," said Marian kindly as Eleanor returned to the kitchen table.

Eleanor focused on the newspaper, trying to temper the flush of heat in her cheeks. This was why she avoided the oven.

"Every time I burn myself I can't help but be reminded of that terrible night...," murmured Mrs. Curry.

But Eleanor had heard her. "August 4, 1889," she said quietly.

"Sometimes I can still hear the shrieks...and the cries...," Mrs. Curry continued, her hand stilling above the vegetables.

"And the heat," muttered Eleanor. It had been inescapable. Like being in an oven.

"I lie awake at night and...oh, it was just so terrible..." Mrs. Curry shuddered. "Thirty blocks devoured in flames, dark clouds, smoke so thick you could hardly see across the street..." She drifted into silence at the memories.

"I was only eleven, but I remember where I was," said Marian softly. "Sitting on the front porch, playing with my dolls, Nain seated beside me, rocking back and forth. It was so hot. And suddenly the night was alive with the sounds of...well... I remember thinking later, as we walked downtown and passed out bread and cheese, that it was like the end of the world..."

Eleanor's hands shook as she gripped the newspaper. She'd almost succeeded in completely forgetting that night and her life before it. She'd set up walls in her mind, blocking the memories so that she could get on with her life. She'd been at the very center of it all, downtown. It really had been like the end of the world. The smoke and ash. It had hung in the air for weeks, been in her hair for months.

But the fire. It had been *alive* that night. The way it had ridden the wind first up one block then down the other, gobbling up whatever stood in its way.

The only thing that had stopped it was the blowing up of buildings. Destruction to stop destruction. It felt...needless and ironic.

She looked at Marian and Mrs. Curry. No one would ever forget where they were that night. An entire generation of Spokane would carry the story forward, but someday, some other destruction would occur and distract from it, and the Great Fire would be forgotten. Like Troy and Atlantis, it would be swept up and washed away in the current of time.

* * *

Marian and Eleanor took their leave of Mrs. Curry with the newspaper and made their way to the carriage house at the back of the drive.

"You live in your own place?" Marian asked.

"Yes. Mr. Sigmund has always been the driver, even when these were the stables for the horses, before the automobile, so it was typical for him to live in the carriage house. And since we're married, which is unusual for those in service, it made sense for us to live outside the main house."

Marian wrinkled her nose as Eleanor opened the door. The odor of manure still permeated the wooden structure. But when Eleanor led the way into the little apartment above, Marian stifled a gasp. She'd never seen a home so clean. Perhaps she'd merely gotten used to the gathering dust in her grandmother's home, since she hadn't found it in herself to brush, wipe, or scrub since her return. Suddenly she felt very self-conscious knowing Eleanor had seen her own home—a home Eleanor herself used to keep as spotless as this—in such disarray.

"However do you find the time to keep your place so pristine?" she asked, noting the pride that spread across Eleanor's face because she'd noticed. She almost looked chipper.

"I like to keep busy," the little woman said modestly.

She led them to two hulking maroon armchairs before a small, spotless fireplace. Although it was not customary for women to sit in such chairs, there seemed to be only one armless chair placed away in a corner. From this simple fact, it was clear Eleanor's husband was the one who did all the entertaining in the house. Marian's dislike for the man was growing with every moment.

She glanced at her friend and realized she was wearing her hair a little looser today so that the bruise she'd noticed yesterday behind her ear was not visible when she turned her head.

Marian suddenly found herself overwhelmed by her original

reason for coming up here to see Eleanor. She might have told herself it was to search out a job together, but really it had been the thought of her murderous husband returning to strike again that had kept her awake all night.

And then fate intervened as her eyes fell on a photograph beside her chair.

"Is that your husband?" Marian asked. It was a portrait of the same man she'd run into just a couple days ago, though it seemed longer. He wasn't wearing that self-satisfied smile, but his eyes seemed to glint evilly.

"Yes," Eleanor said shortly.

Marian ran through her thoughts of the previous night, trying to come up with the best way to approach such a tender and unwelcome topic.

"Eleanor, you know that I'm ever so glad we've reconnected after all these years," she started. "It's like...coming home. Even though Nain isn't here, *you* are, and you're almost as much a part of my childhood as Nain."

Eleanor looked up at her, half a smile beginning to form on her thin lips.

"I haven't felt like 'Marian' in years. It's funny how as you grow older, you seem to grow new layers, like an onion, until it's difficult to recall which layer is the 'real you.' Do you know what I mean?"

Eleanor's brow furrowed, but then relaxed. "Yes, I suppose. I feel younger with you. You take me back to a good time in my life. Seeing you after all this time has reminded me I did have a few happy years...between all the incredibly hard ones."

Eleanor fairly glared at the photograph next to Marian, but Marian tried not to turn her gaze from her friend.

"I haven't had all happiness in my life either. In Seattle, I made some mistakes, and unfortunately there's no escaping some of them. But I decided to accept them, and realize they're part of what makes my life my own. They're part of what defines who I am now. It's like..." Marian paused to gather her thoughts. "It's like I had one identity in Spokane with Nain, another in Seattle, and here now with you, I feel like I've turned a page and begun yet another new identity. But I think everyone is like that. You are a different person with your husband than you are with Mrs. Curry, for instance, or with Miss Mitchell."

Eleanor's eyes flared momentarily, so Marian hurried on past the dead woman.

"I feel like I could talk with you about anything, tell you everything, and I want to, but I also want to keep some of those layers to myself. Does that make sense? I can't possibly explain who I am in Seattle to you, but I've easily slipped back into who I was when I was a child, but I'm also no longer a child." Marian touched her forehead. "I'm sorry, I'm...I'm trying to say something but not saying it very well, I fear." She sighed heavily. "I just wanted you to know that I'm here for you. That if you ever need to talk..."

Eleanor bit her lip. "I know." She looked down at her hands and rubbed her ring finger.

Marian smiled encouragingly.

"Some days are harder than others." Eleanor fiddled with the sleeve of her shirtwaist. "Some days I wish..."

Marian knew what *she* wished. She wished with all her might that Mr. Cecil Sigmund *would* turn out to be the murderer. That he would be caught. And rot the rest of his days in a jail cell. Or even better: be hanged and leave this world, and more importantly Eleanor, altogether.

"I—," Eleanor started and stopped suddenly.

Marian remained quiet, letting her eyes show she was listening, but Eleanor's focus remained on her hands.

Eleanor took a deep, shaky breath, and Marian realized she was holding back tears.

"Mr. Sigmund was having an affair...with Miss Mitchell."

Marian released her breath.

"And what's more, the police seem to think he killed her or that he was a thief, or perhaps *both*!"

Eleanor shuddered and before Marian knew she was doing it, she'd wrapped her arms around the older woman in a soothing hug. She held her for a moment, Eleanor's cries shaking her whole body.

The two stayed like that until Eleanor's breathing slowed and they broke apart.

"I'm here for you, if you need anything," Marian repeated, still holding Eleanor's hand, not ready to break the connection yet. All she could think was that she had to get Eleanor away from here.

Eleanor nodded and squeezed Marian's hand. Then she released it to grab a handkerchief and begin wiping her face.

"Would you like to come stay with me?" Marian asked quietly.

"That's very kind, but no, thank you." She took a deep, steadying breath, but her middle age was showing again in the tired lines around her face. "It's all right. I'll be fine. I'll get through this."

"But what if Mr. Sigmund returns?"

"He won't," said Eleanor firmly. "He wouldn't dare." Her hand clenched around her handkerchief.

Marian was surprised by the look of anger on her friend's face. She was a soup of emotions, swirling between tears of fear and tides of rage. She wished Eleanor would let her help. But some women wanted to do things on their own. She let her gaze drift in search of a new topic of conversation.

"You really must tell me your secret for keeping your fireplace so clean. Mine is simply covered in ash all around the hearth."

Eleanor smiled gratefully at the change in topic, and Marian was thankful to see her friend relax into an easy conversation about cleaning tips.

* * *

The Fernwell Building was a few blocks up Howard from City Hall. A Romanesque six-story brick building designed by Hermann Preusse and built by Rollin Charles Hyde in 1891—a rather sad story as he'd been one of many to lose everything in the panic of '93—it stood alongside the Mohawk Building and the rest of the Rookery Block along Riverside, a permanent reminder of how Spokane had built itself out of the ruins of the Great Fire of 1889.

Any other day, Bernard might have paused to admire the structure, but now he hardly noticed as he pushed open the doors. He walked into the men's clothing store on the main floor and made for the stairs in the back that led to the offices on the second floor.

He found the door marked "L.L. Westfall, Patent Lawyer" on number 13; he hoped it wasn't an ill omen as he let himself into the outermost office. Bernard removed his derby and passed his card along with the returned card to the secretary.

"Yes, he's expecting you." The secretary stood and led him to the main office door, knocking and pushing the door open as she walked through.

"Detective Carew, Mr. Westfall," she announced quietly, before closing the door again as she left.

Mr. Westfall was a slight, mustached Scandinavian with blonde hair parted above a high, proud forehead.

"Welcome, Detective Carew," he said. He stood up behind his grandiose walnut desk and gave Bernard a firm handshake before motioning for him to take a seat.

Bernard waited for the lawyer to sit before he did. "Thank you, Mr. Westfall. And thank you for offering your assistance."

"You're welcome. I always figure help the law when they don't ask and maybe they'll go easy on me later when I need *their* help." He smiled affably.

Bernard half-smiled noncommittally. "You've helped the law before?"

"No, sir, first time." Westfall leaned forward and rested his arms on his desk. "I suppose you're here about her will then?"

"Well, yes, I was, but I couldn't help noticing you've listed yourself as a 'patent lawyer' on your door."

"Ah, yes, that is my primary work, but for Miss Mitchell I was willing to make an exception."

"I'm not sure I follow."

"Well, Miss Mitchell originally came to me for assistance applying for patents. That was where all the money came from, you see."

Bernard nodded like he wasn't hearing this incredibly important bit of information for the first time.

"And because her money was tied up in patents, she thought it simplest to have her will drawn up by the same lawyer."

Bernard continued to nod. "I see."

"I suppose you'd like to see the will."

Bernard's eyebrows rose. He'd never heard of a lawyer so willing and helpful.

"I'd sure appreciate it," he said. As the lawyer stood to find the necessary papers in the drawer of a desk along the wall, Bernard added, "We have yet to discover family members in need of notification."

"She didn't have any. But that's not the interesting part. You should know she mailed me a change to her will on Monday."

Bernard's wits snapped to attention. "On Monday?"

"Yes. She sent me a new will, signed by two witnesses, too, so it's all legal. As that's the day she was killed, according to the paper, I figured that's the sort of thing you police like to know in particular, right?"

"Yes, sir." Thank God Westfall wasn't the type to keep things to himself. "Exactly the sort of information we need. May I see the letter Miss Mitchell sent you?"

"Sure thing." Westfall pulled a thick envelope from his desk drawer and handed it to Bernard with a printed sheet entitled "The Last Will and Testament of Gladys J. Mitchell."

Bernard read through the original will first. She'd left everything to the Ladies' Benevolent Society, which wasn't very surprising, given she had no family.

He laid down the will and turned to the envelope, pulling out three sheets of thick paper that smelled of lavender. He blinked at the smell, recalling the ebony desk where he'd found the same paper in her study.

"Yes, her correspondence always does that to me, too," said the lawyer, noticing Bernard's minuscule reaction. The man was good at reading people.

Bernard started with the first page and skimmed quickly through, his eyes catching on phrases like "I was wrong" and "I want to make things right." Then he stopped and reread a couple words to be sure he was seeing what he thought he was seeing. "Blackmail" stood out in bold letters.

He grunted.

"That's about how I reacted when I read it, too," said Mr. Westfall. "It seems the patents she'd had me write up for her were not actually hers, but belonged to a man who's boarding with her."

Bernard nodded. "And she was trying to change her will to correct the situation."

"So now, as witnessed by Mrs. Curry and Mr. Jennings," said the lawyer, "she's left her entire estate to Mr. Hayate Matsumoto."

* * *

Thomas sat before the imposing stack of account books they'd taken from Miss Mitchell's study. Bernard had decided it'd be better to weed through them back at the station. But by "we" he'd apparently meant Thomas.

Then again, if Thomas was going to prove that Cecil Sigmund was their man—for he'd decided the adulterer would get his attention before the fake butler—what better way to do it than by following the money. He sent one of the underlings to track down the Sigmunds' bank information, thankful that for once he could send someone else to do this rather than being the one sent.

While he waited for the messenger to return, he started perusing the long list of deposits and withdrawals within Miss Mitchell's exceptionally detailed account books. The woman had obviously had a head for numbers. First those diagrams found beside her bedside table, coupled with the organized state of her desk, according to Bernard, and now these neat little numbers all lined up in a row—if Miss Mitchell had been a man she might have been as big a name in Spokane as Amasa Campbell by now.

Every time he saw the name "Sigmund" in the "Name" column, his heart leapt, but it appeared to be the monthly sum paid to the couple for their service, for it was as regular as clockwork.

He sat back and sighed, considering begging Lawson for another cinnamon roll, when the Sigmunds' account information arrived and he was able to get up enough steam to keep rolling.

Almost immediately he noticed an inconsistency. The deposits marked "work" in the Sigmunds' accounts started out matching with the amount listed every month as paid by Miss Mitchell. But then, starting in January, the amount changed drastically.

Not only did it go up, but it kept going up every month from the first of January to the first of April, the last time the Sigmunds had been paid for their work.

Why had their payments gone up? And why didn't Miss Mitchell's accounts reflect such a change?

Thomas pulled out Miss Mitchell's books again. He looked for the January 1901 amount paid to "Sigmund." Then he looked below it. On the next line was a payment to "C.S." for an amount that, oddly enough, would bring the total amount paid to the Sigmunds up to match the amount marked as deposited for "work."

He flipped to February. Again there was the line "Sigmund" followed by "C.S." It was the same for March and April. He grabbed the account book for the previous year. The amount listed in December 1900 was the same, and was *not* followed by a payment to "C.S."

"Cecil Sigmund, you rat," Thomas muttered aloud.

"You're not going to believe what I just learned," Bernard said, approaching Thomas with heavy footsteps.

Thomas looked up at him with a huge grin.

"You're not going to believe what I just found, either," he said, his finger pointing to the account books. "Miss Mitchell was paying Mr. Sigmund extra money every month for something. If she was his mistress, what was she doing paying him?"

Bernard smiled broadly. "Miss Mitchell was being blackmailed."

"That's what I assume, too, but it's a big leap from affair to blackmail."

"Not if that's the news I just learned from Miss Mitchell's own hand."

Thomas's eyes popped. "No."

"Yeah. And it sounds like you just found the blackmailer. I'd thought it might be Jennings since he'd faked his references."

"I would've thought that, too. Wait, let me look."

Thomas flipped through the account book. "Nope. No R.J., just C.S. It's Cecil all right."

"Now if only we could find him."

Thomas pulled out his father's pocket watch and flicked it open. "If we head up to the house now to see if he's returned we'd be just in time for Mrs. Curry's luncheon at one." He grinned and raised his eyebrows.

"Fine, but bring those account books. And the diagrams you found in her bedroom. I want to show them to Prescot, and he said he'd be at the house this afternoon meeting with Matsumoto."

"Yes, sir," Thomas said, grabbing his coat, helmet, the account books, and the paperwork before following Bernard, who was making a beeline for the front exit.

* * *

Bernard marched toward the streetcar stop on Riverside and was extremely irritated when they arrived and could see it already making its way up Howard.

"Come on," he said gruffly. "We'll have to walk and hope to catch the next one."

"Good thing, too. You need the exercise," Thomas quipped.

Bernard huffed and walked faster.

"Slow down. You've still got to tell me what the lawyer told you. How'd you know Miss Mitchell was being blackmailed?"

Bernard handed Thomas a typed copy of the letter from Miss Mitchell, kindly provided by Mr. Westfall's secretary, but Thomas protested he couldn't read and run and carry all the books at the same time. Bernard gave him the highlights.

"Miss Mitchell must have been meeting her blackmailer at the workshop the day she died," Bernard said, huffing even harder as they began the ascent. "Given that you found those diagrams beside Miss Mitchell's bed, when surely she would have filed them in a secret place in her desk, I think she'd left them out for us to find, in case her meeting with the blackmailer went badly."

"You keep saying 'her blackmailer.' You mean Mr. Sigmund."

"Perhaps."

"Now, hang on there, Bernard," Thomas said, hoisting the books into the crook of one arm and grabbing Bernard's elbow, pulling him to a stop. "I know you're the detective, but you asked me to assist you, and I'm trying to do my part. I figured out who the blackmailer was, didn't I? I can show you more clearly if you need more proof. But I won't just stand by and nod and take notes whenever you speak."

Bernard grunted.

"Or grunt."

Bernard smiled. "You're right. Thank you for doing your bit. Your interviewing skills have been invaluable and I couldn't have done it without you."

"Thanks. A bit of honeyed praise, but I'll take it."

They resumed their quick pace.

"So Miss Mitchell was blackmailed over patents?" Thomas asked. "Aren't patents just ideas?"

"Yes. Ideas that you can make money on. But if those ideas originally belonged to someone else, evidently it can lead to a lot of trouble further down the line. According to Mr. Westfall, even the great inventors like Tesla and Edison have been known to fight over the rights to patents. Her lawyer turned out to be a patent lawyer, so he was able to explain some of it to me." Bernard tried to explain what Westfall had told him about Miss Mitchell's money being founded in patents. "Two patents in particular," he said. "See, two years ago she filed for a patent for this funnel thing that focuses sound in a particular direction. Then one year ago she filed a patent for a 'tuning band'—something that could be moved up and down a tuning fork to change its vibration or resonance or something."

"I still don't get it. Those don't sound like the next big thing, Bernard."

"I know. That's what I said. But Mr. Westfall said to consider them to be something like the invention of the fountain pen. Something so simple, and yet revolutionary. Well, with all the advances in phonographs and gramophones and telephones lately, something like these two things could make their inventor very rich indeed, if placed in the hands of the proper investor."

"All right, I'm following. So you're saying Miss Mitchell was *not* the proper investor."

"Right. Mr. Westfall said it's like J.P. Morgan and Edison out east. Only, if Morgan patented Edison's ideas and made the money from them, rather than Edison himself."

"How do we know she *didn't* invent them?" Thomas asked. "Seems like she had a head for science and numbers and that sort of thing."

"Well, for one, she admitted as much in that letter," he nodded to the copy. "And why else would she be boarding an inventor and then suddenly change her will to benefit him, while admitting to being blackmailed?"

"So she had him board with her to patent his inventions without his knowledge?"

"Exactly."

"But she's only had Matsumoto living with her for two years. She's been a name in Spokane for much longer than that."

"Yes, it seems her father was an investor-type who was fascinated by new technologies, which is where she got her love of science and interest in such things in the first place. It was only after she met Matsumoto that it occurred to her to make more money patenting the ideas from the start, rather than simply being an investor."

"And now Matsumoto stands to inherit *everything* from the investor who stole his patents?"

"Yep."

"Think I know why he'd kill the golden goose, then."

Bernard nodded, looking gratefully behind them to see the streetcar heading their way. He held out a hand to flag it down. "He must have figured out what she'd done and heard that she'd just changed her will and thought it was the perfect moment to take his revenge. We need to talk with him before we jump to any conclusions, though. I'm not convinced. Something feels wrong..."

* * *

As Archie approached the workshop from the house, he could hear the smooth scraping sound of metal on stone. He was not surprised to find Matsumoto kneeling in his suit pants outside the workshop, a raised whetstone between his legs, the sleeves of his white shirt turned up above his elbows to keep them clear of the long, beautiful sword he balanced between his hands, slowly pushing it away from himself and back toward himself repeatedly upon the stone, pausing only to sprinkle more water upon it from a jar beside him.

Whish-whish, whish-whish, whish-whish.

He stood and watched for a few moments, somehow certain the blind man knew of his presence, though he didn't pause in his work for several minutes.

"Mr. Prescot." He finally looked up, resting the sharpened sword across his legs.

"How did you know it was me?"

"You breathe through your mouth rather than your nose. Neither of the Carew brothers do this. And as Mr. Sigmund and Mr. Jennings are apparently no longer with us, the only other man who would visit me is you."

"How did you know it was a man?"

"No skirts," said Matsumoto, waving to Archie's legs.

Of course. That one was too obvious.

"May I ask why you're using a stone rather than a wheel to sharpen?" Archie hoped this question wouldn't embarrass him further.

"The wheel is a European tool. In Japan, we use this, and only this. A blade sharpened on a stone like this need not be sharpened so often. Come, I will show you."

Archie approached, setting his satchel on the ground and looking down at the stone.

"You must rub like this," Matsumoto said, taking the sword and doing as he had done before, making a soft *whish, whish, whish* sound. "I know I am holding it at exactly a fifteen-degree angle against the stone because of this sound. If I do it wrong..." He turned the sword just slightly and now Archie could hear *whish-ah, whish-ah, whish-ah.* "You must listen very closely."

"You must be very good at this, then," said Archie kindly.

Matsumoto bowed his head slightly at the compliment, then held the sword out to Archie. "Please."

Archie's eyes widened. "Me?" He hesitantly took the magnificent weapon, certain he was going to slice his hand off, but honored the man trusted him enough to let him hold it.

He took Matsumoto's place kneeling with the whetstone between his legs, though it was quite difficult for him to get down on the ground and he wondered if he'd be able to get up again without grunting like Bernard.

"Now," said Matsumoto, holding his hands parallel directly in front of himself as he stood before Archie. "Hold the blade like this, exactly at a fifteen-degree angle to the stone as you push it away from yourself slowly and evenly."

Archie tried, but immediately knew he was wrong because he could hear a *sheek-ah* that was more like chalk on a chalkboard than sword on a stone. Matsumoto heard it, too.

"Close your eyes, Mr. Prescot."

Archie had known it was coming. It was just like in the front parlor when they'd first met. He'd have to close his eyes and trust his hearing. And his hands, that he wouldn't slice off any important digits.

He closed his eyes. He listened to the sounds around him. To Matsumoto's breathing, which could barely be heard until he closed his own mouth and forced himself to breathe through his nose more quietly.

He heard Matsumoto splash more water upon the stone. Then he held the sword gently in two hands and slowly brought it down until it met the stone, bringing it back up to what he imagined was a fifteen-degree angle, then he drew it across the stone carefully.

At first it sounded like *sheek-ah*, but then steadily it became more of a *whish-ah*, and then finally a consistent *whish-whish, whish-whish, whish-whish*.

He listened to the sound for a long time, its steady rhythm reminding him of the *tick, tick, tick* of his pocket watch. It was rather comforting.

Suddenly he realized he didn't know how long he'd been kneeling there. He popped his eyes open and winced in the bright light.

Matsumoto was seated on the ground to his right, breathing slowly and steadily, his eyes closed—as though that made a difference, and Archie wondered if perhaps it did.

"Thank you, Mr. Matsumoto." He bowed over the sword as he returned it to its rightful owner, because it just seemed like the right thing to do.

"You did quite well, Mr. Prescot. You should know I do not trust everyone I meet with sharpening my swords, but a fellow sound scientist I knew would be capable of grasping the concept."

Archie smiled. It was good to make a friend in these odd times.

Archie stood with a definite *creak* from his knees but no more embarrassing sounds. "I...brought some sketches of my water vibration theory with me." Archie picked up his satchel and swung it back over his shoulder. "I must admit, it's not a new one for me, but something I've been considering for a long time."

"Then we are aptly met at this time and in this place, no matter if it is enshrouded in mystery and grief. I wish I could see the sketches."

"Actually," Archie said with a grin, reaching into his satchel to pull out the pages, "I realized last night that perhaps if I embossed the drawings..." He handed the first page against a notebook to the blind man.

Matsumoto reached out, his eyes widening as his fingers brushed the paper, feeling the lines slowly and methodically.

"Ah, Mr. Prescot, I have the feeling this is the beginning of something wonderful."

Archie smiled with pleasure. It had taken him most of the night to trace over his sketches with a pen pressed down hard into the top of a spare notebook, but he prayed it would be worth it. It was difficult to trust this man, any man, with his ideas when he had been burned before. Many a Seth Thomas clock containing his own musical workings would never hold the Prescot name.

As if reading his thoughts, the quiet, cool voice of Matsumoto said, "Being blind, I have had to learn how to trust others in a way the seeing will never understand. Thank you for sharing your ideas with me, Mr. Prescot."

"You're welcome," said Archie. But he was distracted by the approach of the Carew brothers, marching with determined steps toward the workshop, no doubt intent on ruining his day once again.

* * *

Bernard stomped across the yard toward the workshop. He was especially glad to see that Prescot was indeed there, as he'd said he'd be. Things were about to get very interesting.

"Good morning, gentlemen. It seems we've arrived at a most opportune time. I was wondering if we might see some of your sketches for your work." He held out his hand for the notebook and pages Matsumoto currently held.

"I am afraid these particular ones belong to Mr. Prescot," said Matsumoto, handing the notebook to Prescot rather than Bernard.

He wasn't too sure he appreciated that response.

"May I?" he asked Prescot.

"I—well, why do you need to see them?" asked Prescot. He slipped his notebook into his satchel as though to keep it out of sight and out of mind.

"Gladys Mitchell was not the innocent rich patroness everyone seems to paint her as," Thomas jumped in.

"What do you mean?" Matsumoto asked, directing his question politely back toward Bernard. At least the man was addressing his questions to the right person.

"I mean I bet dollars to donuts some of your notes are missing," Bernard said assuredly.

"Like these." Thomas waved the diagrams he'd found in Miss Mitchell's bedroom.

"Perhaps you would be so good as to describe them to me, Mr. Prescot," Matsumoto said quietly.

Prescot flipped through the pages Thomas handed to him, shuffling them back and forth and taking second and third looks. "They seem to be patent drawings for the funnel and the tuning band I saw you using yesterday."

"Did you say patent drawings?" Matsumoto asked.

Prescot nodded then said yes.

Matsumoto's eyes focused on Bernard. "Who patented these?"

"So you're saying you never did?" Bernard asked.

"No, Detective, I did not."

"Where did you find these?" Prescot asked the brothers, but it was Matsumoto who answered.

"Miss Mitchell had them," said Matsumoto, his voice oddly calm and unperturbed. His blind eyes stared at where the papers rustled in Prescot's hand.

"How did you know that?" Thomas asked quickly.

"No one else at the house would know about them nor understand their worth," the inventor explained.

Bernard grunted. The man could be a detective with that kind of swift logic. Or he'd known already...

Thomas nodded. "I'm afraid it's true. Gladys Mitchell was a thief."

"Wait, Miss *Mitchell* was the thief? She stole from herself?" Prescot asked, clearly thinking of the burglar—the one he'd failed to catch with his clock. "So, then, why did she make a show of it, calling me in, and the police? To make herself look innocent?"

"Oh, no, she stole from others."

"She didn't steal jewels or vases or anything you could see. She stole ideas, thoughts...creations," Thomas added.

"I don't understand," Prescot said. His face had lost all color, however, indicating that some part of him was very aware of the implication.

"Gladys Mitchell made her money stealing inventions from inventors and patenting them as her own," Bernard said slowly, clearly.

* * *

Bernard and Thomas were still talking, explaining how their discoveries had led them to this conclusion, but Archie could only see red.

He thought he might faint again.

"Excuse me." His hand gripped the strap of his satchel as he interrupted Thomas in mid-statement, thrusting the patent sketches back on him and pushing past to cross the yard as quickly as he could.

He was suddenly running. He didn't know where, but he just knew he had to run—or the closest approximation to it he'd been forced to do since he was in school.

The world was a gray blur around him and he couldn't breathe. His ears were ringing and his heart was thumping.

When he was forced to stop he was half-standing, hands on his knees, breathing hard next to Mirror Lake at Montrose Park.

How. Could this. Be happening. To him.

He couldn't think straight.

He collapsed to the ground and continued trying to breathe.

He tried to think about something calming, and the soft, rhythmic *whish, whish, whish* sound of the sword on the stone came to mind. He reached inside his vest pocket and pulled out his pocket watch.

He held it to his ear as he tried to take deep breaths, forcing himself to focus on the steady *tick, tick, tick*.

A splash startled him enough to get him to sit up, his watch still held to his ear.

Tick. A duck swam over to him, no doubt hoping he might have bread to share.

Tick. He focused on the duck.

Tick. On the shine along its back from the sun.

Tick. On the sparkles the droplets made within the oily feathers.

Tick. On the water as it parted around the duck's belly.

The duck climbed out of the water and came closer, hesitantly, practically sniffing him like a dog.

He breathed and tried not to think, slowly lowering his pocket watch to his lap.

Eventually, the duck decided he was all right and nestled herself next to him about a foot away, making herself comfortable in a patch of young grass.

He continued to breathe, but now he wasn't having to think about it so hard.

He let himself review the issue at hand.

Gladys Mitchell was a thief. And not just any thief. The kind that went after susceptible, naive inventors looking for a patron.

"With a wave of my hand I could make all your ideas come true," she'd said. "On one condition: that you be willing to involve me in your process..."

Involve me. And she'd asked him to explain in detail how his clock worked...

What a fool he was. To think *anyone* would be interested in his ideas. To think *anyone* would want to be his patron. To think *anyone* would ever want to hear what he had to say.

He almost cursed aloud but then remembered his waterfowl companion and kept his thoughts inside.

Where they belonged.

Thank God, thank *God*, he hadn't shared his Big Idea with her—his sound engine was so efficient it would make way for a world where energy was not required.

He broke out in a cold sweat just thinking about what might have happened if he had—

But it didn't matter. None of it mattered. God had saved him from absolute destruction at his own hand, and by his own ego, by killing her.

Good riddance, he thought, and then wanted to cross himself, even though he wasn't Catholic, just to ward off any bad omens.

Well, that's that. Time to move on.

He returned his pocket watch to his vest pocket and reached into his satchel to pull out his notebook. The duck didn't move beside him and had apparently fallen asleep in the bright spring sunshine. He rubbed a hand over the front cover, thinking about the Japanese blacksmith.

Could he trust him? Matsumoto was a victim, too. And he'd been a victim for much, *much* longer. He wondered who in the world was already working with that funnel and tuning band, making thousands thanks to the experimentation done by this blind eccentric she'd tucked away and hidden from society, like her own personal researcher.

The gall of the woman. No wonder someone murdered her. It made his blood boil just thinking about it.

He needed to go back. He should talk to Matsumoto and find out how he could help. Together, the two of them might be able to recover from this enormous setback and actually make a difference in the future of their world—*without* the patronage of Gladys Mitchell, or others like her.

* * *

Thomas wished Prescot hadn't run off like that. Matsumoto was trying to explain his work to him and Bernard, and it was all much too involved and boring for him to listen to when the thought of Mrs. Curry's lunch growing cold was on his mind. Hadn't Bernard told Prescot just this morning they wanted him there the next time the inventor started talking, to work as an interpreter?

Finally, he interrupted by shifting the account books to one arm so he could click open his father's pocket watch and declare loudly, "Is that the time? It's nearly quarter past one! Perhaps Mrs. Curry will forgive us if we arrive a bit late?"

Bernard glared at him, but Matsumoto said, "I have not enjoyed one of Mrs. Curry's luncheons in far too long. Perhaps we might continue this discussion at the house?"

Bernard acquiesced with a slight nod of his head.

Matsumoto began walking in the direction of the house without any indication he couldn't see where he was going. The man was a magician. Thomas was tempted to try surprising him, just to see if he could do it.

Thomas adjusted the stack of books in his arms again, apparently playing the role of packhorse in today's show.

"What do you think happened to Prescot?" Thomas asked softly.

Bernard shushed him. "He has the ears of a hawk, that one." He glanced in the direction of the blind man.

Only after the inventor had traveled over a rise in the distance did Thomas dare try again.

"May I speak now, Detective Carew?"

Bernard looked to the sky and rubbed his bushy mustache, but then he nodded.

"So, where do you think Prescot ran off to?"

"Probably to empty his stomach," said Bernard gruffly. "He seemed to take the news that his new patroness might have stolen his work pretty hard."

"Or he realized that meant he was associating with a murderer."

"First Sigmund, then Jennings, now Matsumoto. Is there anyone you're *not* certain is a murderer in this case?"

"Yeah: Prescot," Thomas scoffed.

Bernard grunted.

"You know," he said, as they started the long walk to the kitchen, "Matsumoto did just happen to meet Prescot the day Miss Mitchell was killed—a couple of hours before she was found, in fact. What if, after meeting Prescot, the inventor decided he wouldn't need Miss Mitchell anymore and killed her?"

"And since he's inheriting everything?" Thomas asked. "But that means he must know about the will already. Are we going to ask him about it?"

"I'd like to talk to Mrs. Curry first, as she witnessed the new will. It bothers me that she didn't think to mention it."

Thomas nodded in agreement. He hated to think the lovely cook had been keeping anything from him, other than her secret for making the perfect pie crust.

"Matsumoto seemed strangely calm about the whole thing, didn't you think?" Bernard asked. "Even guessed right away that Miss Mitchell was the one who'd patented his ideas without his knowledge."

Thomas adjusted his grip on the stack in his arms. "What if Matsumoto wasn't alarmed about the whole thing because he already knew? What if he was the blackmailer?"

Bernard stopped in his tracks. "You said the blackmailer was Cecil Sigmund. You were quite certain of the fact at the station."

"Yeah, but maybe he was being paid for something else? Maybe he knew another secret worth paying for?"

"The letter did only say she was being blackmailed over the stealing of patents, but not by whom. And her guilt led her to make it right and leave everything to Matsumoto."

"What if *that* was what Matsumoto blackmailed her for?" said Thomas. "I mean, I get she might've felt guilty about taking his patents, but then why not just leave Matsumoto the patents in her will? Why her *entire* estate?"

"You may have a point there. But then what was Sigmund blackmailing her over?"

"The affair?"

"I suppose. She wasn't married, though, so she might not have suffered too greatly if the truth got out."

"I don't know. Seems those high society sorts take their morals pretty seriously." Thomas shrugged.

They'd have to continue the conversation later, as they were near the kitchen and the smell wafting out the door told him he'd made the right decision bringing them here.

They walked in and were surprised to find Matsumoto seated at the broad kitchen table across from Mrs. Curry and Mrs. Sigmund. The surprise must have been evident as Mrs. Curry quickly explained.

"With Jennings missing, as well, Mr. Matsumoto will be joining us downstairs. He said you'd be along shortly."

"And still no sign of Mr. Sigmund?" Bernard directed his question at Mrs. Sigmund, who merely shook her head and focused on her food.

"Please, join us." Mrs. Curry waved at the extra place settings she'd prepared for their arrival.

Thomas set down the stack of books and papers he'd been carrying for what felt like hours, removed his helmet, and took a seat beside Matsumoto. Bernard remained standing.

"We're honored, but I have a few questions for you first, if you don't mind. Might we adjourn to the hall for just a moment?"

Mrs. Curry smiled and nodded, standing and walking out the door. Thomas was just serving himself a slice of mouth-watering chicken pot pie when Bernard grunted and motioned with his eyes that he required his presence, as well. Thomas stood and reluctantly followed, closing the door to the kitchen and the smell that he hoped would not be all he enjoyed for his lunch.

* * *

Bernard's stomach growled as he turned to the happy cook. Thomas pulled out his notebook and pencil, clearly irritated at having to wait for lunch. It'd do him good.

"Mrs. Curry, it has come to our attention that you neglected to inform us of something rather important that occurred the day of the murder."

Mrs. Curry squeaked. "I don't think I did," she said, her eyes wide and innocent.

"Perhaps something that happened before Miss Mitchell left for her walk?" He wanted to avoid feeding the answer to her if at all possible. A reliable witness needed to come up with the correct answer on her own.

"No, I..." Mrs. Curry's eyes widened even more. "Oh, dear. Perhaps... I did wonder after he said..." She blushed. "Are you talking about that paper I signed?"

Bernard didn't answer.

Mrs. Curry nodded. "You are." She rubbed her hands together. "You see, I thought it was just another food order. Miss Mitchell would always have me sign them after we'd discussed the week's menu. But this one was covered—she had another piece of blank paper over it and just asked me to sign at the bottom. I didn't think anything of it at the time..."

"But then?" Bernard asked.

Mrs. Curry glanced down and then back up again.

"Well...then Mr. Jennings said something after the murder that made me wonder. He mentioned how odd it was that he signed her new will the day she died."

Bernard raised his heavy eyebrows, but before he could say anything, Mrs. Curry waved her hands.

"I promise, I didn't know I was signing her will...but it must have been that... I know it takes two signatures to witness a will, and she'd never covered a food order for me to sign before and when I asked Mr. Jennings about it, he said that Miss Mitchell had told him it was something else, but he didn't believe her, so when he bent down to sign, he pulled on the paper with his pen so it would slide down and reveal the paper behind it." Finally, she paused for breath. "He said it was difficult to miss a heading like 'Last Will and Testament.' Quite clever of him, I thought."

Bernard grunted. If only the clever man hadn't done a runner.

"Did he see anything else? Like the beneficiaries?"

"He said he only saw the top, but naturally I wouldn't know for certain."

All right. If she was telling the truth, then it seemed no one as yet knew the Japanese man was their new employer, perhaps not even the inventor himself.

"What was Miss Mitchell's attitude when you went up?" Bernard asked.

"Quite agitated, I thought," said Mrs. Curry. "She seemed so worried, but I thought it was because she'd forgotten to put something in the normal food order we send out on Mondays. I just wanted to make her happy. I even offered to bring her a cup of tea to settle her nerves, but she said she'd be going out soon and wouldn't require anything. Then dismissed me without even a thank you." Mrs. Curry's eyes saddened at the memory. "I suppose that was the last time I spoke to her."

"Well, thank you, Mrs. Curry, for your assistance," said Bernard. Then, with a smile for the cook, "Now, how about we enjoy some of that pie—I don't think my stomach can wait any longer."

* * *

Rather than returning all the way down the Hill, Marian had decided to take advantage of the glorious sunshine by visiting the park again, since it was on the way. She'd brought her copy of *Maid Marian* with her to finish reading, and so after grabbing a quick bite to eat, she'd found the park bench where she'd last seen Mr. Prescot and settled in to enjoy the revitalizing spring air.

"*Lady Matilda,' said John, 'yield yourself my prisoner.'*

"*If you would wear me, Prince,' said Matilda, 'you must win me:' and without giving him time to deliberate on the courtesy of fighting with the lady of his love, she raised her sword in the air, and lowered it on his head with an impetus that would have gone nigh to fathom even that extraordinary depth of brain which always by divine grace furnishes the interior of a head-royal, if he had not very dexterously parried the blow. Prince John wished to disarm and take captive, not in any way to wound or injure, least of all to kill, his fair opponent. Matilda was only intent to get rid of her antagonist at any rate: the edge of her weapon painted his complexion with streaks of very unloverlike crimson, and she would probably have marred John's hand for ever signing Magna Carta, but that—*"

"Well met, Miss Kenyon."

Marian jumped out of her seat, a hand to her heart. "Oh my goodness! Mr. Prescot, you surprised me."

"I see that I did!" He swept his homburg off his head. "I apologize for my interruption of your reading. You were quite captivated."

"Yes, it's one of my favorite scenes. Matilda—before she becomes 'Maid Marian'—is fighting off a captor."

"The character has a different name in this version?" He pointed to the book in her lap.

"She is the Lady Matilda until she marries Robin and becomes Maid Marian."

"I've always wondered why she's called 'Maid Marian'—do you know why?"

"The answer is clearly offered in Peacock's take on the story," she said, handing her copy to Mr. Prescot. "Robin has taken a vow of chastity along with his men for as long as he remains an outlaw, so even after they are wed in the forest, she remains a maid until the end of the book when all is resolved."

Mr. Prescot sweetly blushed at the suggestion, taking the opportunity to replace his homburg on his head in an attempt to hide it from her notice. He looked at the cover of the book. "Thomas Love Peacock. Now there's a name."

"His is the best version of the Robin Hood legend, and the only one worth reading if one is looking for more personality from the heroine." She'd once tried to read Howard Pyle's rendition and had been greatly discouraged to discover Marian's name wasn't even mentioned but twice in the text. "I prefer to find my namesake engaged in defending her honor, rather than wilting along the hedgerows waiting for Robin to come to her rescue."

"Naturally," said Mr. Prescot kindly, returning the book.

"Why don't you keep it? I take it you've never read it?" Marian said, waving off the return.

"I would love to borrow it!" he exclaimed exuberantly. She stifled a laugh. "I mean, I promise I'll restore...reinstate...*return* it tomorrow," he said, obviously feeling flustered enough to have difficulty finding the right word.

"Oh, there's no hurry. Take your time. I'm certain we'll cross paths again soon enough." She smiled and tucked an errant curl behind her ear. "As you may have noticed, one of the facts of Spokane is no matter where one goes in the world, one always manages to meet someone from Spokane. You could be on a dirt road in the middle of Alaska, and someone would no doubt happen along whom you went to school with."

He laughed kindly at her little joke. "I certainly feel like I've been to Alaska and back today." He adjusted his satchel across his shoulder and pushed his glasses up his nose. "Would you care to take a walk with me?"

"I'd be delighted." She rose, taking the proffered crook of his arm as he went to place her book in his satchel.

The book slipped from his fingers and fell to the ground. He knelt quickly to pick it up.

"I'm so sorry. How clumsy of me," he said.

She took a step back, her boots softly squeaking as they rubbed against one another.

"I'm so terribly—" He stopped suddenly, still kneeling next to her feet, the book in his hand.

"What is it?" she finally asked, but something told her she knew the answer already.

"Your boots," he said quietly.

"Yes, I believe we discussed them the first time we met." Her heart beat inside her chest.

"Yes," he said, "but I've seen them...*heard* them...since then...outside my room."

He was avoiding her eyes. He wouldn't look at her. He just kept staring at the silly gutta-percha boots.

Finally, his puppy dog eyes lifted and connected with hers.

"You're the thief," he said.

* * *

Archie had been on his third circle of Mirror Lake, trying to get his frustration with the day's discoveries stomped out before returning to speak to Matsumoto.

Then he'd spied Marian. He'd thought she looked just as pretty as anything, reading a book, the sun shining down on her red curls beneath a short-brimmed hat, making them blaze anew against the green of her coat.

Now he wished to God he hadn't stopped.

The book was heavy in his hand, the weight mirroring the weight in his chest that was making it difficult for him to breathe.

It couldn't be true.

Her green eyes were meeting his unwaveringly and making his heart thump.

It couldn't be true.

"If anyone was going to figure it out, I hoped it would be someone like you," she said softly.

It was true.

He shook his head. "*You're* the thief?"

"The Red Rogue, at your service," Miss Kenyon said. She bowed at the middle like a man and rose with a wink. "I'm sorry if I've shocked your sensibilities."

"But...you..." Archie could feel his jaw opening and closing and he wished desperately to get himself under control. He looked at the book in his hands and then back at her. The air was getting thin again.

"You're not going to tell on me, are you? It'd be very ungentlemanly for you to do so and I might be forced to return to your room and steal your glasses." Her eyes twinkled and he tried to focus only on them. On the intensity of green in them. Pure green, no flecks.

He self-consciously pushed his glasses up his nose. "I would never, Miss Kenyon," he swore, and he meant it.

"If you're going to know my biggest secret, you might as well call me Marian."

Archie forced himself to relax. "Call me Archie."

"All right, Archie, would you mind telling me what gave it away? I thought for sure I'd gotten off the balcony before you got your glasses on." She smiled at him.

He couldn't help smiling back. He pointed at her feet. "It was the boots. If we hadn't had an actual parsley—er, *parley*—about them, I might not have recognized them. They make a certain squeak sound that I've only ever heard with those particular shoes."

She nodded and twisted her mouth to the side. "I knew I should have dropped another five dollars for a different pair of shoes. But these are just so comfortable!" She laughed.

She had the best laugh...for a thief.

He sat down on the bench, still gripping the copy of *Maid Marian* like a lifeline.

She joined him, but didn't say anything. Just let him think it all through on his own.

He suddenly felt he must be at the epicenter of a whirlwind determined to sweep through Spokane—like in that book that had become a bestseller just last year, the one about the little girl who rode a tornado to another land. Part of him wished *he* would get swept to another land.

Perhaps God was trying to tell him to leave. At the rate things were going, he would next discover his clock tower plans were being cut back and his services would no longer be needed. In just one day he'd discovered his new patroness was a thief, and now the young lady whose company he'd been enjoying was also a thief. There were just too many dangerous coincidences circling his life. Something was bound to break eventually. And he worried it would be him.

"How—," he stopped and tried again. "Why are you a thief?"

"Why are you an inventor?"

"That's not equivocal. That's legal. Why would you...steal?"

She sighed and gazed across the water as he looked at her.

Finally, she spoke: "Five years ago I left home to make something of myself. I was silly; I really did think I could make it in Seattle—such an immense city with so much to offer. It seemed to me the West Coast equivalent of New York City. I couldn't afford it, though, just like my Nain had said. But I'd already pushed her away, so I wasn't about to come crawling back begging for money. Instead, I looked for...alternative opportunities.

There were girls at the boarding house with extra baubles that they didn't even care about. So I helped myself to one or two, pawned them, and got on with my life." She shrugged like this was nothing to worry about. Taking something that belonged to someone else because she needed it, she thought, *more* than the other person. Archie tried to focus on letting her tell her side of things.

"I've always enjoyed photography, and one of my precious possessions I'd brought with me was a camera with a tripod. I decided I'd try being a professional photographer. I studied mostly through books at the library, getting tips here and there from experts who'd answer any questions—like the one I told you I studied with, off the wharf. I was excited to discover I could not only be paid real money for the work, but might eventually find someone who'd cover travel expenses and equipment, should I be contracted on a more permanent basis.

"The photography jobs picked up, and mostly with people who wanted me to photograph their homes—these enormous, luxurious homes filled with so many things they couldn't possibly miss one or two of them... I realized I could use my day job to...research for my night job...and, I guess I just kept going."

She continued avoiding his eyes, fiddling with the gloves on her hands as she spoke. He still couldn't quite believe it. She looked so innocent, even as the words spilled from between her own perfect lips.

"I got caught once. I got cocky. But I escaped on the train—"

"You escaped from a *train*?"

"Yeah." She smiled proudly at the achievement.

He whistled. He had to admit, he was impressed.

"I should have let fate draw me home sooner, but...I just couldn't face Nain. As soon as I saw her, I knew I'd have to tell her the truth. We never kept anything from each other..."

Her voice fell.

He didn't know what to say. What did one say to a thief?

They sat quietly together, Archie thinking thoughts loudly enough she should have heard them, but didn't seem to. Perhaps "the Red Rogue" was thinking thoughts just as loud.

"'The Red Rogue,' eh?"

Marian looked at him and he smiled encouragingly. "That's what I call myself. For the curls," she said, tucking a loose one behind her ear. "It's silly, I know."

"I don't know, I'd say it's almost a little *too* spot on." He chuckled.

"You know," she said with a sigh, "for years I've been living by the motto, 'He travels fastest who travels alone.' It's so nice to unburden oneself."

He studied her. "Thank you...for telling me the truth."

She smiled. "Thank you for listening."

"So, what did you take from Miss Mitchell? I noticed you left the clock..." It was his turn to wink at her.

Her eyes widened.

"Oh! Was that one of your inventions? Of course it was, with that unique chime." She nudged his shoulder lightly. "You know, I almost fell asleep right there in the front parlor!"

"I'm glad to know it worked." He blushed. "Well, maybe not."

She laughed. "I've never been one for sleeping. It takes an insomniac to be able to live out a double life like mine most nights."

Archie's eyebrows rose. "*Most* nights? How often do you rob people?"

She held her finger to her lips and made a *shush* noise. "Not so loud. We're not exactly in a private place."

Archie glanced around. He couldn't see anyone nearby, but she was right. She'd also avoided the question.

"*Whom* do you rob then?" he asked softly.

"Whomever I notice has a little extra to spare. I never take from the poor, and I often find *I'm* the one with extra and leave it on the doorsteps of those who could use it more."

"You're a real Robin Hood—oh, heh, I get it, *Maid Marian*." He chuckled, lifting the book on his lap.

"I think you'll find she's a worthy woman."

"I think I will," said Archie. *At least, I sure hope so.*

* * *

Eleanor ran her fingers through her hair with one hand while swinging the bucket full of chicken bones from the kitchen in the other. She was feeling oddly cheerful at the moment. Her morning conversations with Marian had left her feeling rejuvenated and buoyant of spirit, ready to take on whatever the future might bring.

Outside the potting shed, she set down the bucket next to the Humphrey green bone-cutter for grinding bonemeal for the chicken feed—bought special because it was said to be "so easy even a woman could use it." Mr. Sigmund had clearly known who'd be the one grinding grit.

She didn't pause to grind yet, however. She turned instead to the empty horse pasture which had once housed two brown geldings named Gryce and Raymond after Miss Mitchell's favorite characters from *The Leavenworth Case*, a first edition copy which she'd asked Eleanor to display in the library. But as Eleanor had never had much time nor headspace for her letters—beyond what was necessary to find work in the paper—that was all she knew of the book. That and it'd been written by a woman, which was presumably why Miss Mitchell had liked the book so much: when it first came out, men had insisted it couldn't have been written by a woman because it was too well-researched and engaging. Just the sort of thing Miss Mitchell would find inspiring.

Growing up, Eleanor had always liked the horses best of all the animals on their farm. They seemed the most human. Sheep and goats and chickens had those beady little eyes...

As if knowing she'd been thinking about them, a couple chickens pecked their way over to her feet and clucked about looking for bugs and grit to gobble.

As Eleanor watched the chickens, her mind turned back to the very real mystery in which she was currently living. She could still remember the way her heart had raced when Matsumoto had said he'd found a body in his workshop.

Everything had changed in that moment. But then she smiled. Like Marian had said the other morning: if it hadn't happened, they wouldn't have reconnected after all this time. Even a murder could bring joy in its way.

* * *

Thomas had never seen an automobile up close before. It was a beautiful thing. So elegant. So beguiling. How could such a thing replace the horse and buggy? And yet news from the east suggested someday this was what every man would be driving—no matter his position or class. No more need to own a stable, or rent a horse from downtown. No need to pay for the streetcar, even, if one had an automobile of one's own.

He could hardly imagine a world where one could travel wherever one liked at the push of a button. Sounded like something out of fiction. In fact, hadn't he heard about a book just the other day with exactly such an idea—*The Time Machine* or something like that. Who was the author? Oh, right, Wells. H.G. Wells. He might have to give the book a try after all if the man could see the future.

Thomas ran his hand over the shiny black carriage of this particular model, the one the chauffeur had left in the carriage house. He'd searched the car intricately, even digging his hand between the dark green upholstery and checking the housing for the motor, hoping to land upon a clue as to the driver's whereabouts for Bernard. But all he had to show for it was some oil he couldn't seem to get out of his fingertips.

He climbed in one more time and sat on the single bench, his hands on the two long steering cranks protruding from the floor. He located the starter button, which would begin a series of electrical connections to bring the engine to life, but that was as far as his knowledge went. He knew there were other automobiles that had a hand-crank for a starter, and something called a combustion engine, but he wasn't surprised to find a lady like Miss Mitchell owning an electric car if she hoped to drive it on her own someday.

"Where'd you go, Cecil," he murmured, as though the car might answer him.

Two missing staff members. And both of them with questionable backgrounds. One was certainly a blackmailer, but who knew what sort of secret Jennings was keeping behind his false letters of recommendation. He might be something worse than a blackmailer. Like a politician.

He sighed. Well, nothing for it. Time to try a different route of inquiry.

He left the automobile in the carriage house with a heavy heart, rejoining Bernard in the study of the main house. He'd wanted to look at the butler's references again.

"I telephoned the station and confirmed the names on the letters of reference," Bernard said as Thomas entered. "They all died in 1900. Nothing linking them together other than that, though, so I don't think he knew them. He probably just picked random names out of the obituaries. Unfortunately for him, they were all ones I recognized."

"I wonder what he was trying to hide."

"Could've been anything. We don't even know if that's his real name."

"True. But then, who'd pick 'Reginald Jennings' as a fake name?"

"Someone who wanted to sound like a butler?"

Thomas considered. "It is a very butlery name, I suppose. He'll have to change it if he wants to work in Spokane again, though. You can't keep anything to yourself for long in this town. A person's reputation is all he's got in this day and age. And small towns can kill a person's reputation as cleanly as a hot knife through butter."

"Spoken like a true cynic."

"Said the leader of all cynics."

Bernard gave him a grunt.

"Nothing new in the automobile, either. Though I will say as soon as I can afford one, I'm buying one."

Bernard shook his head. "You'll never be able to afford one. They're only for the rich."

"For now," said Thomas. "But someday, someone somewhere will figure out a way to make them more cheaply and then everyone will have one."

"You sound like an ad in the paper."

"I knew it sounded familiar."

Thomas picked up the account books lying on the desk next to Bernard's hands.

"So, when do we tell Mrs. Sigmund her husband not only had an affair with their employer but also blackmailed said employer."

"I'm not convinced he *was* doing both."

"What do you mean? The hair. She showed us."

"Yes, but that was only her interpretation of the evidence based on what she knew about the man. What if the hair was because he met her to collect the blackmail?"

"You mean, they might *not* have been having an affair?"

"It's possible."

Thomas groaned. "Every time I think I know something for certain, you go and twist it."

"'When a fact appears to be opposed to a long train of deductions, it invariably proves to be capable of bearing some other interpretation,'" quoted Bernard, nailing his point to the floor.

Thomas rolled his eyes.

* * *

Archie decided he'd had enough excitement on the Hill for one day. After saying farewell to Miss Kenyon, he hopped aboard the next streetcar, paying little attention to where it was taking him, only knowing he needed some time to think.

Miss Kenyon—Marian—lived a double life. By day she was an aspiring young woman who loved gardens and reading books in the sunlight, by night she was a thief.

A *thief*.

Dear God, what had he stumbled into.

He'd come to Spokane to build a clock tower for heaven's sake, and so far he'd found a patroness for his hobby, lost said patroness to an unknown murderer, been suspected as the murderer, befriended a blind blacksmith, shared his best invention idea with him even though he might be the murderer, learned the dead patroness had been a thief of such ideas, and now discovered the one woman he thought didn't have something to hide actually *did*.

It was like a punchline to a vaudeville act. "A clockmaker walks into a Western town and asks, 'So, what do you folks do for fun around here?' And a gentleman on the street turns and says, 'Haven't you heard? This is where Edgar Allan Poe got all his best ideas!'"

He wouldn't be surprised at this point to discover there was an orangutan loose in Spokane—hiding in chimneys or forges and beheading young women willy-nilly because it hated the smell of roses.

He chuckled to himself and the woman seated across from

him wrapped her arm around her little boy a little tighter. He tipped his hat to her and smiled what he hoped was a comforting smile, but he wondered what contortions his face must have been making while he thought such thoughts.

He turned his gaze out the window and tried to focus on the sights rolling by instead of those in his head. He'd managed to take the streetcar almost the entire way down the Hill, back into the valley town with its decade-old brick structures. It seemed impossible to ask about the town without someone mentioning how it had almost been erased from the map back in 1889 when what they called the "Great Fire" had swept through, forcing the town to build itself back up from scratch. It was starting to feel like almost every large city in America had been born from flame. The Great Seattle Fire had happened the same year, the Great Chicago Fire in 1871, the Great Boston Fire the year after. Perhaps the people of Spokane should be grateful to whoever started the blaze, for rather than erasing Spokane, it had put the city on the map, ranking it up there with all the other "Greats."

The conductor called out "Riverside" and Archie hopped off the streetcar, meandering the remaining two blocks north to where he could gaze across the channel toward the building of the depot.

No matter what had happened, he was proud to be building the clock for Spokane. He was glad he'd met Marian, too. He might even be glad about the murder, since it meant he'd escaped having his ideas stolen.

But then he froze as an absolutely, positively terrible idea crossed his mind, stopping his breath. How had the thought not occurred to him before?

If Marian was the thief...did that mean she was the murderer, too?

* * *

The Carew brothers decided it was a good night to head home early, after dinner, of course.

Thomas could still taste the rich chocolate orange pudding if he licked the backs of his teeth. Only Mrs. Curry would know where to acquire oranges in April.

Now he sank back into the leather Chesterfield, not completely at ease since their boarder, Prescot, had been invited to join in the nightly discussion.

Fine by Thomas, as Prescot was the only one who didn't seem to have heaps of evidence surfacing against him.

"So, Prescot, who do you think is the evil, red-handed murderer?" Thomas asked nonchalantly, pulling out his pipe and tobacco.

The clockmaker pushed his glasses up his thick nose, seating himself in the overstuffed armchair. He also didn't look completely at ease.

"Well, I know who I don't think did it: Mr. Matsumoto," he said, a little too firmly, like he actually wasn't too certain of his own words but only wished that they were true.

"You would say that." Bernard took a seat at the desk once again and turned the wooden chair so he could see the other two.

"Are you going to tell him or shall I?" Thomas asked, stuffing the bowl of his pipe.

Prescot's eyes looked worriedly from Thomas to Bernard and back.

Bernard twitched his mustache, then rubbed it, then sat forward, obviously attempting to appear as open as possible. The last time he'd questioned Prescot he'd been a bit gruff. "As you know, today we met with Miss Mitchell's lawyer and learned some very interesting things," he began.

"Right, about the patent stealing." Prescot blushed. "I am sorry I ran off like that. I just...couldn't believe what a narrow escape I'd had."

"I'm surprised you didn't stick around to comfort your friend, if you don't think he's a murderer," Thomas put in.

Prescot looked at him. "I was going to return, but...I..."

Something traveled slowly through his mind, first causing him to blush slightly and smile, then to furrow his brow and twitch his mouth before returning to a smile. It was slow enough that Thomas noticed, and he figured Bernard must have, too. But they didn't seem to be hearing each other's silent thoughts tonight. They'd have to practice that.

"I don't see how Miss Mitchell stealing his patents makes *him* the criminal, though," Prescot finished.

"Really? You don't think he'd want revenge for that?" Bernard leaned back and crossed his arms. Maybe he was starting to get Thomas's signals. How could Prescot *not* have reached the same realization?

Thomas wondered if the clockmaker really was that naive and trusting. He certainly played the part with his whole body: wide eyes, fidgety hands, shuffling feet.

"Revenge?" Prescot's expression took a dramatic change. He looked down and to the side, sighed, shook his head. When he looked back at Bernard he said, "You know, I'd understand how you might think that. Look at my own reaction: when I finally had a chance to think it through, I was overwhelmed by a sense of gratefulness toward whoever took Miss Mitchell out of this world."

It was Thomas's turn to raise his eyebrows. "Pretty strong talk for a clockmaker."

Prescot seemed to revert to his usual self, pushing his glasses back up his nose and shrinking back into himself. He reminded Thomas of a giant turtle trying to hide itself in its shell.

"Well, it's the truth. I don't know how much you know about patents...?" He left the question hanging as he looked between the two brothers, who both glanced at each other and shrugged to show they knew next to nothing. "A patent is very important to an inventor, and that's putting it mildly. The patent is meant to protect the inventor and their invention from being used by someone else without paying for the right to use it first. If that makes sense? So, if I invented..." He looked around the room and seemed to notice all the Swiss bear decorations. "If I invented a way to carve a bear out of wood using a special tool, I could patent that tool, so every time someone else wanted to make bears easily, they could use my tool after paying me to use it. That's a patent in its most basic sense."

Both brothers were nodding.

"All right, I understood about that much before," said Bernard, uncrossing his arms and leaning forward again. "But what happens in this case? When the *investor* patented the work, instead of the inventor. Is there any way for the inventor to get the patent back?"

Prescot shook his head and shrugged. "Not much they can

do, from what I know. They could pursue it in court, I suppose, but the cost of that would most likely outweigh the purpose. It sounds to me like Miss Mitchell found a way to cut out the middleman, and got away with it for two whole years."

Thomas puffed on his pipe. Sounded like something worth killing over to him.

* * *

Sounded like something worth killing over to Bernard.

"There's something else I'd like your help with, if you're willing," he said, trying to keep his posture open.

Prescot eyed him warily but nodded. "If I can."

Thomas shifted on the Chesterfield and drew his attention, shaking his head in disagreement, as if he knew what he was about to share with Prescot and didn't think he should do so. But who was the detective on the case anyway?

"Mr. Prescot, I think you should know, we went to speak with the lawyer originally to ask about Miss Mitchell's will."

"That makes sense." Prescot nodded, then shrugged. "I don't see how I can help with that. It's not like she would leave anything to me. As I said before, I had just met her."

"No, no. Not to you. But she did leave her entire estate to Mr. Matsumoto."

Prescot's jaw dropped. The man certainly knew how to show surprise. Or any emotion, for that matter.

"No," he said slowly.

"Yes. She'd known the inventor for two years, had stolen from him, and felt guilty about it."

"So she left *everything* to him? My goodness," he shook his head, "maybe the woman did have a conscious after all."

Bernard glanced at Thomas, who was focusing on his attempted smoke rings and purposefully avoiding his eye contact. He wondered why Thomas, who had declared Prescot to be the only person he *didn't* think guilty in this case, was acting like Bernard had made a mistake in telling him.

"It goes without saying that what's been said here must remain in confidence."

"Little late for that," muttered Thomas from the couch.

Bernard glared at his brother.

"I understand," said Prescot, "of course I won't say anything to Matsumoto. But I do wonder why she'd leave everything to him. Nothing to the staff?"

"Perhaps she assumed the inventor would be a better person than she was and gift them a little something, or keep them on."

"Or she was in a rush to be off to meet her blackmailer," Thomas offered from around his pipe, evidently deciding to add his share.

"Blackmailer?!" Prescot jerked his head in surprise. "Is there anything this woman wasn't tied up in?"

"Nope," said Thomas, puffing another ring.

* * *

Archie was getting a headache. It might have been the smoke from Thomas's pipe, or it might have been that he was regretting the Carews taking him into their confidence. They were telling him everything. But he knew he couldn't reciprocate. There was no way he was going to reveal what he'd learned this afternoon about Marian.

Even if she was the murderer. He'd been considering this matter ever since Bernard invited him to sit in. So far, however, it seemed they were distracted enough by the mystery of the murderer to ignore the mystery of the thief.

The brothers went through their day, filling him in on all their discoveries, laying out substantial proof against the missing Mr. Sigmund and Mr. Jennings before circling back around to Matsumoto.

"So, now that you know a little more, do you still think the blind blacksmith is innocent?"

"It doesn't really matter what I think, does it? I mean, you're the police. In the end, you'll make the decision."

"Man's got a point." Thomas started cleaning out his pipe over a tray. "The way I see it, we've got three secret-keepers. Sigmund: blackmailer, possibly affair, missing. Jennings: false references which were hiding something, missing. Matsumoto: inheriting estate—does he know, stolen patents—did he know? Did I get everyone?"

"The thief," said Bernard.

Archie's heart stopped. And there it was. *She* was.

"I thought we'd removed the thief from suspicion because of the coat?" said Thomas.

"The coat?" Archie interjected, trying to avoid sounding hopeful, but then realizing it was the same coat Bernard had woken him to that morning. Had it really been this morning? "Oh, right—Miss Mitchell's coat."

"We figured if the coat was returned to the house," continued

Thomas, "it must have been a member of the staff or her boarder who killed her."

"Yes," agreed Bernard, "but then I've started wondering if the thief still might have done it."

Archie decided now would be a good time to distract his hands and eyes by cleaning his glasses.

"What's to say he didn't return the coat precisely because then we'd think it was a member of the household?"

He. Bernard had said he. And why not? Who'd ever heard of a female thief?

"That'd be mighty clever," said Thomas.

"We're definitely dealing with a clever thief. Someone smart enough to strangle her, then behead her, and why not escape in the dead woman's coat, too, so if anyone saw him, they'd think it was someone from the house."

"But why would the thief come during the day? Don't most burglars wait until dark to attempt a break-in?"

"I don't know." Bernard leaned back in his chair and shrugged. "That's a valid point."

Archie tried not to blow air out in relief.

"Plus there's the question of how the thief would fit Miss Mitchell's coat over his burgundy one."

Archie put his glasses back on and sat up straight. "How do you know the thief wears a burgundy coat?"

"You told me, Mr. Prescot."

Archie glanced from side to side, trying to recall when he'd said so. That had happened this morning, too.

"Wait, you think the thief who broke into Miss Mitchell's

house was the same thief who tried to break in here?" Archie hoped he'd made the suggestion sound ludicrous enough.

"Why not?"

"Seems like quite an auspicious leap. You don't think there's more than one burglar at work in Spokane?"

"I agree, Bernard, that's quite a connection to make," said Thomas from the couch. Archie was thankful for the support, even though he knew Bernard was actually correct.

"And yet, possible." Bernard said, pulling out a bit of red fabric from his vest pocket. "I found this in the wood chute of Miss Mitchell's house. I'd say that's burgundy. Wouldn't you, Mr. Prescot?"

He held the bit out to Archie, who pretended to give it a good look before shaking his head. "I still think that'd be quite a concurrence. This could have come from anything." He handed it back to Bernard. "Do you have anything else to connect the two, other than suspicion?"

Bernard twitched his mustache. "Just the fabric really." With a grunt, he waved his hand. "But there's still the problem of the coat. If the murderer walked away wearing Miss Mitchell's coat, it must not have been our burgundy-coated thief."

Archie nodded vigorously. "Yes, yes, the coat! That's right. That must mean the murderer was from the household, not the thief."

"But why wear her coat back?" Bernard murmured.

It seemed Archie had successfully swayed Bernard off the thief for the moment. He glanced at the mantel clock and let out a sigh, thankful to see there was a worthwhile reason for him to excuse himself. "Well, I've got to call it a night. It's been quite the day for me."

The brothers stood and said good night but then reseated themselves, as though they would be continuing their conversation for a while longer.

No matter. So long as Archie didn't have to sit there any longer, listening to reasons why his friends were guilty—when they very well might be. Sometimes ignorance really was bliss, and he wished he could return to the ignorance he'd been enjoying before this evening, or this day, or this week had begun.

* * *

At the end of the long day, Eleanor sank into the deep armchair before the fireplace, letting her voluminous skirts create an unladylike pillow around her knees, revealing her ankles and calves. She didn't care. Mr. Sigmund wasn't here, so she could sit wherever and however she wanted, no matter what society might say. It was moments like these Eleanor couldn't give a fig for society. She stared at the armless chair tucked in the corner, behind another armchair. *Her* armless chair, the chair for a lady, the lack of arms providing a more lady-like seating: legs crossed, hands clasped demurely upon the lap or beneath a cup of tea.

Eleanor wanted to throw something at it.

A sudden knocking at the door made her jump to her feet, arranging her skirts politely around her legs, adjusting her hair, and ensuring her shirtwaist was tucked into her skirt. Her heart pounded in her chest and she subconsciously rubbed at the bruise on her wrist.

She walked slowly down the small hall calling out, "Who is it?"

Only silence answered from the other side of the door.

"Hello?" she called out, the fear rising within.

"It's me, Eleanor."

She breathed out a sigh, bringing her hand to her chest in relief. It was Jennings.

But what was Jennings doing here at this time of night?

She quickly unlocked the door, peeking out before opening it fully so he could step out of the shadows and into the light from the Argand lamp.

He made straight for the fire, only turning to face her once there, his broad shoulders backlit by the flames. He was not the man she'd known. He was still dressed in a suit, high collar, and tie but his manner was as shaken as a rug she was cleaning, and his demeanor about as beaten.

"Where have you been?" she asked, coming to join him, standing just out of arm's reach.

"It doesn't matter. I came back to take you with me."

"*Me?*" She took a step back before realizing he might think her reaction was incredibly rude. The look on his face told her it had been. "I'm sorry," she apologized, rubbing her hands together nervously. "I...I didn't mean for it to come out like that. I was just so surprised. Why did you come back for me?"

"I think you know why." His face was stoic, but his eyes...his eyes were looking at her in a way Mr. Sigmund's never did.

"You...*love* me?" The word surprised her as it leapt from her lips.

"Yes," he said. His voice was deep and sincere.

He took a step toward her, lifting his hands as though to take hers. But she took another step back, and then turned her back on him completely, lowering her head, only to have her eyes land on a picture of her and her husband.

"I can't," she sighed, tears welling in her eyes.

"Yes, you can. Cecil has left you already. Don't you see that? He's either a murderer or a coward, but either way, he's left you to the wolves. *I* came back. Doesn't that mean anything?"

She turned the picture frame face-down, so she could no longer see her husband's judging gaze. She closed her eyes and took a deep breath before turning around to face Jennings.

"Reggie, I..." Her eyes connected with his. He was a completely different man from Mr. Sigmund. In every single way. But she couldn't dare. Not again. She couldn't risk loving another man. They were all the same.

Her eyes hardened as her heart did. Look at him. He was willing to have an affair with her, to steal her from her husband. But she wouldn't stoop to that level. It didn't matter if her husband had already done so.

"No," she said firmly. And then again, as though to give herself the strength to believe her own words, "No."

Jennings's face fell. His shoulders fell. His whole body seemed to crumple.

"Are you certain?"

"Yes." She paused. "I'm sorry."

He nodded once, pulled himself up, and made for the door to leave as surely as he'd entered. But when he got there, he paused, his hand on the handle, and turned to her.

"I didn't kill her, you know," he said.

"I'm sure you didn't," she said. "That isn't...that's not why I said no."

"I know," he said, his mouth becoming a firm line. "I know."

"Where will you go?" she asked.

He sighed. "I'm not sure. I lied, you see, about who I was, about my past, in order to get this job. So I suppose the smartest thing would be to leave town. But if I do that, I'll only look even more guilty than I probably already do—disappearing like I did."

She nodded.

"You could turn yourself in," she said quietly. But she knew he wouldn't. He had too much pride for that.

His eyes said as much in response. "I don't know if I'll see you again, Eleanor, but...thank you, for believing in me at least."

"You're welcome. I wish I could do more."

"No," he said, "you don't," and he turned and left her.

* * *

"So, Bernard, where does that put us?" Thomas asked, grateful their boarder had excused himself for the evening so they could get back to theorizing properly.

"Same place we've been for three nights now. Stuck with a body in a blacksmith's workshop."

"I keep coming back to the blood. With Prescot gone, can we talk a little more about the blood?" Thomas chuckled darkly. They certainly couldn't talk about such things with the fainting inventor in the room.

"The blood spot or the blood spray?"

"Let's start with the spray and see if it takes us somewhere."

Bernard scratched his chin. "Well, there was blood spray

everywhere, all around the anvil and along the sides of the forge. It must have gotten all over the murd—"

He cut off abruptly, staring into space.

"What?" Thomas demanded.

Bernard gave Thomas a self-satisfied grin. "I have an answer for the coat."

"Already?"

"The murderer must have gotten blood spray on themselves, removed their clothes, then tossed Miss Mitchell's coat over themselves as they ran back to the house, probably to burn the clothes."

"Why burn the clothes at the house when they could do it in the forge?"

Bernard's eyes widened and Thomas had to admit he felt a bit of pride swelling in his chest. See, even he could think of solutions.

"That, dear brother, is exactly what the murderer did." Bernard pointed at Thomas and shook his finger. "Our murderer already had the basis for a nice fire going—we know that for certain because Matsumoto said he never puts the forge fire out. So our murderer just had to build up the heat—crank the bellows a few times, throw a few more coals on the fire—it doesn't take an inventor to figure out how to make a forge work. And," he raised his finger to the ceiling triumphantly, "that explains the poker."

"Poke her? I hardly know her!" Thomas grinned.

Bernard rolled his eyes. "When we were there the night of the murder, I noticed a poker in the sandpit of the forge, but when I returned the next day after you spoke with Matsumoto, it was lying beside the forge. If you didn't move it—"

"You know I would never."

"And Matsumoto didn't, either?"

"Neither of us moved it. It was like that when we walked in. And he didn't touch it while he was with me. In fact, I asked him if he'd left anything out and he said no. But I didn't tell him it was the poker—"

"So you didn't touch anything? He didn't move the poker?"

"No," said Thomas, his turn now to roll his eyes as he repeated himself succinctly. "No, we did not touch the poker."

Bernard nodded shortly. "Then it must have been the murderer. They must have used the poker to push their bloody clothes into the forge to burn the evidence."

"Or to push something else in. There's still that large blood spot we were circling back to."

"Don't say it."

"I'm telling you, it was the Baker of the Great Fire!"

"The Baker returned to Spokane just long enough to strangle Miss Mitchell, begin to dismember her to bake, then stopped and thought better of it? But not before taking the time to burn his clothes and then run off in Miss Mitchell's coat?" Bernard asked sarcastically.

"Who said anything about returning? We just confirmed that the coat must mean someone at the house is the murderer."

Bernard held up a hand. "Hold on. You're saying one of the people living at Miss Mitchell's house could be the self-same Baker of your preposterous legend?"

Thomas smiled and pointed at Bernard. "Yes."

Bernard shook his head. "Nope. Not possible."

"Wait, so it's completely feasible that one of them strangled and beheaded Miss Mitchell, but not that they intended to bake the body to hide the evidence?"

Bernard scratched his chin.

Thomas looked around for inspiration. His eyes landed on Roslyn's magazines. Perfect.

"You should talk to Roslyn about it. I bet she'd have an article picked out in no time. You know how she prefers *Scientific American* over *Homemakers United*, or whatever it's called."

"*Good Housekeeping.*"

"Funny that you should know that," said Thomas. "But my point is, it sounds like something she's mentioned before. Wasn't she just telling us about an article about dual personalities?"

Bernard grunted. Always a good sign. "Actually...yes. But it wasn't in any scientific magazine. That was in reference to an old newspaper clipping a friend of hers from Pullman sent her. Something about dual personalities in sane people."

"Well, there you go. Obviously, that's what we have. Someone completely sane doing a very insane thing."

"Isn't that the very definition of murderers?" Bernard asked.

"Point taken," said Thomas. "It seems to me we have an intelligent murderer who was very careful, had it all planned out, until he was interrupted. Baking a body seems like a perfectly understandable explanation for a way to hide a body until—" Thomas stopped. His wheels were spinning faster than a taffy puller.

He stared at the floor, visualizing the blood spot. That blood spot would probably remain indelibly, sinking minute by minute deeper into the dirt-packed ground.

Poor Prescot had said the sight of blood had taken him by surprise. He hadn't expected such a large spot to still be there.

Such a large spot of blood.

"What now, Thomas?"

Perhaps by speaking he could latch back on to that erratic thought. "There's something about that blood spot... I just know it."

"She *was* beheaded."

"Right. But...first she was strangled."

"Yes, yes, she was, we know that now," said Bernard.

"So," Thomas started slowly, "shouldn't there be *less* blood if she was dead already? And we arrived so soon after Matsumoto claimed he found the body... Wouldn't it take awhile for so much blood to drain out? I mean, why would there be a *large* blood stain?" Thomas asked, just fingering the tail end of the thought that had leapt through his mind. "And so much blood spray..."

And then it snapped into place and he looked up at Bernard's face.

"Gladys Mitchell wasn't the only one murdered that afternoon. There's a *second* body!"

In the silence he could hear the *dun-dun-dun* coming from the orchestra pit. Maybe he should be the detective.

Bernard grunted. "How do you figure that?"

"When Miss Mitchell's body was discovered she was found in a pool of dried blood the length of her body—"

"I was there, go on."

"But we know now she was strangled and *then* beheaded."

"Yes, right."

"Then why so much blood?"

Bernard seemed to stare at the spot on the floor, too. "So...you're saying...there's *too* much blood?"

"Right."

"So there must have been someone *else* killed before Miss Mitchell?"

"Yes."

"Who?"

"I don't know. Blood is blood. You can't tell from blood who's dead—that'd make it too easy. So we still have to figure out who it is."

Bernard grunted.

"But I think you're missing the more important point." Thomas walked across the room and clapped a hand on Bernard's shoulder. "What happened to the second body?"

Four

Thursday, April 18, 1901

Spokane, Washington

The Red Rogue wondered if she'd done the right thing telling Mr. Prescot—Archie—the truth. Not that she'd had much say in the matter. He'd figured it out from a mere chance glance at her boots.

Marian had stopped in at the Crescent Department Store on Riverside on her way home from the park to buy some new shoes—she wasn't about to take that chance again. She'd told the salesman she needed something for bicycling—this being the most strenuous sport she could think of for a lady that might not cause raised eyebrows—and he'd helped her pick out a ready-made pair that fit even more comfortably than the gutta-percha boots.

She'd taken the new pair out for a trial run this evening, tucking her red curls under a driving cap and wrapping herself in her burgundy driving coat as she'd done almost every night since her return to the city of her youth.

The new shoes drew her back to the Mitchell home, but this time she didn't enter the firewood door to sneak into the main house. Instead, she circled the woods and entered the lawn toward the back of the property, turning to the right and loping across the yard until she found the low stone building Archie had described to her as being the workshop where he'd been meeting with the inventor-blacksmith. She quickly found her way inside and took a look around.

She didn't think Archie had made the connection yet, but she felt certain the police had: it was possible the thief and the murderer were the same person. Except she knew she wasn't the murderer.

Maid Marian would never have let such a connection persist. She'd have figured out the murderer herself, cleared her good name. Originally Marian had thought she'd solve the case for Eleanor's sake, but now it was much more personal.

The workshop was pitch black, however, so it was impossible for her to see much of anything. What had she been thinking? Of course it'd be too dark, as there were no windows. The only glow was a rather muted one coming from the still-red coals resting in a sandy divot. She was surprised the blacksmith would risk such a thing with a wood roof. Flames and wood did not mix in her memory. The Great Fire leapt to mind.

Even with eyes that were used to working at night, she'd have to light a candle in order to give the place a proper looking over, and she couldn't see well enough to find even that. When she got home she'd add a candle and matches to one of her numerous pockets, just in case, but that was little help at the moment.

There was nothing else to do but return in the daylight, and that would take careful manipulation of friends, which she hated to do. Of course, now that Archie knew the truth, she supposed she could just ask him.

As she returned to her home, hid her Red Rogue garb, and took a seat in her rocking chair before the fire, she considered her next step.

She hated to think it, but it might be time for the Red Rogue to retire for good. The thought sickened her. To lose the Red Rogue would be akin to murdering a part of herself. Then again, so long as the Red Rogue was being hunted by the police as both a murderer and a thief, it was much safer to give the night life a rest. Until they found one, they'd never rest searching for the other, convinced that they were one and the same.

If she stopped her nightly trips, she'd definitely need to find an alternative source of income. She could always pick up photography again, but she still thought it'd be helpful to her friend if she could find a place for both of them.

What would Maid Marian do in this situation? "The world is a stage, and life is a farce, and he that laughs most has most profit of the performance."

Sounded like something Nain would say. Of course, Nain would also say, "If you don't make mistakes, you don't make anything."

She sighed. Such deep thoughts for the middle of the night. She glanced about the room and her eyes landed on the black-eyed daisies.

"I certainly made plenty of mistakes, didn't I, Nain?" She shook her head. "I should have told you," she whispered. "I should have come home the moment I stepped off that train."

I might have forgiven you.

"You might have understood."

A pair of brown eyes behind thick glasses and beneath an ill-fitted hat passed before her mind's eye. Archie had understood. In fact, had taken the whole matter rather well. It might be quite fun to have someone who knew her secret.

And as Nain would say, "Better the devil you know than the devil you don't know."

* * *

Eleanor found herself cleaning. She was on her hands and knees, scrubbing a large spot that wouldn't come out.

"You're mental." He was angry, again.

"Why must you constantly clean?" Mr. Sigmund was standing up at the table, coming toward her. "Can't you see I'm hungry? Can't eat a broom can I?" He was raising his hand, ready to strike her.

Eleanor turned away. She was in a room. Her bedroom. It was a mess. It wouldn't have looked dirty to anyone but her. She couldn't help it. She had to clean it.

She bent down to sweep beneath the bed but she stopped.

Beneath the bed were rows and rows of shoes. Women's shoes. They weren't her shoes.

They were shoes belonging to his women.

Didn't he realize she knew? She knew about all of them?

Why? Because she loved to clean.

And when you love to clean, you notice the lipstick that didn't quite come off the edge of the glass.

You notice the hair on the bedside table that's not yours.

You notice the rows and rows of shoes hidden beneath the bed.

So many shoes.

She tried to count them, but there were more of them every time she went to count.

So many. So many.

She started to scream in frustration but then she realized he was back, standing over her, his anger dripping off him like condensation off a milk bottle.

"I just want you to be all you can be. You do understand that, don't you?" he said coldly.

There was almost a tenderness in his voice, beneath the anger.

That was why he hit her. Because he loved her. He knew that if he hit her enough, she could someday be more. Someday she would fulfill her destiny, become the person he wanted her to be, and he would stop, and rejoice with her, and be happy with her.

It was her fault he had affairs.

He had affairs because she wasn't good enough for him.

So he had to look elsewhere.

But someday, someday she'd be the woman he wanted her to be.

Someday she'd be enough for him.

And all those shoes beneath the bed could be hers.

If only she'd stop cringing. If only she'd stop crying. If only she'd stop cleaning.

And listen for once!

He screamed at her.

She awoke, and wept.

* * *

Archie returned to the workshop early the next morning feeling sheepish after his running off suddenly the day before—again. But Matsumoto comforted him by completely looking past it, not even questioning why, and inviting Archie to join him for a walk through the forest. Apparently, he did this most days, finding a need to stretch his limbs and mind with nature and her sounds. Archie liked the idea and joined along happily, hoping this might become a regular thing.

Unfortunately, what was on the inventor's mind was not the future, but the past.

"Detective Carew read to me from Miss Mitchell's letter," Matsumoto said, his voice barely rising above the crunching of leaves.

Archie had ridden the streetcar up with the Carews, whom they'd left behind at the workshop while they went on their walk. This arrangement seemed to please them since it gave them time to look around without the blacksmith present, and Archie had no interest in seeing the inside again until it'd been properly cleaned.

"The letter was most apologetic in regards to the stealing of my ideas and selling them. She told herself it was just business, but then something made her feel guilty enough to admit it to her patent lawyer."

"That was all?" Archie asked. The Carews had read the letter to Archie, too, last night, but he doubted they'd shared it in its entirety with Matsumoto.

Matsumoto paused in his steps. "That was all, according to Detective Carew. I did wonder if he was keeping something to himself, though. You would not happen to know what it might have been, would you, Mr. Prescot?"

Archie wanted so badly to tell Matsumoto everything. He felt torn between the two groups. He knew he couldn't tell Matsumoto that Miss Mitchell had felt so guilty she'd left him the entire estate to make up for it, even though he'd find out soon enough. Bernard had made it quite clear this morning that he wanted to find out what Matsumoto knew first before telling him anything else contained in the letter. Archie was glad he could report back that the inventor didn't seem to know anything, not even about the blackmail.

Archie decided to avoid Matsumoto's question. "I suppose it means something that she apologized. I'm thankful I was fortunate enough to...well...escape the arrangement before it was to my detritus."

Matsumoto shook his head and absent-mindedly pushed his rolled sleeves up above his elbows as though they'd slipped down. "Yes, I handed over two years' worth of work to her..."

He sighed heavily before starting to walk again, Archie beside him, once again easily forgetting the man was blind. He seemed capable of avoiding every tree in their path without his guidance. It was only when he was very close to Matsumoto that he realized the man was making soft clicks with his tongue as he walked to determine his location.

Both men walked on quietly for awhile. When they came to

one portion of the woods that looked the same to Archie as every other portion so far, Matsumoto stopped and pointed out past where the trees ended, back into the open expanse of yard that was Miss Mitchell's property.

"This is where I heard the person in the overcoat the night of the murder," he said.

Archie looked. There was nothing to mark this location as different from any other. "How do you know?"

"I walk the same path every day. I know my own steps." The blind man smiled. "And I placed this large rock in the path to mark where it happened, it being an odd thing to occur." He chuckled and pulled back his shoe a little to reveal a stone beneath his foot.

Archie laughed. "That's what I would call a blind man's bluff!" He'd start turning into Thomas if he wasn't careful. Archie looked past the trees. "Let's walk out into the yard to see where we are in relation to the house."

Once they passed the treeline, Archie could see they were closer to the house than to the workshop, back near where the stables and chicken pen were hidden beyond the ornamental garden.

"It must have been someone from the house you heard," said Archie. "Given their direction."

He still wondered about the thief, though, and wished and hoped Thomas had been right about the significance of the returned coat.

"I suppose we might head back now," he said.

Matsumoto nodded and they turned back to walk along the treeline.

"So, why the hidden workshop back here anyway?"

"I suppose it was simply an available location away from prying eyes. It was an abandoned building all covered in ivy when I was first given ownership," said Matsumoto. "It smelled of age and decay. Miss Mitchell had it renovated into a blacksmith's shop per my instructions. I will admit, Miss Mitchell never hesitated when I asked for anything for research."

The location *was* ideal for keeping the inventor's work secret. But part of Archie also wondered if it had something to do with the Japanese man walking at his side. He'd seen signs downtown put up by the Anti-Chinese League of Spokane—though he guessed that probably included any and all Asians—and heard whispers that Chinatown lay on the south side of the river, next to where his clock tower would be standing. Out east, it was standard to find Chinese, Japanese, Italians, Mexicans, Irish each living in their own quarters. For some reason he'd thought—hoped—maybe out west the lines might be a little more blurred.

He glanced again at the Japanese man at his side. At least they were blurred for them.

* * *

Bernard stared at the blood stain and the blood spatters on the floor and forge of the workshop. The wheels in his head were turning at a rate that was much too slow for the new theory his brother had come up with the night before.

A second body. Could there really be a second body somewhere?

He looked around the room.

"There's no way I've missed an entire body hiding somewhere in this room the last three times I've been here," he remarked.

"I don't know. You might be going blind in your old age," Thomas replied.

"I'm two *minutes* older than you, smart aleck."

"Hey, there's no need for name calling. Besides, we know where the second body is—you just haven't accepted the fact yet."

"Because there are no facts. It's just a theory. A ludicrous theory based on a story." Bernard pointed to the sandpit where the coals still glowed red. "Look at that forge and explain to me exactly how you'd fit a second body in there."

"A *second* body?"

Bernard whipped toward the doorway and realized they'd been rejoined by Matsumoto and Prescot, the latter seemingly happy to wait outside, a little farther from the bloody scene.

"Yep," said Thomas before Bernard could suggest they might want to keep this theory to themselves for now. They really needed to work on their silent communication skills.

"But where is it?" Prescot asked, throwing his voice into the discussion. He sounded worried, like it might appear next to him and make him faint again.

"Only one place it can be: in the forge!" Thomas said theatrically, no doubt loving the fact that he had an audience now.

"What?" said Prescot, his voice somewhat higher than usual.

"It is possible," Matsumoto said coolly, his eyes focused on the forge.

Bernard grunted, he hoped sardonically.

"It is apparent to me that someone used my forge while I was gone. The poker was left out—I noticed its empty space but did not mention it to you, Officer Carew, since you seemed reticent to share everything with me—and the coal barrel was half empty. And then there was the mess that you did mention." His focus turned to the brothers. "I told you I could smell the death from outside my workshop. Did you smell anything when you were here that night?"

Bernard nodded and said, "Roses," as Thomas said, "Bacon."

Thomas threw back his head and laughed.

"See," he said, hitting Bernard rather hard on the shoulder, "I *told* you the Baker did it!"

* * *

"I'm sorry, I'm missing something. Who is the Baker?" Archie bravely took a step into the doorway of the workshop beside Matsumoto, making sure to keep the large anvil between his line of sight with the...thing that had made him faint before. "Not Mrs. Curry?"

"Certainly not!" Thomas said emphatically. "At least...I hope not..."

"He meant the Baker legend connected with the Great Fire," explained Bernard, shaking his head.

Archie's brow furrowed questioningly. "I haven't heard that particular version of history yet. By 'legend' do you mean 'theory'—what people suspect caused the fire?"

Bernard glanced at Thomas and waved his hand. "Oh, you tell him."

Archie didn't like the sound of that, or the way Thomas

grinned at Archie as though about to share a marvelous ghost story. Did Thomas *want* to make him run away again?

"Most folks blame it on the lack of water pressure, but that's just why the fire spread so quickly before they could get it under control," Thomas began. "And even that's just a theory. There's another story about why the fire started in the first place." He paused.

"Go on," said Archie with a deep breath, putting a comforting grip on his satchel strap.

"Well, it's rumored the fire started in a lodging house above Wolfe's lunch counter—an oven left unattended. Once they got the fire under control, they traced it back to that point. And when they opened the oven, they found," he paused dramatically, "a body."

"A *body*?"

"Thomas," muttered Bernard, "you needn't scare the man."

"It's the truth! Or at least, it's what's been told to me."

"But—how did—how—," Archie started and stopped.

"How did someone get it in there?" Thomas finished for him, glancing at Bernard as though he'd asked the question. "Must've chopped it up into pieces, right? Only way to make a body fit."

Archie gulped. He would *not* faint again. He would not faint *again*.

"And now you think—you think—"

"The Baker has struck again!" Thomas's eyes were alight with the story.

"'Again'?" Archie asked. "They never caught the person who did it?"

"Back in '89? Nope. Least, no one's told me when they've told me the tale."

"That's all it is, Mr. Prescot," said Bernard comfortingly, "a tale."

Sure sounded like it fit their current situation to Archie.

"So...how are you going to prove something like that?"

"Only one way," said Thomas, rubbing his hands together gleefully. "Bones."

* * *

Thomas turned toward the forge.

"Is it cool enough to touch?" he asked Matsumoto.

The blacksmith walked in and Thomas helped guide him around the blood spot to stand with him at the forge. "I have not used it since the day of the murder, as you requested," he said, reaching a clean yet burn-marked hand into the brick enclosure and waving it about before setting it down in the sand. "Yes, you may touch it. It is warm, though—always is. You will have to scrape out the ash bit by bit, away from the coals, to go through it. Here, let me capture the flame. Then you may put the whole thing out and sift through without fear of getting burned."

"Capture the flame?" Bernard repeated.

"Like I said, it is a blacksmith belief. You cannot ever let the heart of your forge go out, and that is the flame."

"Sounds like something the Greeks would've done," grunted Bernard.

"It's all Greek to me," said Thomas with a shrug and a smile. Bernard gave him a glare.

They all watched as the blind blacksmith moved smoothly

about his work, using the tongs that still hung in their proper place to reach in and grasp the burning coals from the pit. But then he fumbled as he reached for something to his right.

"Interesting," he muttered. "There should be a bucket next to the forge beneath where the poker, tongs, and shovel are, or should be, hanging. Would you be so kind as to hand me a bucket, Mr. Prescot?" he asked over his shoulder.

Prescot scrambled outside for a moment before holding out a large metal bucket just beneath Matsumoto's tongs. Matsumoto released the coals into it with a *clunk*, Prescot keeping his eyes on him and not on the spot of blood as though his life depended on it.

"Thank you," said Bernard. "I think that's enough help for now. Perhaps you and Mr. Prescot might return to the house for the remainder of the day."

"I understand, Detective," said Matsumoto with a small bow of his head.

Prescot led Matsumoto back around the anvil to the doorway.

"But before you go," Thomas put in, "is it even possible? I mean, do you think someone could bake a body in this forge?"

The blacksmith turned and stared at his forge. "A lost bird once made the mistake of flying into my forge while I was working. It died almost instantly upon touching the coals, but it was much longer before the body was burned away completely, only bones remaining." He bowed again and left, carrying his hearth fire with him.

Prescot tipped his hat at the detectives and followed, no doubt quite happy to escape the fun of digging through soot for evidence.

"Only bones," Bernard repeated. "That means we should be able to sift through the ash and find some proof, *if* that's what happened. And I still think it's a pretty big *if*. The big ones may be gone, but there's bound to be a few little ones that escaped notice."

* * *

Marian had found one intriguing listing in the classifieds and decided she'd follow up on it before telling Eleanor, figuring it best not to get her hopes up before she knew anything certain.

The advertisement in her hand read: "Wanted—Female companion to invalid, live-in, general housework may be required. Apply Mrs. Carew 1423 W Mallon Ave."

What Marian hoped to find was that the lady in question would be open to hiring a companion and a maid as two separate people.

It surprised her, however, to find she'd visited 1423 West Mallon Avenue once before. But it had been at night. And she'd been wearing a driving cap and her modified burgundy overcoat.

She almost turned away but decided she'd just leave her card for now and could always pursue other inquiries before returning.

She walked up the front steps of the simple home with green siding and red-painted shutters, noting the ramp on the side that led up to the front porch. She tucked the ever-loose red curl behind her ear and put on her best smile before knocking politely.

After several moments, the door opened and Marian looked down to see a middle-aged woman seated in a wheelchair. Her pale blonde hair was pulled back tightly above kind blue eyes, and her striped pink dress was cut in the latest style as it flowed down her legs.

"May I help you?" she asked.

"Mrs. Carew," Marian bobbed politely. "I apologize, I had merely intended to leave a card in response to your advertisement in the paper." She held up the page where she'd circled the description. "I'm Marian Kenyon." She handed over her card.

"Miss Kenyon, a pleasure to meet you. Won't you come in?" Mrs. Carew replied, wheeling herself back from the doorway so Marian could enter.

"Thank you."

Marian stepped in and closed the door behind her before following Mrs. Carew into the front parlor. It was simply furnished in a Swiss design complete with bears climbing, crawling, hugging, and holding up furniture. Mrs. Carew waved toward an armless chair with two carved bear cubs climbing up the chair legs. "Please, have a seat."

"Thank you. You have a lovely home." Her Nain had often said, "Praise the child, and you make love to the mother," but she'd found in her time photographing people's homes that it was a very similar matter when complimenting a woman's rooms.

"Thank you. So, tell me a little about yourself," said Mrs. Carew, parking her wheelchair smoothly beside a leather Chesterfield.

Marian appreciated that Mrs. Carew was a woman who got straight to the point. She'd never interviewed for a permanent position before, but she felt she must like Mrs. Carew as much as Mrs. Carew must like her if she was going to take the position.

Especially as it had been listed as a "live-in" situation. Marian hadn't let her thoughts go quite so far as to consider what that would mean for her, whether she'd sell Nain's place or rent it out or simply close it up as Eleanor had said, but she'd always felt it best to eat the cookie one bite at a time.

"Well, I'm from Spokane originally, but I've spent the last five years in Seattle photographing homes."

"Oh, I love photography!" Mrs. Carew smiled. "The photographs are what make my favorite magazines so intriguing." She waved a hand toward the ones stacked on a table, and Marian was surprised to see they were not fashion and home mags, but *Century Magazine* and *Scientific American*.

Marian returned the smile and continued. "I've recently returned to Spokane and am seeking employment, though I must admit, I'm hoping to find somewhere both my friend and I can be of use."

"Oh? Where's your friend today?"

"She's still working her current job, and as your advertisement seemed to be looking for only one person, I wanted to meet with you first. I was thinking I might be your companion, while my friend, who currently lives as a maid-of-all-work at a large house, might assist in the cleaning."

"I see." Marian watched Mrs. Carew consider this for a moment. She realized she was being somewhat impertinent and was grateful when Mrs. Carew continued the questioning. "Are either of you married?"

"I am not, but my friend is...at the moment."

"At the moment?"

"I'm afraid I shouldn't say more without her present."

"I see. And children?"

"None. Neither of us has any children."

"I see. You said your friend is currently working. May I ask why she is seeking new employment?"

Marian hesitated. "I suppose I might tell you her current job was with Miss Mitchell. You may have read about it in the paper?"

Mrs. Carew's eyes widened. "My husband is the detective on the case!"

Marian didn't think it smart to let Mrs. Carew know she knew this already, not wanting to get Mr. Prescot in trouble for letting her into his confidence. She tried to indicate surprise by letting her eyebrows rise to meet her curls. "Really? Then you must know Mr. Prescot?"

"He's our boarder!"

The two women sat smiling congenially at one another.

"I've only met Mr. Prescot on a couple occasions in Montrose Park, but he's seemed quite a kind man," said Marian. "I haven't had the pleasure of meeting Detective Carew, as yet."

"Yes, he's been quite busy with the case." Mrs. Carew nodded. "So your friend is—was—working for Miss Mitchell?"

"Yes, she's quite mixed up in it as her husband has been missing since the murder and I imagine that means something terrible."

"Ah, your friend is Mrs. Sigmund?"

"Yes." Marian nodded sadly. Detective Carew must have kept his wife abreast of the case.

"I'm so sorry. Well, once the case is over, I would love to meet her with you. Perhaps we could come to an agreement of some sort."

"Thank you!" Marian smiled. As her Nain would say, "Adversity makes strange bedfellows."

* * *

Bernard sighed, his hands covered in black and gray soot. He looked over at Thomas, whose forehead was smeared from wiping the back of his hand across a rather furrowed brow. It was clear he was thinking the same thing: this was not only quite disgusting, digging through the ash for a body, but one of the messier things he'd ever had to do in his life. Made him appreciate chimney sweeps.

"This is one of the best days of my life," said Thomas.

Bernard grunted before he could stop himself.

"First I figured out that there were two bodies, then I figured out that the second body was baked, and now I get to go on a dig like one of those archaeologists searching for mummies. And I'm even looking for a mummy of sorts!"

Bernard had to admit, when he looked at it that way, it was kind of exciting. "Or like digging into the center of the earth through a crater entrance found in a volcano?"

"Ah, *Journey to the Center of the Earth*. That's another great thing to happen today! Or maybe it was yesterday? You don't think Miss Mitchell would mind if I borrowed some of her books from her library? Or took home for safe-keeping?"

Bernard looked up from his current pile of ash to give Thomas a glare.

"I was just kidding!" Thomas waved two gray-black hands in defense. "Sort of," he muttered, returning to his work.

But not for long.

"Ah ha!" shouted Thomas, pinching something between his pointer and thumb. He blew on it in an attempt to clear some of the warm gray and black particles still clinging to it before dropping it into Bernard's palm.

Bernard held it up to the light of the sun streaming through the doorway. He turned it this way and that, but there was no denying what it was. He couldn't tell what part of the human body it belonged to, but it was definitely a bone.

"Unbelievable. You have all the luck," he said with admiration and not a hint of jealousy. He set the bone on the anvil. "Well, that's one, but we're going to need larger bones to prove a second body. Smaller bones like that one might just be what's left from Matsumoto's lost bird."

"I'll see what else these blessed fingers can dig up for you." Thomas linked and pressed his hands forward to crack his knuckles before going back to sifting.

Sift. Sift. Sift.

Bernard quietly finished his pile and then stood to shovel out another batch to sift through. It was slow and meticulous work, and it suddenly occurred to him as he looked at the size of the pit in the forge that they might be here sifting all day. The cone-shaped hole seemed to go down so far that it just might reach the center of the Earth. Even then, it was clear there wasn't a whole body's worth of bones hidden beneath the ash. Just a few swirls with the shovel showed that.

But what was this?

"You're not the only one on a lucky streak today," he said, feeling a bit relieved he had at least found *something*. He pulled out a piece of sooty leather that had been buried in the sand alongside where the burning coals and ash had made their nest.

Thomas stood and came closer as Bernard held it between his hands, pulling it as taut as he could and holding it up.

"It looks like it was once a glove. I doubt Matsumoto would burn clothing in his forge," said Thomas.

Bernard agreed and handed the leather glove to Thomas. "I feel like I remember Father saying blacksmiths don't wear gloves when they work. It's actually safer for them to use bare hands so they can feel the true heat of an item."

"You mean so if they touch something hot they react quicker?"

"Something like that." Bernard shrugged. "You've surely noticed Matsumoto's hands. I assume that as a blind man he must unfortunately rely on his touch more than your average blacksmith. I highly doubt, given the scars, that this is his."

"So let's move forward as though it doesn't belong to Matsumoto."

Bernard pointed to the glove. "Can you tell what kind of glove it is?"

Thomas flipped the piece of leather back and forth but shook his head. "It's burned too much to tell anything other than it once enjoyed a life as a pair of gloves."

Bernard nodded. "All right."

"Is there another?" Thomas looked over Bernard's shoulder.

Bernard turned and started swirling the ash again with the shovel. "I don't see anything."

"How did it survive the heat?" Thomas shook his head in amazement. "Don't forges get to white-hot temperatures?"

"I suppose because it's leather?" Bernard glanced at the leather blacksmith's apron hanging by the door. "And it was buried in the sand, so it might have escaped the most intense points of heat. I think we were just lucky."

Thomas handed the glove back to Bernard. "Good find, Bernard." He slapped him on the shoulder, no doubt leaving his sooty handprint on Bernard's back. "It seems to me that this is confirmation of our theory that the murderer burned his blood-soaked clothes in the forge and then high-tailed it back to the house in nothing but Miss Mitchell's overcoat."

Bernard nodded. "Yes. Too bad people don't write their names on the insides of their gloves like they do their clothing. Then we'd know for sure who we're dealing with."

"That still wouldn't tell us whether it belonged to the body being baked or the Baker," Thomas said, kneeling back down by his pile to continue sifting. "If only someone would mutter, 'Now, where did I leave my gloves?' like in a story. Then we could say, 'Ah, ha! You're under arrest for murder!'"

Bernard twitched his mustache. "If only it was so easy."

* * *

Archie meandered alongside Matsumoto as they made their way toward the house.

"Let us adjourn to the garden, Mr. Prescot," Matsumoto said as they neared the natural pathway into the ornamental garden. "Have you had the pleasure of discovering the beauty of this particular area of the estate?"

"I have not."

They entered along a natural dirt path, their shoes softly padding on the earth, winding their way amongst beautifully curved bare branches, up and across an arched wooden bridge that brought them from one side of a small pond to another.

Matsumoto took a deep breath. "There is nothing quite so fulfilling as the scent of a *Sakura* in bloom." He pointed to a cherry tree to his right. The short tree's branches seemed to weave back and forth laden with an explosion of tiny pink and white blossoms.

"I've only ever seen cherry blossoms in Japanese artwork," said Archie in awe.

The path continued to wind, sometimes *over* roots of large trees, as though unafraid to embrace its surroundings. At one point it branched off toward an ornate iron structure that curved and arched upward as though trying to be a tree itself, though in Archie's opinion, it failed miserably. He had yet to find a piece of art that captured the beauty of nature only God could create.

Finally Matsumoto led Archie to a simple wooden bench beneath a cherry tree, but Matsumoto didn't seat himself on the bench. Instead, he removed his sword and gun from his belt and seated himself on the soft moss growing on the ground, crossing his legs, resting his hands on his knees, and closing his eyes.

"Join me," the blind man said in a soft whisper.

Archie looked about him. "Join you in what?" he asked carefully.

"Listening."

Even as he spoke the word, Archie could hear other, softer noises in the "silence" all around him.

Birds chirping. Leaves rustling. Water spilling over rocks.

Archie sat down as quietly as he could, removing his satchel and placing it beside him, and took in his surroundings. The world was still except for the whisper of a spring wind breathing through the cherry blossoms.

Even with all that was happening in the workshop on the other side of the property, here, in this garden, the earth was at peace.

Long moments passed in semi-silence as the world moved around them. Archie closed his eyes and let his ears listen.

There was such peace in stillness. In a world full of noises that would only get more distracting and boisterous as technology advanced, he understood why many people were finding themselves drawn back to the tranquility of nature.

To be alone, or almost alone, out here felt like discovering a sort of privacy that couldn't even be found in one's own bedroom.

A wave of sadness passed over him at the loss of such calm and he opened his eyes. Matsumoto took a deep breath beside him and, opening his eyes, turned his face toward Archie.

"Thank you," he said. "Sometimes I find the conflict of sounds in this world becomes too much for me, and I find it most rejuvenating to take a few quiet moments to breathe in nature's harmony."

Archie nodded, then said, "Yes," though he knew the man had probably heard his nod.

He took a deep breath, savoring the semi-solitude a little longer.

* * *

Sift. Sift. Sift.

Thomas sat back and wiped his hands off on a rag before pulling out his father's pocket watch to check the time. They'd been sifting for an hour and so far all they'd found was one small bone and a leather glove.

He blew out between his lips and regretted it immediately when the remainder of his pile of ash blew across the floor. But then he leaned forward quickly and picked up something small and white. He grinned. Damn, he was good.

"Well, I suppose that was one way to be sure there was nothing else in that pile," he said. "Of course, there *was*."

Bernard looked up hopefully but went right back to work when he saw the bone's size. "Still not big enough to not be a bird's."

Thomas shrugged and stood, clinking the bone next to the other one on the anvil.

Then he stretched his back and shoveled out another pile to sift through. He was going to find that proof of a second body in the fire if it took him all day. He needed to know he was right.

Sift. Sift. Sift.

Then again, once they did find proof, they'd still need to find the rest of the body. It was probably buried like the mummies he'd been thinking about earlier.

"So," Thomas began, "where do you think the rest of the bones are buried?"

Bernard looked up at him from his own pile of ash. "Why do you say buried?"

Thomas shrugged. "What else do you do with bones? Dogs bury them, people bury them..."

"True. You're thinking maybe the first body was chopped up, baked, and the bones buried, and then the murderer returned to do the same to Miss Mitchell, but was interrupted?"

"Yes. It's possible the blind Matsumoto actually missed something and didn't realize the murderer was still there with the body the first time he 'discovered' it—before running to get Jennings to tell him who the body was." It was so rare Thomas got to be the voice of reason, he quite enjoyed it.

"Except Matsumoto heard our coated murderer fleeing to the house *before* he returned to the workshop and smelled the dead body."

And there went Thomas's puffed pride. "Oh. Right." But then it blew right back up. "The murderer needn't have wasted time burying the bones before we arrived. They might have held onto them, stuck them behind a pile of wood outside, and come back to bury them later that night. We didn't do a thorough search of the area, and certainly not of the house, till the next day."

"Maybe you didn't, but I searched this workshop top to bottom," said Bernard, clearly irritated at Thomas's implication that he'd missed something.

"Well, they've got to be somewhere, Bernard. That's all I'm saying."

"For now," muttered Bernard.

* * *

Sift. Sift. Sift.

"*If* there's a second body, my money's on Sigmund," said Bernard. "It would explain a lot."

"I really wanted him to be the murderer," said Thomas sulkily.

"You can't pick a person to be the murderer and then hope the facts line up. It never works out that way."

"And it's never the guy who's beating his wife."

Bernard looked up from his pile of ash. "You noticed the bruises, too?"

"Of course."

"We can't do anything about it, Thomas. There's no way to prove that sort of thing. And Mrs. Sigmund is the type who'd never tell on her husband."

"I know, but we're the police. Shouldn't we be able to do something?"

"Perhaps someone already has." Bernard pointed to the blood on the floor.

"In that case, I hope the second body *is* Sigmund," said Thomas. "Then at least he got what was coming to him."

Bernard agreed but kept his thoughts to himself.

Sift. Sift. Sift.

"You know, Bernard, you might be on to something with what you said earlier."

Bernard realized it cost Thomas something to admit that, so he politely looked up and waited for his brother to continue, though he didn't yet know what he'd been right about.

"You called the second body the first body. But the question is: which came first?"

Bernard sat back on his legs. "Go on," he grunted.

"All right, so, I figure there's a second body because of the blood pool beneath Miss Mitchell. As it's *beneath* Miss Mitchell, I assume someone was killed *before* Miss Mitchell and the body discarded somehow. Right?"

"I'm following."

"So what we think of as the 'second body' because we realized its existence *after* Miss Mitchell was actually the 'first body.'"

Bernard shook his head. "I think you can just say Miss Mitchell and Sigmund for clarity's sake. He's the only person who's been missing since we got here, so he must be the...whichever body...the missing body."

"All right." Thomas continued to sift as he talked. "So that means Sigmund was actually killed *before* Miss Mitchell..."

"Where are you going with this, Thomas?"

"I'm just clarifying the order of events. I think it's important we think of them in the correct order to understand what happened here."

"You're starting to sound like me."

"Dear God, I wouldn't want that."

Bernard grunted. "If that's true, I wonder how long Sigmund was out here before Miss Mitchell. He'd been missing almost all day..."

He thought back through his notes.

"Oh! I've got it," said Thomas, clapping his hands together and releasing a cloud of ash that made him cough a couple minutes before continuing. "All right, so Miss Mitchell came out here to meet Sigmund—"

"Why?"

"Because...of the affair or the blackmail, it doesn't really matter which. Maybe she was going to tell him the deal was off for the blackmail and she'd written to her lawyer... The point is, she happened across someone burning his body to hide the evidence. The someone turns around, strangles her, then drags her over to burn her, too."

"But then why stop? Why not finish baking Miss Mitchell too?"

"Because it was really Sigmund he wanted dead?" Thomas offered. "What about Jennings?"

"What about him?" Bernard replied.

"Well, whoever did this really didn't want us to find out one body was burned. So maybe it was Jennings, and he only burned Sigmund so we'd think Sigmund was the murderer and dig up his past and discover he was blackmailing Miss Mitchell. Wait, maybe he *knew* Sigmund was the blackmailer! Maybe he set up the meeting between Sigmund and Mitchell so that he could kill them both."

"Why? Why would he want to kill his employer and the man blackmailing her?"

Thomas paused to consider. "To save Mrs. Sigmund? The faithful knight errant to the rescue and all that?"

Bernard nodded. "And he's staff, so it covers the coat problem." He sighed. "I wish he hadn't disappeared before we could question him further. We need proof for one of these theories. Something more than random attempts to pull everything together."

He stood and shoveled more ash out of the forge.

But what clue could possibly bring all this together? So far they had affairs, blackmail, thievery, strangulation, beheading, and now baking. What more could one ask for in what had started as a simple burglary case?

Bernard chuckled lightly to himself as he continued to sift through his pile. "Too bad we're not panning for gold. Remember that story we made up as children? Where we discovered gold nuggets in the creek bed and then lay on the grass dreaming of exactly how we'd spend it?"

Thomas smiled. "Yeah. As I recall, we were going to spend a good portion of it on building our own sweets factory."

"Too bad we were panning in the wrong creek. If we'd lived in Idaho we might've had better luck."

"Maybe we should try panning for gold later today," said Thomas, holding up something small and white, "before all this good luck runs out."

It was unmistakably a tooth. And birds definitely didn't have teeth.

* * *

Eleanor's eyes were puffy and tired from the lack of sleep and crying. It was hard to believe it had only been three days since that terrible night. All she wanted to do was curl up in bed and let it all fade away, but it seemed even when she closed her eyes only horrifying images floated before her.

Cleaning wasn't even helping, and it had always been her way of coping with the most disastrous of days. She'd walked the entire property line twice now, in an attempt to keep active and distract her mind from brooding. Even Mrs. Curry was running out of ways to use Eleanor's help.

She stopped outside the stables and watched the horses in her mind's eye as they bent their long necks to the ground and nibbled at the new grass at their feet. Such placid, simple lives. She wished she believed in reincarnation so in her next life she might return as a horse. Such freedom. Perhaps she'd start believing just for that reason.

She was startled out of her reverie by Mrs. Curry of all people.

"What are you doing out of the kitchen?"

"I'm not chained to the stove, dear. What are you doing staring at an empty horse pasture?"

Eleanor sighed. "I've always wished I could be a horse."

"Why? There aren't many differences between them and us."

Eleanor looked at the graying older cook, waiting for her to explain.

"Horses think they're better than other animals," she said. "But in the end, they spend their lives in hard labor, some of them ridden into the ground. Seems like a lot of folks these days."

She gave Eleanor a look that made her return her focus to the pasture beyond the fence.

"They say things will get better," said Eleanor softly. "That the future is bright and full of technologies, like the telephone, that will make the world a better place."

Mrs. Curry nodded. "Yes, but I often wonder: better for whom?"

Eleanor agreed. The automobile in the carriage house hadn't made things better for her and Mr. Sigmund. Had only, perhaps, enhanced the relationship between him and Miss Mitchell—providing them with more time to talk and laugh, seated together on a single bench as he drove her around town, her clutching his arm with one beautifully gloved hand while the other held onto her wide-brimmed driving hat, making even driving goggles look attractive as only she could...

She ground her teeth.

"Sometimes I long for the simplicity of the early days," said Mrs. Curry, thankfully dispelling the image in Eleanor's head. "You just don't find the same genuine fellowship one used to. Cooperation between people—friends and strangers—it just doesn't exist anymore. Instead, folks spend half their time yelling at one another to move faster, as though a horse's pace isn't fast enough."

Eleanor nodded again. With each passing year she found more reasons to agree completely with that sentiment. Sometimes she wished the world would just stop spinning for five minutes so she could catch up. Instead, it just seemed to spin faster, as though trying to throw her off.

"Seems to me," Mrs. Curry continued, "these days, folks'd rather ignore the problems their neighbors are facing. It's easier that way. Sure, they'll crack open the paper and absorb the world's problems, but the problems of their neighbors? That's a mite too close to home." Mrs. Curry looked at Eleanor and said softly, "But there's still them as want to help."

Eleanor turned to Mrs. Curry, but then looked away quickly.

"I know these past couple days have been difficult, Eleanor. Especially with your husband disappearing in the midst of it all. But maybe that's for the best? Maybe, in the end, it'll be better that he's gone."

Eleanor shook her head, tears welling in her eyes as memories threatened to overtake her.

"A husband is supposed to love and cherish," said Mrs. Curry, and suddenly her hand was on Eleanor's, giving hers a little squeeze. "You must find it within yourself to stand your ground."

Eleanor choked on the tears she held back. "What if I can't? What if that's not the sort of person I am?"

"All I know for certain is: the sort of person you are deserves better than the sort of person he is." Mrs. Curry squeezed her hand again and let go.

Eleanor studied her hands. "What if it's too late? What if some of us are not meant to get what we deserve?"

"In the end, it's the Lord's will that decides. Not us. Our bodies simply end up in the ground, food for the grass that feeds the horses."

"Unless you're cremated," said Eleanor.

"Cremated?" Mrs. Curry asked, sounding shocked.

"'Dust to dust, ashes to ashes,'" Eleanor quoted.

Mrs. Curry eyed her as though she'd just told her she'd cleaned the oven with lard. "I plan to be buried, not burned, as the good Lord intended."

"And what if He intends you for Hell?"

The cook's brow furrowed and she shook her head, reaching forward and grasping Eleanor's hand once more. "Then why start early?"

* * *

After lunch, Archie decided he should probably begin making his way back home, and was just heading down the drive when who should be coming up but Marian Kenyon—the Red Rogue herself.

He stopped where he was and considered trying to make a dash to hide behind the line of pines, but then compared his girth to the width of the trees and gave up the idea. When she looked up and saw him he pasted a smile on his face—the first time he'd ever had difficulty smiling in her presence.

As he approached, he tried to sound jovial. "The Red Rogue is making visits in broad daylight now, eh?"

Marian's cheeks blushed as she laughed. "Of course not. I'm here to speak with Eleanor—I may have found us a job once this whole affair is wrapped up. With Mrs. Carew, no less!"

Archie's eyebrows rose. "Really? Doing what, may I ask?"

"She placed an advertisement in search of a companion and a maid—roles I think Eleanor and I might fit quite well if given the chance."

He bit his tongue to keep from saying, "I'm not sure how glad Mrs. Carew would be to have a thief for a companion." Instead he just nodded and continued his fake smile.

But she noticed.

"Archie," she said slowly. His heart skipped a beat as she spoke his first name.

"Yes?"

"If I didn't know better I'd think you were nervous around me for some reason."

"Me?"

"Yes." She crossed her arms and shifted her weight back on one foot, looking him up and down as though sizing him up for a roast.

"It's nothing," he said. But he could feel the sweat beading on his forehead.

"Archie," she said again, slowly, a half-smile playing across her lips.

He looked at the ground and shuffled his feet, his hands feeling out of place at his sides, like they didn't know what to do with themselves.

She stood straight and came closer. He could smell her now. She smelled like...the color green. Like a freshly cut pine tree at Christmas, and new, green grass on a summer's morning.

"Archie?"

He could hear the concern in her voice.

"Archie, is it because I'm a thief? I'm sorry I told you the truth. If it's too difficult for you, I understand. I'll leave you alone. I just have to find this murderer, first."

He looked up and found her green eyes.

"I can't leave Eleanor before I help her, and I need to clear my own good name."

"The good name of a thief?" He hated how judgmental he sounded, after he'd told her he could handle it yesterday.

He could tell he'd hurt her.

"I didn't murder Miss Mitchell," she said softly. "I didn't even know the woman. I admit I stole from her home, but that was the night before she died."

He nodded but looked down at his feet again, fidgeting with the strap of his satchel over his shoulder.

"Well," he took a deep breath, "actually, Detective Carew doesn't think the thief is guilty anymore. Something about a coat which means it has to have been a member of the staff."

"See?" He could hear her smile.

But he didn't look up until she reached out and placed her hands gently around his.

"I want to make one thing very clear: I am not a murderer. A thief, yes, by all means." She waved one hand as though this was a trivial admission. "But I've never hurt anyone, and I hope I never will." She studied his eyes and he tried to believe her. He wanted to so badly.

He glanced down at where their hands connected and tried to pray the sweat away from his palms. When he looked back up she said firmly, "I swear to you, Archibald Prescot, that I, Marian Kenyon, am not a murderer."

Archie tried not to think about all the societal implications if someone saw them together right now. Instead, he focused on her face. Her lovely face with eyes so green they would surely reveal any and all impurities hiding within.

"I believe you," he said.

She smiled and gave his hand a squeeze before letting go. He tried to smile back but he wished she was still holding his hands.

"I sincerely hope you do," she said, taking a step back and sweeping a roguish red curl behind her ear. "Now, do you think we can move on and solve this case? Mrs. Carew mentioned you were all up here. How is it coming along? Any sign of Mr. Sigmund, do you know?"

"No, but apparently he was blackmailing Miss Mitchell."

"No!" Marian said, eyes wide, the green in them sparkling in the sun.

Archie nodded. "Yesterday we learned she made her money

from stealing and selling other peoples' ideas. Apparently, Sigmund was blackmailing her over that information."

"Oh dear! She didn't get any of your ideas did she?"

Her concern was so heartening.

"No," he said, smiling. "Thankfully, she did not."

"Oh, good."

Archie looked down and fiddled with his fingers. He was suddenly aware he was telling her everything. "I shouldn't say anymore, I'm afraid."

"I understand. Where is the detective now, may I ask?" Her voice was so sweet, like the most melodic wind chime.

He looked up. It was so difficult not to tell those eyes everything.

"They're in the workshop digging through the ash from the forge fire. They think there was a second body. They're looking for bones right now."

His hand flew up and covered his mouth in an attempt to stop himself, but it was too late.

Marian's eyes were wide with interest—more interest than he'd expect from a lady, but then again, she *was* a thief.

"Bones?"

"Yes," he mumbled, shaking his head at himself. "I shouldn't have told you that."

"It's all right. Who am I going to share that with other than you?"

"Mrs. Sigmund?" suggested Archie, glancing toward the house.

Marian also glanced in that direction, but then she looked

back at Archie and put a hand on his arm. "I would never betray your trust. *I'm* trusting *you*, aren't I?"

Archie nodded. His throat too dry to speak at the moment.

"Bones, eh?" she said. "I'd think the best person to question on that account would be the cook, wouldn't you? I'm sure Mrs. Curry wouldn't mind if we popped in for a quick hello."

* * *

Sift. Sift. Sift.

Bernard was beyond done sifting through ash, but his meticulous nature wouldn't let him leave the job half-finished. It was clear no larger bones—leg, arm, skull—were in the forge, but he still wanted to find more proof. Their theory of someone "baking" someone in the forge was so crazy it sounded like the answer to a Poe story.

Sift. Sift. Sift.

A second body. How had he missed it? He was finding it very difficult not to compare himself to Thomas today. His brother seemed to have all of the brains suddenly.

He recalled those first moments when he'd just arrived to find Miss Mitchell dead. The large pool beneath her and blood spatter all over everything had ended up belonging to someone else. The smell of revolting roses had turned out to be the smell of perfume mixed with a baked body. The area beyond the forge was devoid of blood spatters and evidence because someone had contained the mess and then thrown their own clothing into the fire.

And yet, they'd left the body of Miss Mitchell. Why? Why leave the murder unfinished, if the plan was to bake her like Sigmund? It must have been a matter of time. At most, their suspect had three or four hours to murder two people, butcher one, bake one, and discard the bones. The math didn't work out in his head. He looked back at the pit in the sand of the forge. It was maybe a foot in circumference. The body would have had to be baked in stages. Perhaps bit by bit as he was...disassembled. And then the bones pulled out as quickly as possible, cooled, and hidden somewhere. Yet all the staff were back at the house, seemingly busy with their chores by the time Matsumoto ran up to tell them his discovery.

He should have questioned them each as to what they thought the *others* were doing, not just what they claimed to be doing. Perhaps one of them had lied about where they were.

What was he thinking? Of course one of them was lying. One of them was the murderer!

He shook his head. Maybe he wasn't cut out to be a detective. After all, it was Thomas who had figured out the second body and the baking and the blackmailer. What had Bernard done, really?

But there was no use getting bogged down in who solved what. It didn't matter. He sighed and rolled his neck.

As he did so, his eyes snagged on the barrel of coal.

The barrel of coal had been full when he'd first laid eyes on the scene, and yet was half empty the next day. If Matsumoto hadn't used the forge, someone else had, and they'd have needed a lot of coal to keep the fire hot enough to bake a body.

He stood.

"Are we done?" Thomas asked eagerly.

"Not yet...," Bernard said slowly.

He reached the barrel and looked in over the side.

"Thomas, there's only one reason why there would be blood stains inside a barrel of coal." He looked back at his brother happily. Finally, he'd figured something out on his own. "The murderer must have hidden some of the body parts in here until he could return that night to finish baking."

Thomas wrinkled his nose. "Ew. You mean parts of Cecil Sigmund were hiding under the coal while we were here that night? How did we miss the smell?"

"How did we miss the smell of baking human flesh?" Bernard shook his head. "You and I just weren't blessed when it comes to sense of smell, I guess."

"Ugh. I can't believe I'm going to say this, but I think I won't be eating bacon or pork for awhile. I'll always wonder if what I'm smelling is really—"

"Don't say it." Bernard returned to his ash pile. He knelt back down and went back to sifting, feeling much happier about his brain now.

Sift. Sift. Sift.

So, how did the murderer get Miss Mitchell to land directly over the pool of blood left by Sigmund? They must have strangled her and then pulled her over to the pool.

But if that had happened, why couldn't the order have been the reverse? Why couldn't Miss Mitchell have been strangled, and *then* Sigmund? But then why bake only Sigmund? Why make his body disappear?

Interesting. He'd wondered the same thing about the strangulation marks. He'd wondered if someone had sliced her head off only to hide the strangulation because that revealed something about the murderer.

If the same murderer who wanted to hide the strangulation also wanted to hide Sigmund's death...

Why? It always came back to why.

* * *

What had started as a treasure hunt had since lost its excitement for Thomas after the first few pieces of tiny bone and teeth were discovered. It was time to move on to bigger bones, now they knew they were on the right track, he thought, yet Bernard insisted they sift through every bit of collected ash from the bottom of the forge, just to be sure.

They'd been sifting through ash for the better part of three hours now. Bernard hadn't even let them stop for lunch. Thomas's stomach growled for the missed enjoyment of delicacies created by Mrs. Curry's hands. Maybe once they solved this murder they could hire her to replace their home cook? She'd be in need of a job, wouldn't she?

He sighed again, hoping he'd draw Bernard's attention, but his brother stubbornly declined to look up from the pile of ash before him.

"If you're done sifting ash, you could always start searching the woods for buried bones," Bernard growled.

This time Thomas grunted. "Not alone, thanks. I can wait for you."

He stood and stretched his back, reaching for a rag to wipe his hands.

As he wiped, he chuckled to himself. "It just occurred to me:

we've got a butcher," he waved at the blood spot, "and a baker," he waved at the forge. "Makes me wonder where the candlestick maker fits in."

Bernard looked up long enough to give Thomas a good long glare. "If you're just going to stand there, perhaps you'd be so good as to shovel out another pile of ash for me?"

"Sure thing," said Thomas. But as he went to grab the shovel, he noticed the poker again.

Why didn't the murderer use the poker to kill Miss Mitchell? It was so handy.

What if the poker had been used, but not for her. For him. Perhaps the poker was used to take Sigmund down, and that was how the murderer came to the idea of baking the body?

Or perhaps they really were about to discover the identity of the original Baker, and baking Sigmund came to them because they'd done it before?

He looked back at the poker, then at the shovel in his hand, then at the brush and tongs hanging in their places. Something was missing. Matsumoto had said the ash bucket was missing.

"I think I know what I should be doing," said Thomas.

"There's a surprise," muttered Bernard sarcastically.

"The ash bucket," Thomas said, ignoring his brother because he knew he was on the right track. "The murderer had to carry the larger bones out of here somehow. To be buried or whatever was done with them. So instead of looking for bones, perhaps we should start by searching for the ash bucket."

* * *

Archie knocked on the door to the kitchen and entered, blinking after walking in the April sunshine.

"Good afternoon, Mrs. Curry," Marian called out.

"Good afternoon, Miss Kenyon, Mr. Prescot," Mrs. Curry replied from where she stood beside the range, dressing a leg of lamb. "I wasn't aware you two knew each other."

"Oh, you know Spokane," laughed Marian. "It's difficult *not* to know everyone."

Mrs. Curry chuckled politely. "So what brings you my way this afternoon?"

"I'd come to see Eleanor and happened to cross paths with Mr. Prescot. I was wondering if you might know where she is?"

"I just saw her out at the old horse pasture, but she was headed to the potting shed afterward. She's seemed quite lost lately. I'm glad she has you for a friend during this difficult time." Mrs. Curry bent down to open the oven door on the range, sliding the dressed lamb in and firmly shutting the iron door behind it. "While you're standing about, Mr. Prescot, would you mind emptying that pot over there? It should be cool enough now. Don't dump it into the sink, though, please. There's a refuse bucket just there for scraps."

"This one, Mrs. Curry?"

"There's two there: one for scraps and one for bones. Miss Kenyon, would you mind dumping the tea grounds, too, please. Yes, into the scrap bucket. They may be small, but they expand when given the space and water. I don't need a plumber muddying up my kitchen just to fix something that could have been prevented."

"Might I ask what happens with the refuse bucket when it's full?" Marian asked.

"Oh, it'll be fed to the back of the fire later, and all the drafts thrown open, to be burned away."

"The bones, too?" Archie asked.

"Oh, heavens, no. Bones and fire don't mix. Only thing to do with them is to take them to the potting shed for use in the garden."

Archie glanced at Marian, who nodded toward the door.

"Might I deliver those bones for you, Mrs. Curry?" he asked, picking up the bone bucket. "I'm heading out that direction, it seems."

"Why, thank you, young man, that would be most helpful."

"I'll go with you, Mr. Prescot. Perhaps Eleanor will still be there."

"Just listen as you get closer," Mrs. Curry said. "You'll hear the bone-cutter grinding before you see it."

"'Bone-cutter,' Mrs. Curry?" Marian asked.

"Yes. It grinds the bones into bonemeal: fine enough to be used as grit, or finer still to be used as fertilizer."

"Grit?"

"Yes," Mrs. Curry chuckled. "You're not a farm girl, so I wouldn't expect you to know. Chickens don't have teeth, so they need to eat grit along with their food so it all gets ground up in their stomachs. The calcium in the bone benefits the egg production—makes more of them and stronger besides. It's one of those ways that nature makes a full circle."

"I see," said Marian politely.

But Archie still had a question. "That sounds like a ponderous piece of equipment. If the groundskeeper is missing, who's running the bone-cutter we'll hear?"

"A farm girl," said Mrs. Curry with a smile. "Mrs. Sigmund."

* * *

"Sounds like something your detective friends should know about—a bone-cutter," Marian said as they walked. "Handy way to make bones disappear, and here they are sifting through ash looking for bones. Perhaps Eleanor can tell us more. She grew up with a father who made her do a lot of farm chores," Marian explained as they rounded the shed. "I'm sure she learned a lot of things—"

She stopped at the sight of Eleanor working the wheel on the bone-cutter, leather work gloves protecting her hands. Several images flashed through her mind at once.

Eleanor feeding chickens from a bucket full of feed and grit. Eleanor saying, "I've done everything from grinding bonemeal grit for the chickens to chopping wood to scooping out the stables." Eleanor's broad, strong shoulders and arms. Eleanor self-consciously touching a bruise inflicted by a brutal husband. Eleanor sobbing into her shoulder over the discovery that her husband had been having an affair with Miss Mitchell. Eleanor saying her husband, "wouldn't dare" return.

And now Eleanor with a self-satisfied grin across her face as she ground through a pile of rather large bones beside her.

Almost like the bones belonged to her missing husband.

"*Be he alive, or be he dead, I'll grind his bones to make my bread...*" Her head cocked to the left and right as she sang and ground.

Marian's gaze fell on the bucket a little behind Eleanor's feet, from which she was replenishing the pile of bones. It was covered in soot and ash, not kitchen residue. Inside were leg bones, but they were much, *much* too long to have once belonged to a chicken.

Before she could stop and think, Marian reached out and grabbed the kitchen bucket from Archie, switching it with the bucket from behind Eleanor, then pulling Archie's arm.

"To the workshop," she murmured.

"But—"

"Now."

She half-ran across the yard, using her skills honed as the Red Rogue to move swiftly while exerting little energy, dragging the much slower Archie alongside her.

When they reached the small door, she led the way through and found two policemen cleaning their hands beside an anvil, on top of which lay a collection of small white bone fragments...including a couple teeth.

"Miss Kenyon, this is Detective Carew and Officer Carew," said Archie by way of quick introduction as he entered, puffing, behind her.

The policemen looked surprised to see her there, but she didn't leave them much time to wonder at her appearance.

"Are you missing an ash bucket?" she asked, holding out the bucket she'd stolen from Eleanor.

She focused on the detective.

The mustached, hairy man grunted. "Where did you get that, Miss?"

Before she could respond, she heard running footsteps behind her and turned.

* * *

Eleanor stood in the doorway. Her eyes took in the scene. She'd been reaching back for another bone from the bucket when she'd seen Marian running off with it toward the workshop. Why would she do that? But now she locked eyes with Marian.

And she could tell Marian knew. Somehow...she knew.

Eleanor slowly pulled off her work gloves, gripping them in her hands to give her something to hold onto, gathering her thoughts.

"He was having an affair," she said softly, still holding her gaze with Marian.

Marian nodded slightly, a strange look of fear mixed with confusion in her eyes.

"She wasn't the first, but..."

Eleanor realized the policemen were still standing beside the forge, but the fat inventor had come up alongside Marian. All four of them were staring at Eleanor with dawning comprehension in their eyes.

Eleanor sighed, focusing on the ground, and twisting the gloves.

"I'm innocent, really. It's not like I meant for it to happen."

She looked again at Marian, and not at anyone else, her eyes searching Marian's. And then something broke inside her and the truth came spilling out before she could stop it.

"It was tea time and Mr. Sigmund hadn't joined us, as he usually does, so I went looking for him. I don't know why I thought to check the workshop. But I did. And I found them. They were together, just standing there. It was clear they'd been fighting. I couldn't see Mr. Sigmund's face, but I could see the fear in Miss Mitchell's eyes. She knew she'd gone too far..."

Eleanor swallowed and looked down, her hand rising to rub the last bruise he'd ever inflicted upon her.

"I'd known the violent side of my husband for years." She'd trembled before it, had cried out for mercy, had begged him to forgive her. "The first time I'd caught him in an affair and asked him to stop, he'd beaten me so badly I hadn't left the house for weeks. He might have killed me. But he hadn't. Which was his mistake."

She felt her fists clenching around the gloves. "I'd seen the women he'd had affairs with—especially the day after they tried to call it off with him. I'd pitied them." She'd also been pleased by their pain, in a way, since it meant he'd hit them, rather than her. She'd always felt terrible for feeling that way. "But now...now was my chance to do something about it."

She stared at the spot where her husband had stood, just in front of the anvil, facing away from her and toward Miss Mitchell. Poor Miss Mitchell. But it took two to make a marriage. And two to make an affair. So two must pay.

"Mr. Sigmund—he was so quick. His hands were around Miss Mitchell's throat. He strangled her so efficiently—before she could do so much as scream."

"I knew he was the murderer!" cried the officer.

The detective silenced him with a hand, his eyes never leaving Eleanor.

"I stood there. Watching," Eleanor continued, so immersed in the memory now she felt her body making the motions.

"My hand covered the scream that threatened to erupt from my mouth. I knew if he saw me, if I didn't act fast, he would kill me, too."

She glanced toward the forge.

"I grabbed the closest weapon: a simple iron poker. And he..." A smile crept across her mouth. "He never knew what hit him."

Her clear blue eyes met Marian's and her smile fell. But she had to finish it.

"I killed him. With one swift *whack* over the head." A laugh bubbled out of her and her eyes lit, suddenly—but then her brow furrowed as she wondered where the laugh had escaped from.

She looked down at the ground. "He fell beside the forge and...the rest of it just...fell into place."

A full grin scurried across her face and disappeared. She looked up and saw the horror in Marian's eyes that she could not mask. Eleanor's brows furrowed again. Why didn't she understand?

"It was self-defense, Marian. Surely you must see that. It was for the best."

Marian took a step back, standing closer to the policemen and the inventor than to her. Eleanor looked at all of them.

"I'm innocent."

The big detective grunted. "I suppose Miss Mitchell just fell on your hatchet then?"

Eleanor studied the ground, twisting the gloves tighter, tighter.

"No, I...I do admit, I tried to cover it all up..." She tried to stop the grin that began to spread again across her face, but it couldn't be done. It wanted to be free. Something inside her longed to burst out of its cell.

Her eyes shifted to the forge. She focused on the memory. The wonderful memory. She couldn't have done it on her own. She didn't have the strength, the willpower. The courage. But there was another part of her that did, the part that had defended her against her first husband all those years ago, in their lodging house above Wolfe's lunch counter. The Great Fire, they'd called it. There had been something great about it after all.

And so, Eleanor straightened, her grin splitting her face like that first slice through fresh cake, her eyes an icy blue. Time to explain herself. Time to become the Baker once more. "My first husband was a cremationist. He taught me everything I know. He was my first successful bake... It's because of him I learned the most important thing to remember when cooking a body: smaller pieces cook faster. It's true of any baking one does. Thus, the first step was to butcher Mr. Sigmund to get him in the fire."

The Baker smiled at the memory. It was so much fun crumbling a cookie.

"I pulled on his gloves and used the hatchet for a nice, clean slice. The right knife is the most important weapon in a cook's arsenal, you know." She pulled on the gloves, slowly. Then she clasped her hands, letting them fall before her as she continued. "It required patience, baking him a piece at a time. But the meat sloughs off rather quickly, you know, when fire is given his head, so it was simply a matter of removing the bones as they were cleared and cooling them in the slack tub. It was rather fun playing blacksmith!"

The Baker laughed happily. "Unfortunately, it became clear I wasn't going to have adequate time for a proper bake, so I was forced to store some of my ingredients in the coal barrel until I could return that night." She waved a hand in that direction. "And then once I'd finished clearing Mr. Sigmund I realized I had a new problem: all that blood and spatter. So, I simply dragged Miss Mitchell's body over and plopped it down in the middle, so they would think it was her blood, and that there was only one dead body. I knew that would throw them off the scent for a little while.

"But as I looked at the scene I'd set, I realized I'd made another silly mistake. Miss Mitchell had been strangled, and yet she lay in a pool of blood. I would need one more detail for my disguise to work." She grinned. "I grabbed the hatchet."

Marian flinched, her face drained of all color. She didn't seem to like the Baker for some reason.

"There's really nothing quite like a successful bake," she tried to explain. "A well-done pie. A well-done body. Cooked to perfection. The way a man should be...

"Once Mr. Sigmund was well-done, I scraped out what bones I could into the ash bucket, and threw my apron and dress in the fire, since there was quite a bit of blood on them. I heaped them all with the coals so should someone return before I had a chance to finish cleaning, they would only find a burning forge and a beheaded body. I threw his gloves in the fire, then looked around for something to cover myself. Miss Mitchell's coat was hanging by the door—perhaps she'd removed it thanks to the sweltering heat of the workshop. I pulled it over myself and ran back to the house. It wouldn't do to be seen running practically naked through the woods...as much as I might have enjoyed that..."

The Baker gave them all another winning smile.

The policemen just studied her, moving closer inch by inch, as though ready to nab her once she was finished confessing all. She took a step back toward the door. She wasn't finished.

Marian was pale and looked like she was waiting for her to yell, "Fooled ya!" like they were young and at play again. But they were very far away from those days now.

"I came back to finish the bake late that night, and I cleaned out the oven after everyone had gone, though I suppose I missed a few." She waved her hand toward the small pile on the anvil. "Not bad for night work."

"Where are the rest of the bones?" the detective asked gruffly.

The Baker looked at him and cocked her head.

"Where does anyone put bones?" she asked, giving him a quizzical smile like she'd just given him a marvelous riddle.

"She ground most of them into bonemeal grit for the chickens," Marian said softly, nodding to the bucket that still hung in her hand with what remained of Mr. Sigmund's legs.

The detective grunted again.

"Clever," said the patrolman to his left, nodding in admiration.

"Thank you," said the Baker, glad someone finally appreciated all the work she'd done. "I ground his skull first, since that was the most recognizable bone among all the other animal bones collected in the potting shed. Mr. Jennings found me soon after I'd finished." She laughed, her eyes sparkling. "He just stood there and talked about how late Miss Mitchell was for dinner while I ground my adulterous husband into grit beneath the wheel."

"He wasn't having an affair," came the low voice of the detective.

The Baker cocked her head, raising a questioning brow. "What do you mean? I saw them...," she faltered.

"No. You saw your husband attempting to blackmail Miss Mitchell for the last time. She turned him down. That's what caused him to kill her."

Her heart stuttered. She caught her breath. "But...the hair...," Eleanor finally got out.

"I have no doubt he'd had affairs in the past. But this time, he'd chosen a new sin: blackmail."

Eleanor started to breathe quickly.

"Eleanor?" Marian dropped the bucket with a *clatter* that seemed to reverberate inside her skull. She came to Eleanor's side, catching her as she started to fall.

Eleanor looked up at Marian as she gripped her hand and held it tight.

"I still did the right thing—didn't I? I had to stop him. He would've killed me."

She watched the conflict cross Marian's face and focused on her eyes, willing her to see the truth.

Finally, her friend answered, "As my Nain would say, 'Innocence is a matter of perspective.'"

THE END

TO BE CONTINUED IN *CUPBOARDS ALL BARED...*

Historical Notes

I've always loved books that weave real history alongside fictional events, from historical fiction like Alison Weir's *Innocent Traitor* to time travel fiction like Connie Willis's *To Say Nothing of the Dog*. I so enjoy flipping to the back of the book to discover just how much was real and how much was imagined—or for some of you, this is the first part you read! I knew when I wrote this novel, it was going to have historical tidbits interwoven with fictional characters and events. Where possible, I have used real people from history and have attempted to remain accurate and true to the city and its people circa 1901. So, here you go: some of the real history I wove into *Butcher, Baker, Candlestick Taker*.

Let's begin with the characters. When it comes to the Spokane Police Department, I only created two new people: the Carew brothers. Everyone else is a real person from history, thanks to the hard work done before me on the book *Life Behind the Badge: The Spokane Police Department's Founding Years, 1881-1903* by Suzanne and Tony Bamonte with the Spokane Police Department History Book Committee.

William W. Witherspoon was the 9th Chief of Police beginning July 12, 1899. The other detectives named in the text, Dougald McPhee, Alexander MacDonald, John McDermott, and Martin Burns, are the documented detectives serving Spokane in early 1901. The desk sergeant, George Hollway, the patrol wagon driver, Walter Lawson, William Shannon, "the Terror of the Tenderloin," and Captain James Coverly were also real historical figures.

Outside the police force, I threw a few other real people into the paths of my creations, including Coroner Nathan M. Baker and Patent Lawyer L. L. Westfall, who could be found in 1901 at the locations described in the book. A few names that were mentioned in passing, but were also real figures from history, include Dutch Jake, Amasa B. Campbell, and Kirtland Cutter, a well-known designer of several hundred homes and buildings in and around Spokane, including the Campbell House.

This brings us to locations, almost all of which are places that can still be visited today. I've marked them on a map which can be found at my website. For my descriptions of downtown Spokane circa 1901, I relied mostly on some marvelous photographs taken by Marinus Crommelin during his stay in Spokane from 1901-1902. His images capture everyday details and are collected along with his incredibly descriptive letters into a book entitled *Dear Mother*. Many of the nuances of life at that time came from the letters, including special little details like Marian's gutta-percha boots.

The Great Northern Railroad Depot clock tower is the only part of the depot that still stands at what is now Riverfront Park. The weight-operated clock within the clock tower was designed by the Seth Thomas Company in Connecticut, though Archie was a creation for story purposes. Frost and Granger of Chicago and Charles Johnson of G.A. Johnson and Son of Chicago were the lead architects for the depot. A complete description of the new depot can be found reported on the front page of *The Spokane Daily Chronicle*, October 30, 1900. This and more articles and information on the depot can be found at my website.

Montrose Park lives on but is known by another name now: Manito Park (changed in 1903). Francis Cook, the owner of the land, named it "Montrose" because of the wide variety of wild roses. Although today there are numerous gardens within Manito—Duncan Gardens, Japanese Gardens, and Lilac Gardens, to name a few—the park would first pass through many phases, including being home to a zoo from 1905-1932. What is today known as "the duck pond" was called "Mirror Lake," and was large enough people would ice skate across the shallow surface in winter. The Japanese garden at Miss Mitchell's estate was inspired by the one you can visit at Manito today. It is a beautifully quiet oasis in the middle of a bustling city.

Browne's Addition, where Nain's house is located, is a beautiful area of Spokane where you can still experience the Campbell House for an immersive historical tour of a Spokane home circa 1910. It is located next to the Northwest Museum of Arts and Culture and the Ferris Archives, which are staffed by people who were invaluable in the writing of this book. The Campbell House was a major inspiration when designing Miss Mitchell's mansion home and when describing the lifestyle of those who lived in such luxury at the turn of the century. I look forward to sharing more about the Campbells in the next book...

City Hall is no longer at the location in this book, Howard

St. and Front St., as this is currently where you can visit the 1909 Looff Carousel in Riverfront Park. The 1894 City Hall was built to house the fire department, city hall, and police department, which was located on the first floor. The Fernwell Building, however, which housed the lawyer Westfall in 1901, as well as many other businessmen, is still located a few blocks up Howard from the old location of City Hall, and is exactly as described by Bernard.

As regards true events in the book, the biggest one would be the Great Spokane Fire of August 4, 1889, which was the worst fire in Spokane's history. The source of the flame was said to be the upstairs room of a lodging house located above Wolfe's lunch counter. Only one man was reported dead. There were many theories bandied about as to why the fire started and why it spread so quickly, but the cause could never be verified. The Baker is my own theory created for this story. You can read the original front page report from *The Spokane Falls Review*, August 6, 1889 on my website.

Many of my descriptions of chatelaines, corsets, mattresses, and everyday life were inspired by Sarah A. Chrisman's *This Victorian Life*. The Chrismans are modern-day "historical ambassadors" who live their lives as close to an 1889 lifestyle as possible, from clothing to furniture, baking to cleaning. You can learn more about them and their fabulously interesting life at ThisVictorianLife.com.

When it comes to Eleanor's cleaning skills and Mrs. Curry's menus and cooking tips, these were taken from cookbooks of the time period. Check out Fannie Farmer's *Boston Cooking-School Cook Book* published in 1896, Mrs. Simon Kander's collection entitled *The Settlement Cook Book* published in 1901, and *Mrs. Rorer's Cook Book* published in 1886. Links to these and many more, along with some of my favorite etiquette manuals of the time, can be found at my website.

A fascination with all things Japanese really did sweep through America at the turn of the century. Japan opened to international trade in 1858; until then, it had been bound by a policy known as *sakoku*—"the secluded country." Most of the items described in Gladys Mitchell's home are real, based on descriptions found online or in books. For more information, I recommend Lionel Lambourne's *Japonisme: Cultural Crossings between Japan and the West* and *The Illustrated Encyclopedia of Victoriana* by Nancy Ruhling and John Crosby Freeman. Cherry trees, however, did not enter America until 1906, and even then were only brought as far as Maryland. For purposes of this story, I brought cherry blossoms over early to appease Miss Mitchell's draw toward all things Japanese.

Regarding Bernard's fascination with Sir Arthur Conan Doyle's Sherlock Holmes: *A Study in Scarlet* was published in 1887 and was the first appearance of Sherlock and Watson. In "The Final Problem," published in 1893, author Conan Doyle killed off Holmes. Although Holmes would make an appearance in "The Hound of the Baskervilles," serialized in August 1901, it was set before his "death." Conan Doyle would not bring Holmes back to life until 1903 when he published, "The Adventure of the Empty House."

The other highly inspirational detective mentioned was Anna Katharine Green's Ebenezer Gryce. *The Leavenworth Case* was published in 1878, nine years before Sherlock, and was considered so well-written and researched many readers at the time believed it couldn't have been conceived and authored by a woman. Agatha Christie has her own renowned detective, Hercule Poirot, mention *The Leavenworth Case* in *The Clocks* (1963), and Conan Doyle himself visited Green when he came to America in 1894, so inspired was he by her writing.

Finally, although the term "echolocation" didn't really come into use historically until 1944, I've referenced the idea back in 1901 for story purposes. One of the most fascinating things I learned during my research was the ability of people to use a form of echolocation to move about. This is actually a real thing! Certain blind people have mastered the ability of making a clicking with their tongues to almost "see" their surroundings.

And if that's still not enough historical tidbits for you, I've logged my research in-depth, complete with images of people and places, important news articles, and more on my website at Patricia-Meredith.com.

Thank you so much for listening and reading!

Acknowledgements

First, I offer praise and gratitude to my Lord and merciful Savior, Jesus Christ, with whom nothing is impossible, for giving me a gift, a passion, a talent with which to spread his love.

To my husband, Andrew Meredith, who said I should move my murder mystery to Spokane and thereby set something in motion which has only just begun. Thank you for your never-ending encouragement and love even when I've been writing into the wee small hours of the morning.

My kids, who can look back on this book someday and realize that's why Mommy was so busy sometimes, and who said I look like Mary Poppins in my 1901 clothing—which just totally made my day.

My parents, who have championed my writing ever since I wrote my first book at age nine. I am so very thankful to be blessed with such incredibly supportive, encouraging, and faith-filled parents.

My mother- and father-in-law, who offered such a loving home for us here in Spokane that we realized there would be no better place to set down roots.

Special thanks to Corin Faye, my editor and writing partner whose critiques made this book better with each revision.

Also to Rebecca Cook, whose voice has breathed life into this story and its characters—literally! (If you haven't listened to the audiobook, I can't recommend it enough!)

To the entire Crommelin family, but especially Miff, Mariad, and Patrick Serné, for compiling the letters of Marinus Crommelin into *Dear Mother*, a collection of letters sent home from Spokane in 1901, which was invaluable in my research and descriptions. Special thanks also to Jeff Sims for pointing out *Dear Mother* to me, and to Bob Yoh for tracking down the Crommelins so we could "meet."

Logan Camporeale for his enthusiastic help with research into the specifics of 1901, down to lighting a circa 1900 Majestic range for me and pointing me to his own informative Spokane history blog TheLocalHistory.com. And to all the staff at the Ferris Archives, who opened their doors and minds, offering so much information I couldn't possibly include it all!

The Campbell House docents who always gave a wonderfully informative and enlightening tour. (You really must visit the place yourself!)

Susan Walker, the Spokane Regional Law Enforcement Museum Secretary-Treasurer, for opening up her files and directing me to the correct museum displays so I could find hands-on research, as well as answering all my questions with aplomb.

Robert Silvan, whose expertise as a blacksmith and study of Japanese culture greatly influenced the character of Matsumoto.

Sherri, Lois, and all the staff at Heavenly Special Teas for providing, if not a room of one's own, the next best thing in a private place to write, drink incredible blends of tea, and enjoy the best scones and cream in town.

My amazing Beta Readers: Carrie Anderson, Ben Armstrong, Jason Armstrong, Noelle Austin, Paula Biesen-Malicki, Kathy Buckmaster, Linda Chase, Anne Fischer, Jacquie Gramlow, Randy Haglund, Patti Hammond, Leah Humenuck, William H Keith, Kenda Kellawan-Shafer, Kimberley Lackey, Heather Lionelle, Cindy Matson, Brenda McCosby, Maggie Meredith, Renae Meredith, Scotte Meredith, Su Meredith, Diane Meredith-Gordon, Blaine Pardoe, Lydia Pierce, Sarah E. Pounder, Jennifer Pullen-Caldwell, Andy Rizzo, Beth Rizzo, Catie Rizzo, Dean Rizzo, Jessie Rizzo, Julie Rizzo, Sue Rizzo, Kathy Sharp, Carol and Jim Strobeck, Jessie Wickham, Rebecca Writz, and Kim Yoh. Each of you made this book better for your input!

And you, dear reader. I look forward to sharing the next book with you soon!

Thank you all!

Photo by Angus Meredith

About the Author

Patricia Meredith is an author of historical and cozy mysteries. She currently lives just outside Spokane, Washington on a farm with peacocks, ducks, guinea fowl, chickens, and sheep. When she's not writing, she's playing board games with her husband, creating imaginary worlds with her two children, or out in the garden reading a good book with a cup of tea.

For all the latest updates, you can follow her as @pmeredithauthor on Goodreads, Instagram, and Facebook, and sign up for her newsletter at Patricia-Meredith.com.

CPSIA information can be obtained
at www.ICGtesting.com
Printed in the USA
LVHW040514230921
698482LV00001B/108

9 781087 885940